SCENT OF DANGER

A DALE KINSALL MYSTERY

SCENT OF DANGER

DORANNA DURGIN

FIVE STAR
A part of Gale, Cengage Learning

GALE
CENGAGE Learning

Detroit • New York • San Francisco • New Haven, Conn • Waterville, Maine • London

Copyright © 2008 by Doranna Durgin.
Hitchhiker's Guide to the Galaxy and, within that work, the motto "Don't Panic" are creations of Douglas Adams and © Douglas Adams in the United States, and their use herein shall not be deemed to imply Adams's endorsement or sponsorship of this work.
Five Star Publishing, a part of Gale, Cengage Learning.

ALL RIGHTS RESERVED

Set in 11 pt. Plantin.
Printed on permanent paper.

LIBRARY OF CONGRESS CATALOGING-IN-PUBLICATION DATA

Durgin, Doranna.
   Scent of danger : a Dale Kinsall mystery / Doranna Durgin. — 1st ed.
     p. cm.
   ISBN-13: 978-1-59414-675-6 (alk. paper)
   ISBN-10: 1-59414-675-6 (alk. paper)
   1. Veterinarians—Fiction. 2. Dog owners—Fiction. 3. Beagle (Dog breed)—Fiction. 4. Asthmatics—Fiction. 5. Hantavirus infections—Fiction. 6. Arizona—Fiction. I. Title.
PS3554.U674S28 2008
813'.54—dc22
                                      2008037873

First Edition. First Printing: December 2008.
Published in 2008 in conjunction with Tekno Books and Ed Gorman.

Printed in the United States of America
1 2 3 4 5 6 7 12 11 10 09 08

DEDICATION

Dedicated to my pal Julie Czerneda, for all the inspirations along the way, little and big. Not to mention some great reading fun!

With thanks to:

Jim Maciulla, DMV (Any mistakes are in spite of his efforts! And besides the dogs love him.)

Roxanne Willems Snopek (any mistakes are in spite of her efforts!)

Suzanne Thomas of Cedar Ridge Beagles (Beagley mentor extraordinaire!)

Lucienne Diver (*another* book that's all her fault—! "What if you . . . ?" she says, slyly planting the idea and walking away, as if it *won't* take root. . . .)

And with love to:

Xtacee's Carbon Unit CGC, Resident Evil Matriarch Genius, so dearly departed

Cheysuli Jean-Luc Picardigan OJP NAP OJC NAC CGC, Cardigan schoolmaster, brain-injured but game

Cheysuli's Silver Belle CD RE PAX MXP3 MJP2 EAC EJC CGC, Cardi Comeback Girl

Ch. Cedar Ridge DoubleOSeven CD RE MX MXJ EAC EJC CGC, Beagle Q-Hunter, AKA ConneryBeagle

CHAPTER 1

Come daylight, Dale Kinsall still expected to open his eyes to lush Ohio fields—summer humidity closing in around him, song birds trilling him awake to rolling corn rows. And each morning, the dry bite of high-desert air still somehow came as a faint and welcome surprise. The scent of hot Ponderosa pine, the acrid bite of ancient volcanic cinder dust, the dry sting of single-digit humidity—they were all reminders of a new home, new job, new friends . . . new life.

Dale sighed, wiggling his toes at the end of a bed not quite long enough as he admired the bright splash of late summer sunshine against the adobe textured bedroom wall. *Bare* bedroom wall. Pretty much past time to hang his pictures. *But not there.* He hadn't even realized the sun hit that spot, because he was always up and gone before it had the chance.

Up and gone. . . .

Dale snatched up the alarm clock, scattering change, three battered paperbacks, and his cell phone. *Way past time to get up,* it informed him. Dale made a strangled noise. Any day but a clinic surgery day, oh please! "Why didn't you wake me?" he demanded of the tightly curled bundle of Beagle in the corner dog bed.

One eye cracked open to regard Dale without concern. *sleeping.*

"Up," Dale said, mercilessly brusque as he rolled out of bed, groping for yesterday's jeans along the way. New jeans, worn

7

once . . . they'd do. *"Up,"* he repeated, snagging a short-sleeve button-down from the closet without even looking to see which.

Sully Beagle gave a languid yawn, stood up, shook off, and trotted to the recently installed dog door in the corner, right through the wall to the buffered outdoor storage closet on the porch and into the yard. He returned as Dale emerged from the bathroom, toothbrush in mouth, to scoop up his wallet, paw through the sock drawer, and hunt the errant cell phone.

food.

"Later," Dale muttered, dashing toothpaste from his chin before it caused a change of shirt.

Wrinkles of woe appeared, most effective over black-lined chocolate brown eyes and a white-blazed face, long ears set to Flying Nun mode. *staaaarving.*

"Busy," Dale told him, stretching beneath the bed and hoping the black widows hadn't found this space yet. *"C'mon, phone. . . ."*

It rang. Right beside his ear, it rang. Dale jerked in surprise, smacked his head on the bedside table, lost the toothbrush, and snatched up the phone from behind a stuffed fuzzy smiley face, not bothering to check caller ID. "I'm coming!"

"Doggy neuterectomy in forty-five," Sheri said, undeterred by his brusque tone. "Snap, snap, snap!"

"Be there!" he said around the toothpaste, as if neuterectomy was really even a word anyway. He hung up on her, tossing the phone on the bed and tossing the smiley face to Sully. His wrist and hand, freed from the cast of this spring, gave its usual single morning twinge and then gave it up for the day.

Dog hair now coated the toothbrush. Dale dropped it in the bathroom trash, spat out the remaining paste, ran wet fingers through his dark hair, and at the last moment remembered to snap up his jeans.

From the bedroom came a half-hearted smiley face squeak. *food.*

"Later." Dale emerged from the master bath at a near trot. "Time for work."

Sully froze in an instant of quivering glee and then shot past Dale to reach the back door first. No dancing in excitement for Sully Beagle, oh no. He crouched motionless, every fiber of his twenty-two pounds focused on the door knob. Waiting . . . waiting. . . .

Late or not, Dale couldn't resist. He could never resist. He let his hand hover over the knob, not . . . quite . . . touching.

Sully glanced away from the door in disbelief, pinning Dale with a reality check. His astonishment burst out in an explosive *"Bawhh!"* of demand. His eyes bugged out only a little.

Dale grinned and pushed the door open into the warm morning heat, listening to claws scrabble across garage concrete to the back of the Forester, where he dropped the tailgate so Sully could leap up and crate himself for the short drive to work.

Foothills Clinic. Dale Kinsall, DVM. Soon enough, Dale hoped, Laura Nakai, DVM would be on that sign, next to Brad Stanfill's name. What with the clinic expansion and remodeling under way, they'd have room for a third vet. They'd *need* a third vet to pay off that loan. . . .

Dale pulled into the parking lot with the careless speed of familiarity, leaving the rest of traffic to commute into Flagstaff. The clinic itself sat in West Winona, the not-really-a-town outside the eastern edge of Flagstaff, Arizona. Seven thousand feet high, one volcanic range, and more Ponderosa pines than a man could shake a stick at, whatever that meant. For Dale it meant escaping Ohio, where a fiery past had damaged his lungs into asthma. Of course, it had also meant immersing himself in the most bizarre series of murders to hit this area since. . . .

Well, since ever.

Didn't matter. That was over, life had settled—as much as it ever did—and he'd met Laura in the process.

Yeah.

Dale glanced longingly at the neighboring RoundUp Café as he slipped a martingale collar and lead on Sully. *Not today.* He'd grab office coffee and hope for something stale in the new upstairs break room fridge.

But after negotiating the construction detritus in the parking lot, the painter's truck and the ladder leaning askew against the truck, he stopped short—coffee notwithstanding. With Sheri gesturing impatiently at him through the recently installed storefront-type window—*get in here!*—and his hand on the knob of the outer door, Dale instead squinted suspiciously at the note jammed into the tight space between door and jamb.

Notes. Never a good thing. Never said *you've won the lottery,* only *sorry I lost that winning lottery ticket.*

bored. Sully abandoned his obedient dog guise and tugged at the lead, sniffing around the doorway to find the very best place to lift his leg.

"You'd better not." Dale plucked the note free. "You're a year and a half now. You should be setting a good example for Beaglekind everywhere." In the background, Sheri had subsided to angry hands-on-hips mode, her brightly flowered and tightly tailored slacks largely—and mercifully—obscured by the tunic-length scrub smock she'd taken to wearing lately. More professional, she said, though how she thought it could offset the slacks or even the bright pink streaks currently slashing through her highly coiffed hair, he wasn't sure.

Sully, too, subsided. *poop.*

And Dale opened the note to read a neat little handwritten verse.

> *Due to your expertise,*
> *This should be a breeze.*

Say what?

Sheri stared at him, a glare of demand, her veryvery red lips pressed together in stark contrast to her dark skin. Dale waved the note at her in mute question and she shrugged in an exaggerated fashion and stabbed a finger at the door. He shrugged back and stuffed the note in his pocket, pulling the door open to the surprise of the high-perching painter inside the air-lock space.

To Sully's surprise as well. Up close and personal, the ladder and the pile of painting gear beneath it clearly resembled a dog-eating monster. His hackles went up all the way down his back and his tail disappeared, an extra wary hunch in his back making sure it stayed hidden. He skittered to the far side of the small space. Brave dog.

"Oh, hey!" The painter straightened, a careless hand on the texturing trowel. Innumerable layers of paint had turned his once-white bib portion a muddy black, stiff enough to stand up on its own. Maybe even to walk away. He was surprisingly short of stature even near the top of the ladder, and he had a thick monobrow that turned his developing frown into something truly alarming.

But Dale knew that look, especially of late, and especially aimed in his direction. Recognition. *Dark hair, dark eyes, taller than most, just barely ever grew out of lanky, a Beagle by his side. . . .*

"Hey! Aren't you the one who—" The painter gestured to fill in his words, and texturizing glop flew through the air to land at Sully's feet.

evil! danger!

"*BAWHH!*" Sully cried, completely fixated on the splot of goop. His prodigious hound voice reverberated in the air-lock space, and if the painter had anything else to say, it was lost. Dale, well aware of the futility of any other course, bent to swipe it off the floor with stiff fingers, flipping it aside.

11

"There," he said, as Sully stared at the floor with wrinkles of profound suspicion on his forehead. "Gone. You vaporized it with your noise." And then he swiped his forelock out of his eyes without thinking about it until the very moment it was too late. He met the painter's eyes steadily, a dare of sorts. *Go ahead. Say something about it.* The man pressed his lips together, suddenly mute. Good. "Yes," Dale said, with much forbearance. "That was us." *We got tangled up with the bad guys. We brought them to justice. We are mighty.* "You didn't happen to see anyone hanging around out front, did you? Say, posting a note?"

The man responded in patent relief at the new subject. "Sorry, been working up on the ladder. Can't see anything from here except the fake fire hydrant."

A touch Dale had blatantly, unrepentantly, and gleefully stolen from Laura's clinic.

"Something wrong?" the painter asked.

Dale shook his head. Nothing but weirdness . . . and weirdness had pretty much become his life since his arrival here, so . . . no big deal. *Due to your expertise, this should be a breeze.* Apparently not. "Nothing, thanks. You'll be done with this before office hours?"

"Planned it that way." The man gave him a narrow-eyed look of impending resentment, and dug back into his bucket of texturizer. Dale beat a retreat. Sully squirted out the door ahead of him, still unconvinced of their safety.

"*Gawd,*" Sheri said. "Took you longer to come inside than it did to get here in the first place." She reached over to her domain—that which everyone else called the reception desk—and swiped several folders from the surface, slapping them against his chest. "Neuterectomy is here and being prepped by Jade. Nasty cyst-dog just arrived. Isaac is considering a trank gun and I don't blame him."

From behind the double swinging doors of the procedure

room, Isaac's bass voice rose several octaves into a yelp of dismay.

Sheri didn't miss a beat. "Guess he went for the hands-on approach. Now gimme that cute little dog and go get to work." But when Dale handed Sully over, Sheri's eyes strayed to his hair and stayed there; she forgot to reach for the leash. "Gawd," she said again. "White men. You just don't know what to do with *product.*" She helped herself to his hair—not the first time—quickly arranging it first this way and that, then nodding with some resignation. "Best that can be done. Now gimme."

"He needs breakfast," Dale told her, and headed for the procedure room. Lab work, surgery, emergency trauma cases . . . it all happened here, with two central stainless steel tables and the walls lined with equipment, supplies, and two massive sinks. At the end of the renovations there'd be a small separate surgery room off the back of this area, and a supply pantry with neat wire shelves higher than even Dale could reach without a stool.

For now, there was Isaac and a small Maltese mix whose crooked bite sneered out the end of the tiny cloth muzzle. Dale imagined he saw a hint of blood staining the disarrayed white mustache. Isaac held the dog gingerly, like a living pillow; an IV catheter trailed from the dog's shaved front leg. "Him first," he suggested, his long swoop of a curved nose emphasizing his current hangdog expression. "So I don't have to start over again with the muzzle. I've got Midazolam and Butorphanol ready to go . . . I'll get him clipped up really fast once that's on board."

"All right," Dale said, "Cyst dog it is. Maybe he won't be so cranky once that thing is off his hip." He gave the dog a quick scritch and pretended not to notice when it tried to bite him through the soft muzzle. "We'll be using Medetomidine and Fentanyl to start off the castration—lay that out for me, will you? And is Dru here?"

"Of course," Isaac said, his expression changing into something like dread. Dru, their kennel master—grandmother, as abrasive as Brillo and irrepressible as the pink battery bunny. "Out in the kennels. You want me to get her—?"

"No, no," Dale said hastily. "Just thinking that if we're fast enough, we can get through at least one castration without—"

"Oh." Isaac nodded. "The earrings trick. Well, *she* thinks it's funny."

Dale couldn't help a wince. Women always thought that one was funny. "Let's see if we can avoid it."

No, of course not. Dru had pounced at just the right moment, dangling the two excised testicles at her earlobes just long enough to get Sheri in on the act. They cackled together on the other side of the double doors, and Dale knew he'd best check the toppings on the pizza he intended to order for lunch. Sheri would get there first; she always did, taking a slice as toll for accepting the pizza in the first place. And that cackle sounded. . . .

Just a little bit too satisfied.

He left the Maltese mix wrapped in towels and growling to himself, and the castrated young mix barking his way out of the anesthesia. Sheri handed him the afternoon appointment folders, looking entirely too innocent. It was not a convincing look, not with those knowing eyes. "I'm ordering pizza," he told her. "Will you see if anyone else wants to get in on it?"

"Sure," she said. Too innocent and too compliant. She ought to have assessed him the pizza toll on the spot, not smiled brightly at him.

Dale leaned over the top of the two-tiered corner counter—a standing level for the clients, and a lower work surface for Sheri and the techs. His height could be imposing when he wanted, and at the moment . . . he wanted.

"Just so you know," he said, his voice low and confidential.

"I'm not ordering mushrooms. Cheese and pepperoni. And I intend to inspect it."

Sheri was good. She barely blinked. "Good for you. You want this afternoon's folders, or you want to wait till you've inspected the pizza?"

"I'll wait," he said. "I've got enough to catch up on in there. And I need to get a new alarm clock." He turned away, aiming for his office down the long hall that clients never saw—but stopped himself short, fumbling in his pocket for the now-wrinkled note. "You know anything about this?"

Sheri took the paper, muttering the words under her breath as she read them. "Buncha nonsense. Where'd you find—" But she stopped in mid-word. Her eyes narrowed; her nostrils flared slightly. Uh-oh. "That painter asked me if you'd figured out your weird note and I had to pretend like I knew what he was talking about. You think there are any circumstances around here where a painter should know a weird note and I don't?"

No safe answer to that one. "Check," Dale said, sidestepping the whole thing. "Don't know anything about the note." He plucked the paper from her hand before she could protest and resumed his trek to the office.

"*Better* check that pizza," she grumbled after him.

He placed the order as soon as he hit the office, knowing Sheri would pay from his pizza fund. One of these days he'd have to start packing his lunches.

Heh. Right. Ha ha ha.

Dale found his dog curled up in the Sullybed, pretending not to notice Dale. Not the usual. "Hey, dog. Sheri feed you?"

no. But Sully didn't so much as lift his head. *i'm staaarving.*

It only took Dale a moment to locate the small metal food bowl, shoved behind the door and licked clean of every molecule. "Liar," he said, putting the bowl back on the shelf beside the small bin of food.

pout.

"You okay?" Not yet worried, Dale checked out the contents of his desk for the first time that day. A new puzzle—yet another version of Neuschwanstein castle, and he knew right away that Laura had left it here, evidence of her understated humor. She'd never quite gotten over the number of Neuschwansteins available in puzzle form. The sticky note attached confirmed his guess; she said she'd call him later.

It would, he hoped, be a call in which she accepted his offer to work at the clinic.

He put the puzzle aside, perused the neat stack of papers waiting for his attention—bills from the remodel, mostly—and played briefly with the latest fancy pen left by the pharmaceutical drug rep. "You ready to go outside?" he asked without looking.

Sully arrived at his side with no discernible travel time, one foot beseechingly propped against Dale's calf and his head tipped back to provide Dale with a clear view of his Most Earnest Expression.

Also a clear view of the Sullybed, which proved to have one of Dale's old bandanas in the center, ironed flat—the reason behind Sully's so-casual-but-determined occupation of the bed. "Uh-huh," Dale said. "Nice try."

Sully gave him wrinkles of woe, looking from the bed to Dale and back again. *mine.*

"Not so much," Dale told him, and rescued the bandana, flapping it out to the tune of much dust and dog hair. Instantly, he held his breath. *Stupid, stupid.* His asthma had never tolerated flying dust, not even now after he'd finally gotten it under control again. Childhood asthma secondary to smoke inhalation, he once thought he'd outgrown it—but that was before the clinic fire in Ohio, the one that eventually drove him to this high, clean-air clime. And now with the construction, he was back to best behavior. Being good.

So he grabbed Sully's leash from his desk—the same desk that held Big Blue 2, the office rescue inhaler—and ducked out of his office and out the back door. Lunch should arrive in short order, and then, he thought, he might just be able to fake his way through the afternoon as though he hadn't skipped a shave this morning.

o smells! o dusty lovely smells! all piled up around the people junk. o musky dusty critter smells, living in the people junk! o stranger man who smells of musky dusky critter smells—

dale! dale! let's go this way! why are you heading the other way, down to the—

oh! the woods! let's go to the woods! o lovely green sap smells! o dead stinky things! hurry hurry hurry, daledaledale!

Chaos ruled the entire clinic office property, from the new patient housing off the back to the piles of junk discarded from the remodeled interior. The now-retired Dr. Hague had initiated the project . . . his final stamp of influence on Foothills Clinic. And Dale had known about it when he signed on as senior vet, had known he'd be taking on the financial burden of it, had even managed to revise the plans to his own sensibilities.

He just hadn't known it would be so unrelentingly loud and messy.

He took Sully past all of it, out to the back of the property where it butted up to national forest. Sully inspected his favorite trees while Dale breathed deeply of the hot noon pine needle scent and pondered the advisability of earplugs in an environment where he actually did need to hear what was being said. Then he pondered the sky and the building clouds—monsoon-like, in this mid-summer, but not quite looking serious about rain. On the way back they detoured to a pile of scrap wood and drywall and Dale stood by as Sully found the scent of something interesting and inhaled hard enough to stir every atom of air in the pile.

A voice spoke out of the blue. "Better be careful with that."

Sully essayed a tentative paw into the pile, stirring wood.

"Nails?" Dale guessed, finding that they'd gained a companion. The man was broad-shouldered and barrel-chested, his features distinctly Navajo; his shirt said *Mountain Air.* Good, the duct guys were finally getting to work.

"That's just the kind of place for mice." The man gestured at the debris, where Sully had jammed his head beneath a piece of drywall to yodel *wantwantwant.* "They carry all kinds of diseases."

"Not usually the sort dogs get," Dale said absently, untangling the lead in preparation to bodily remove Sully—lunch was waiting, after all. "But I'll keep it in mind." And anything else the man might have said was lost in Sully's protests, yodels gone to full-blown wails as Dale pulled him out of the rubble with a veritable *schlurp* of breaking suction.

wantwantwant!!!!

"Me, too," Dale told him, untouched by the drama of the protest. "Want *lunch.* And a nice quiet afternoon. And a phone call from Laura telling me we've got a new partner."

Pizza waited in his office, minus the toll piece. Dale grabbed a soda from the upstairs fridge, double-checked the pizza toppings every bit as thoroughly as he'd warned Sheri he would, and came back down to eat several pieces in quick succession. Then he poked himself in the stomach and decided against another piece. Still flat enough . . . but he'd seen how his uncle—almost as tall as Dale, almost as hollow-legged—had put on weight in his early forties. Dale still had half a decade to go, but planning ahead seemed like the thing to do.

Besides, then he'd have enough left for dinner.

Swigging down the last of the soda, he ambled into the waiting room to snag the client folders Sheri had offered him earlier, standing at the counter to flip through the first appointment. Allergies. *'Tis the season.* . . .

"Hey," Sheri said, stomping down the stairs—not through lack of grace, which she had aplenty for a lady living large, but because Sheri never failed to announce her presence in every way. "Call came in. I picked up when I heard the machine. You know the Wilsons?"

How could he not? They'd brought in their aging shepherd mix several times over the summer, dealing with his increasing allergies and dietary issues, visibly worrying about the dog's prospects even as they just as visibly adored him. An old certified therapy dog, he'd raised their kids . . . and was now the only one who hadn't flown the coop.

"Nancy had a tone," Sheri said. "And you know they're not panickers. So . . . I told them to sneak in before the first afternoon slot."

Dale glanced at his watch. "That would be any moment now," he said. "Better get the door." He glanced down at Sully, who was investigating a corner, and pointed down the hall. "Back to the office."

busy.

Dale made a quick move, an exaggerated step, and Sully scooted on down the hall, glancing only once over his shoulder to see if Dale still watched. Dale did. Sully hastened his pace and disappeared from sight, although not without the distinct *poomf!* of a body leaping on the Sullybed.

When Dale turned back, he found that Sheri had opened the door just in time. Tom Wilson staggered through the door under the load of his seventy-pound shepherd mix, followed by his wife. *Both of them.* It alerted Dale as much as the dog-toting; both worked in town, and couldn't have found it easy to coordinate this sudden visit.

"Can he walk?" Dale asked them, standing back rather than rushing up to the dog. First impressions. . . .

Tom Wilson carefully set the dog on his feet. "He can walk. I just couldn't bring myself to make him." He hooked a finger through the dog's collar and urged him on a circuit around the waiting room. His wife, Nancy, watched only a moment before closing her eyes.

Dale schooled his face, watching the dog stagger, head tilted, barely staying on his feet. He moved close enough to support the dog's lower jaw in his hand, tipping it so his eyes caught the light.

Deep, brown dignified eyes, jerking in uncontrollable nystagmus. Dale stroked the dog's head and stood. "Take him right on in to the first room," he told the Wilsons. "We'll have you in and out before things get busy in here again."

The moment the door closed, Sheri said, "You got *the look.*"

"Brain tumor," Dale said, scrubbing a hand across his suddenly tense forehead as he flipped through the dog's records, hunting any sign that this had been coming. And he'd need a CBC and a chem panel; he'd need to rule out toxin exposure. . . .

"Hey, no!" Sheri leaned back in her chair, accusing and startled at the same time. "You can't know that. Just because you got *the look* doesn't mean you know for sure. Maybe it's that ear thing. That gets better in a few days sometimes."

"Vestibular syndrome? Yeah, maybe." Dale found nothing in the records that looked like warning in hindsight. Some iffy liver panels, yeah . . . the dog was getting old. Increased allergies this summer, ditto.

Sometimes a tumor just plain came on fast and hard.

Sheri squinted at him. "But you don't think so."

Frustrated, he scrubbed a hand through his hair, through the stiff spot from the paint texturizer. *Thinking* about it wasn't the same as reacting to it . . . as knowing somewhere deep inside that he'd seen what he'd seen. "We can do X rays, but I don't know that our machine will be precise enough to visualize the bulla meaningfully. It really needs an MRI . . . which would show a tumor. But the nearest machine is—"

"In Phoenix," Sheri finished for him.

"If it's vestibular, it'll improve," Dale said. He scooped up the folder and steeled himself to enter the treatment room.

It wasn't vestibular, and he knew it.

The Wilsons had taken the news well, all things considered. They'd chosen to wait a few days rather than rush the dog to a specialist clinic in the valley; by then the situation would be more obvious, and they weren't planning to subject him to extreme measures in any event.

Dale gave them some anti-emetics in case the old fellow became ill, suggested that they hand feed and water him as best they could, and said he'd call them to see how it was going.

But he knew how it would be going.

"Damn," he sighed, sitting heavily in his desk chair. It creaked in warning. Lanky wasn't the same as lightweight, not once you reached a certain height.

Sully rose from the bed and put his paw on Dale's leg. *pet me.*

"C'mon, then," Dale told him, beckoning with a finger. Sully leaped lightly onto his lap and instantly took advantage of the opportunity to shove papers around Dale's desk with his face. Dale tugged gently on a soft ear and let Sully have his way. Just at the moment, he didn't have the heart to scold him, even if at eighteen months Sully well knew the rules he was breaking.

The afternoon schedule held puppy visits and a diabetic cat and a handful of allergy cases. And then he'd head out for Sully's new obedience class, the perfect antidote to the day.

Or this part of it, at least.

The phone rang, startling Sully into extreme hackles and a little soprano growl. "Not manly," Dale told him. Sheri wouldn't have put the call through if it wasn't important—she hadn't even yelled down the hall to see if he'd take it. He grabbed it before the second ring finished. "Hey," he said.

"Sheri told you it was me." Laura's voice. All it took was Laura's voice to see Laura's face, heart-shaped and strong, refined bones, thick black hair all the way down to the middle of her back. . . .

Whoa. Dale shook himself out of it. He supposed that an objective observer wouldn't find her beautiful, wouldn't be so drawn by the mix of cultures there—Castilian mother, Navajo father—or besotted in her presence.

But then, he was far from objective. And he wasn't sure, at any given time, whether the besotting was mutual, or whether she found him a good—*shudder*—friend. He cleared his throat. "I guessed. Now, tell me I can get out the sign paint."

She said, "We're on for dinner tomorrow, aren't we?"

Wow, direct deflection. Probably not good. "Sure," he said, as if he was really that casual about it. "I've got some grass-fed beef steaks set aside. I put a good sunset on order, too." It might not have kicked over to the official monsoon or blessed them with rains yet, but the clouds regularly gathered to tease them nonetheless, spreading drama over the San Francisco Peaks.

"The thing is," she said, as if they'd been talking about it all along, "I'm in a different place here, now." A different place, she meant, than in the late winter—when she'd applied for the open position at Foothills. *The one Dale had gotten.* "When Jake left Pine Country, I renegotiated terms with Marlee. I've got more say in how things go . . . more influence."

"Better money, I hope," Dale said—just a little too hearty, because even if he tended toward cluelessness, he could see where this was going. He winced, glad for the visual anonymity of the phone.

"Ha," she said. "That's for me to know. The thing is—"

"No, it's okay—I get it." That meant the sooner this conversation was over, the better. Dale had always been a Band-Aid ripper.

Laura's voice softened. Typical of her, that quiet . . . and when she got mad she only got quieter. But this was soft, and apologetic, and dammit, it only made things worse. "It's been sudden, Dale. *T'ah ñê'ê*. I didn't know it would work out this way."

"Hey," he said. "How about those Diamondbacks?"

She got it, then. Only one of the reasons he found himself drawn to her. How fast she got it. "My cousin's been trying to reach me, so I've got to give her a call. Don't you feed my steak to Sully."

"I would prefer to feed it to you." He didn't mean to let that sort of thing slip, the constant giveaways of his hard crush. She wasn't a woman to be pushed.

And indeed, she went sideways again. "I know someone in Albuquerque who might be interested in moving here," she said. "I'll bring some information with me tomorrow. Stay out of trouble."

Instant protest rose in his throat. Just because he hadn't always been so good about keeping on the asthma regimen, just because he'd stumbled into a murdering ecological oligarchy within days of his arrival here, just because it had almost gotten him and her and even Sully killed. . . .

Some things were hard to live down, it seemed. Come to think of it . . . he'd been in trouble more than he'd been out of it, as far as Laura knew. But the last couple of months had been quiet enough. Nothing more than the occasional dry storm rumbling through to light up the evening. Still, he said, "Good plan," and "See you tomorrow," and "Have a good one," before hanging up the phone. Then he looked down at Sully, who'd propped both front feet up on the desk to survey the office territory from this lofty angle, and said, "You'd better be good in obedience class this evening. Otherwise, the only thing left to do with the day is to get to the end of it."

Out in the sun-heated Forester, the end of the long summer day within reach and only Sully's obedience class left to go before the long summer . . . and something didn't smell quite right.

Sully circled in his crate, nose jammed up against the mesh, inhaling loud enough to hear as Dale slid into the front seat, his nose not all that far away in a modest SUV with the back seats habitually turned down to make way for the crate and guy gear. The pizza sat beside Dale, but that wasn't it. Pizza was a *good* smell. Dale sat with the keys inserted in the ignition, not quite turning the key.

Sully gave a sharp little bark. *smells!*

"Yeah, I know . . . I just don't know—"

Oh yes he did. There, in the corner of his eye. Dangling from the rearview mirror like a pair of shriveled tan fuzzy dice . . . only not fuzzy at all.

"Alrighty, Dru," Dale muttered, groping in his pocket for the little knife that would cut the string holding the wee little testicles to the rearview mirror. "Ha, ha, ha." He opened the door just enough to toss the tidbits out to the lurking ravens, then turned the ignition and cranked the air-conditioning on high. "Now we're going to find out just how much you like testicle tea."

heel heel sit turn heel.

dog class. I like dog class! butt sniffing! tail wagging! dale makes proud noises. and there are *cookies*. i feel much bigger than the other dogs. i *am* much bigger than the other dogs. all of them. heel heel sit stay heel—

what's that smell? o stinky! o mouse! beagle sniff! beagle pounce!

pouncepounce*pounce!*

Oh yeah. The only thing left to do with this day was to get to the end of it.

Dogs barking, Sully baying, one woman still making noises of vast dismay, another in complete retreat, the only other man in the class trying to pretend like it had only been a matter of time. "Well, what can you expect?" he said, his voice coming through loudly in a brief gap in the chaos. "Beagles aren't exactly smart."

Dale stiffened, pricked by one of the few things that could do it. The other man seemed to sense he'd crossed a line; he took a hasty step back, his perfectly obedient Australian Shepherd at his side. The instructor—slight, boundless energy, dark hair cut perky—seemed to realize it, too—she removed her attention from the noises of vast dismay and said, "He was bred to hunt on scent. He was also bred to think and act independently, so his motivations in training are different from non-hunting breeds. Big for their inches, that's what they say about a well-bred Beagle. And of course if I'd *known* there were mice under that shed—"

At least, Dale thought that's what she said, as he knelt to extract Sully from the hole beneath said shed, the leash a thorough tangle between them. It was hard to tell.

Sully didn't say much. But when he said it, the whole world heard.

And as Dale's hands closed over Sully's straining, digging,

bawhhing little Beagle self, the noise grew desperately louder, and, quite unbelievably, went into a register so high even Sully couldn't even sustain it.

Instead he began to squeak.

Dale thought how convenient it was to be crouching beside this shed. A nice solid wall against which to beat his head. But he finished extracting Sully—

mousemousemousemouse!!

—which only made the noise louder, and then Dale said to Elaine the instructor, "We'll go regain his composure." He pointed at the parking area outside the fenced yard, just in case she couldn't hear any better than he could. She nodded, and off they went, Sully still bawling at the top of his lungs.

About halfway to the Forester he subsided to a mournful yodel and quit squirming, still tucked securely under Dale's arm. Almost all the way to the Forester his tail started to beat against Dale's back, and Dale followed his attention with surprise. "Laura!" He blinked in a double take that should have amused her—but her expression remained serious. He dropped Sully lightly to his feet and the dog immediately added to his transgressions by jumping on Laura, tail flagged and wagging.

She crouched to greet him, rubbing those floppy brown ears in just the right way to turn on his adoration face. "I'm sorry to interrupt your class—"

"Is something wrong?" He closed the distance between them. Of course something was wrong. Laura was good at hiding her feelings, but not that good. "You should have called—I would have come—"

She waved away the words. "I had errands to run anyway. My cousin is on the way down from the res. She'll be staying with me, and I. . . ."

She trailed off, a slight frown marring her forehead as she looked away, over to the yard where the obedience class was back into footwork drills, taking advantage of the cooling evening. Dale suddenly thought of how seldom she mentioned her family—make that never—and kept his voice as neutral as possible as he asked, "You need help with something?"

Relief was clear enough, whether or not she meant to hide it. "Moving furniture. We . . . don't know each other very well. I want her to feel welcome. The east bedroom has my office in it."

The east . . . ? Dale didn't ask it, but he knew his face showed it. His face was not always his friend.

But Laura just smiled. "The rising sun," she said. "She may not even realize. But it'll matter."

"I didn't even know you had a cousin," he admitted.

She stood, dusting off her trim khaki cargo pants, and chagrin was the last thing he expected to see. "I'm not sure I've done it right, the family thing. You wouldn't even know I spent my first years on the res, would you?" The surprise on his face was apparently answer enough; she gave a short laugh. "Not that I remember all that much about it . . . just those things that settle inside you and live there, so much a part of you that you don't even realize they're there."

Like the faint pattern in her speech, her quiet demeanor, her acceptance of others . . . and of his various quirks.

Such as the way questions came out of his mouth when maybe they shouldn't. Part of his own early patterns, the asking . . . the hunting answers. He'd never gotten those answers, and he'd never stopped asked the questions. "Why did your parents leave?"

"My mother left," Laura corrected him. "After my father died in a car accident. Someone had been drinking, of course. And the family . . . she was welcome to stay, I know it. She never said otherwise. But it was not a life that called to her."

"But you remember," Dale said.

27

"I remember enough." Laura looked back to him, meeting his eyes squarely for the first time. "I want her to feel welcome—and cared for. Her son—my cousin of something removed, but we just say nephew—may have hanta . . . he's been flown to Flagstaff Medical Center. And her husband died in the army, so . . . she's dealing with this herself."

"Hanta?"

"I know," she said. "It's not a big year for it. But any year will do it, if you stir up the wrong dust."

Dust laden with mouse poop and urine, that was. Since the reservation-based epidemic in '93, hanta virus had become part of the Southwestern milieu. Classic scenario, to go clean out the toolshed one day and have hanta the next.

Dale looked over at the obedience class, the dogs and owners frolicking around in a praise party next to the shed. Maybe Sully had done their instructor a favor at that.

CHAPTER 2

"He knows better than to mess around in outbuildings without wetting the dust down first," Laura said, standing in the middle of her living room. "Not that any ten-year-old is in danger of a sudden urge to clean any outbuildings."

Dale staggered under the load of the short wooden file cabinet. "Where?" he grunted. Seldom had he been in Laura's home; he couldn't even guess where she might want it. And rather than settling on a likely place, his eyes flitted over the rug collection adorning her walls—walls otherwise bare, respecting the beauty of the weavings—the practical but classy fixtures, and the quiet lighting on the large snake aquarium and—

And damn, this thing is getting heavy.

"Over here." Laura patted the end of the couch, quickly moving aside a basket of sewing materials. "I'll turn it into an end table."

Dale obligingly plunked it into place, staggering only a little, and then he plunked himself down on the couch, lifting his face slightly to the overhead fan. Tidy, well-kept, and built before the recent spate of unusually hot years. No central air . . . just plenty of overhead fans and wide-open windows.

"Okay?" Laura asked, and they both knew she meant the asthma.

"Fine," Dale said. "Want to come to the dog show in Prescott?" Whoa, there went his mouth again.

Laura didn't answer right away, but she gave him a surprised look, glancing around the disrupted room, her thoughts obvious enough. A dog show, when she had this going on?

"It's in early fall," Dale added hastily. "Thought I'd give it a try, since he took Winner's Dog at the local show last month. Not that I'm not too tall to be out there in that ring, handling classes or no. And especially in the thirteen-inch class—" The smaller of the two Beagle varieties, since Sully was a hair under thirteen inches at the withers, but now he was just babbling, inside and out.

Understanding dawned. "Ah," she said. "Yes, I'd like to see that. I'm still sorry I missed his win."

A major, it had been, giving Sully a little collection of points toward his championship and making it one of the two major wins—wins over a significant number of dogs—he had to earn.

Oblivious, he now had a rare treat of pressed rawhide, and he crouched with it under the aquarium, blithely unconcerned with the snake once he'd sussed out the unfamiliar smell and dismissed it. Not a snake dog.

"So it's only right you should come," Dale said. He reached up to tug her hand, pulling her down into the couch. "Take a break. You might as well—I am."

She resisted, but only for an instant. Then she sat, more genteelly than he had, sinking into the comfortable cushions with a sigh. Not Laura-like.

He went one further. He put an arm around her shoulders and pulled her in so she leaned against him instead of the couch back. If she'd resisted he'd have given her space, but she didn't. It gave him a perfect view of the back of her neck. Unintended bonus.

But he wasn't distracted by the view for long . . . not once he felt the tension in her body. "Laura—"

"I know," she admitted. "This isn't about me. She's not going to be taking notes . . . she's going to spend every possible moment in the hospital with her son."

"She's going to know she's welcome. She'll know you made this place for her to recharge."

After a moment, he felt her relax. They sat together in conversational silence for a few minutes, listening to Sully chew. A few more minutes and Laura took a deep breath she probably wasn't even aware of, letting it out in a sigh; her weight settled more completely against him. *Yeah.*

Sully hesitated in his chewing just long enough to belch into the contentment. Dale stifled a snort; Laura laughed outright and shifted away from Dale, climbing out of the comfort zone. "Way to go, son," Dale informed Sully.

Sully offered a wrinkled forehead of thought, but only for an instant. *chewing.*

"The desk, I think, can go in front of this window. I'll just put the plants around it." Laura's moment of weakness was over; she helped Dale shift the small desk and left him to arrange plants while she headed to the kitchen for last-minute touches.

"Seriously," Dale told Sully, his voice low as he crouched to tug a giant pot into place, ducking the voluminous leaves and hoping his brown thumb hadn't touched it long enough to kill it. "Next time, I'm booting your butt outside."

Sully took it as an invitation; he leaped to his feet and brought the gooey chew over, dropping it on Dale's hand. Dale scooped him up, giving the gooeyness back to Sully to carry. "Might be time to get out of your hair." Cousin Mary, after all, should be arriving at any time.

"*Out of my hair* isn't how I'd put it," she said, her voice filtering out of the kitchen and punctuated by a cupboard door. "But I think my cousin will be tired and worried, and probably not up to meeting anyone." She appeared briefly in the arching kitchen entryway to lean against the wall and add, "I'll let you know how the boy is. My nephew." She said it as if the thought had truly just occurred to her, that she had someone to call nephew at all.

"Tomorrow," Dale said. "When you have time." And he let himself out.

But when he arrived home, he discovered himself too restless to settle down. Too excited, in some weird way, that Laura had reached out to him for help. He ate the final piece of pizza, hovered over the puzzle table for a few moments, placing three pieces and then removing the one that hadn't been quite right, and ended up out in the back patio area, enclosed by stucco privacy walls and darkness. Sully met him there and Dale joined him at the oversized dog bed that had no place indoors but was just perfect as a stargazing platform. Dale lay back and wiggled a bit to get comfortable, gazing out at Leo heading west and knowing Scorpio was lurking just below the opposite horizon. Without even looking, he groped around in the patio storage bin and pulled out the old sleeping bag against the fast-cooling night, throwing it over both Sully and himself.

And there, because he had no alarm clock, he fell asleep.

Dale scooted into the clinic as the wall clock hovered on the last few seconds of leeway. "I'm not late!"

Sully scooted along in his wake with wary glances around the air-lock entryway, expecting the ladder or the painter to appear out of thin air. Dale left the door open so Sully could give the space an accusing eye until it got boring, and then the whole air-lock thing would be done.

Sheri regarded them both with hands on hips. "I need to get you a new alarm clock for your birthday, or what? And when is your birthday, anyway?" But she waved him off before he could not-answer, beset by instant visions of Sheri's idea of a birthday party. "No, no, never mind. If I can't learn that little goodie, I don't deserve to sit here in my position as queen of all."

"My alarm clock is fine," Dale informed her, a pathetic attempt at distraction.

She let him know it with a sideways cut of her eyes, then slapped a printout on the upper counter for him. "Today's schedule," she said. "Got you a ferret and a baby goat. Can't beat that."

"Not with a stick," Dale agreed faintly, not quite trusting Sheri's sudden turn to cheer. He slipped off Sully's lead and pointed down the hall. "Office," he said, sliding the sheet closer with a cautious finger to take a look for himself. "I'll be along." And Sully went, but after a few feet he disbelieved and stopped, checking to make sure Dale really, truly meant it.

But Dale's attention was well and truly caught, and not by a hopeful Beagle. "Hank's coming this morning? He's bringing that temper with teeth and you didn't warn me?"

"Hard enough to get you here on time as it is," Sheri said wisely, crossing her arms over her generous bosom, which bore serendipitously placed giant flowers this morning. So much for the tasteful scrub shirts.

Dale was about to give her a cross look. "*One* day I was late—"

Outside, a car door slammed. Outside, even through the single door closed between them, Dale heard the distinct sound of a very specific individual dog, growling to itself as it trotted along. "Grff—grff-grff!"

And the voice of Hank the mailman, once known as Humping Hank for his inexplicable attraction to dogs. For Hank never got bitten on his rounds . . . he only got humped. At least, until he'd adopted the little terrier mix who'd been orphaned by the spring's eco-killers. The same terrier mix who'd lived in the walls of this very building, ensuring that the remodeling went ahead with much purpose and vigor.

The same terrier mix who'd held them all hostage to its

temper. . . .

"Grff-grff-grff!"

Through the door, Hank's cheerful voice struck a note of adoration. "That's a good boy!" And when he opened the door, Dale abruptly realized that the dog was not on a lead. The animal bounded stiff-legged into the room. "Grff-grff-GRFFF!"

Dale found himself up on the high counter, working hard to maintain his dignity even as he fought the impulse to lift his legs higher. Just around the open corner, Sully's ears flattened; his tail tucked. He knew that challenge, and he knew he wanted nothing to do with it. He scuttled down the hall and into the office.

"Aww!" Hank gave the little terrier mix an affectionate glance, laughing as if he was sure the world would share his appreciation for its assertive claim of the world. The dog had gained a significant amount of weight in the past months, enough so Dale had him on weekly weigh-ins; he looked more like an expanding football with sandy wisps of terrier hair and jutting teeth than, say, a dog.

Hank had named him Frank N. Privileges. Great. Just what this dog needed, a terribly clever name. Now it looked up Dale and displayed its crooked bite in a snarl. "Grrrrrrrff!"

"Geeze, Hank, did you *tell* him he was coming in for heartworm testing today?"

"What? Oh, ha ha!" Hank's thin grey hair—long at the sides and back to make up for the fact that there wasn't any on top—was today drawn back in a straggling ponytail. His employee ID tag dangled jauntily off the collar point of his spiffily embroidered USPS navy polo shirt; it hung off his lanky shoulders and bumped off his hard, round little pot belly—which wasn't quite as big as it had been. Frank had apparently offered up new opportunities for exercise.

Hank and Frank. Dale barely restrained himself from slapping his forehead, and instead cleared his throat. "If you can get him leashed before anyone else arrives. . . ."

"Oh, right! Ha ha! Sorry. I thought that inside door would be closed . . . I was gonna get him then." Hank made a dive for the terrier. Expanding football or not, it had no difficulty skittering aside, nails loud on the tile. "Independent little fellow, isn't he?"

Dale wondered if he dared suggest a nail-clipping to go along with the weekly weigh-ins. He pondered his fingers. Then he pondered Dru. She could do it. She and the terrier were two of a kind.

"Here, now," Hank said. "I'll just slip this little piece of hot dog into my hand . . . you just watch."

Frank's beady little black eyes watched Hank's fingers dip into a sandwich bag of hot-dog pieces; as soon as the fingers were loaded, the dog took a few steps forward. Hank tossed the hot dog as a reward and went back for more. The dog skillfully acquired half a hot dog before moving close enough for Hank to put a slip lead over his head. "There," Hank said in triumph. "You see?"

"Yeah," Sheri said. "Lookit that."

"Suddenly," Dale said, eyeing the dog's barrel shape, "it all becomes clear to me."

"Works like a charm," Hank confirmed, all blithe pride. "This dog thing is working out so well, I'm thinking maybe Frank would like a little friend."

"I'm not so sure Frank is into sharing," Dale said.

"*I'm* sure." Sheri shifted on her chair and Dale suddenly realized that she'd somehow managed to get her feet up on the seat, cross-legged and out of Frank's reach, even though she was behind the counter and even though she substantially filled the chair even without adding feet.

Now that Frank was under control, Hank got that look in his eye. The Gossip Look. Little blue-haired old ladies at kaffeeklatsches had nothing on Hank. "Hey, did you see that kid in the paper this morning? The one with hanta? They don't know if he's gonna make it, poor little guy. Happens every year—kinda surprised we haven't seen more of it before this. Of course they're saying everyone should clean up their sheds and such. With precautions. What do you figure is precaution enough?"

"Misting down the area helps," Dale said, his thoughts on the boy. On Laura, and the tight worry in her eyes as he'd said good night the evening before. "Wearing a mask with a carbon filter lining, if you can keep it tight around the edges."

"You knew!" Hank looked at him with wounded accusation, and at first Dale thought he meant the precautions, and then he realized that Hank's specialized gossip sensor had detected not only his lack of surprise, but his inner grimness.

"You're right." Sheri narrowed her eyes. "He definitely knew. And that makes *another* thing he knew around here that I didn't. This isn't a good pattern, Dr. Dale."

"Laura's nephew," Dale said shortly. "He came in last night by chopper. They didn't diagnose him in time to be on top of the pulmonary phase of it."

Sheri startled as though he'd hit her; her bright red lips pressed together. She touched the picture stuck to the edge of the monitor . . . her son, Tremayne.

"And here I thought it was just more of your detective work in play, ha ha!" Hank said, not quite in synch with the changed mood. He did a double take of the bulletin board, the one in Sheri's domain, on the wall against which her counter butted up. "Hey, what's this?" He squinted, leaned forward, then back again as he found just the right distance for his bifocals. "Due to your expertise, this should be a . . . breeze?" He looked at Sheri. "What's that supposed to mean?"

"Dunno," she said, glancing at Dale to see how, in his current mood, he would take to the fact that she'd filched this note from his office. Dale widened his eyes at her in a way that should have been both warning and alarming, but apparently wasn't either. She relaxed visibly. "Figured if I put it there, someone would figure it out."

"Hmm," Hank said. "Hmmm. I know someone in the sorting room who's good at word games. I'll ask—"

"No," Dale said. Two quick, long-legged steps and he'd reached the note, snatched it, and backed out of the terrier's range again. "Seriously. I. . . ." *I really don't want the whole postal system spreading the word that the vet who solved those murders can't deal with a simple word game.* "I'd rather have some time to figure it out myself. You know . . . it's no fun when someone tells you the answer before you're ready."

He and Sheri both watched to see how Hank would take this. It percolated through Hank's consideration in an obvious journey, and then he gave a decisive nod. "Let me know when you're ready, then."

"Thanks." Dale tucked the note away in his back jeans pocket, giving Sheri enough of a hairy eyeball so she'd know she wasn't off the hook. If he hadn't been there, he could well imagine her making a copy of the thing for Hank to take with him.

And then he headed down the hall to make sure Sully was settled in before he came back to deal with Frank N. Privileges, taking the opportunity to tuck the note away in the file cabinet, the folder marked for Sully's records. When he turned around, expecting to see Sully curled into a tight Frank-deflecting ball, instead he found the dog sitting bolt upright on the Sullybed, fully attentive with his long ears pulled forward into Flying Nun mode and his forehead wearing Wrinkles of Thoughtful Attention. A square of white paper stuck to his lip.

just tasting. really.

Dale rolled his eyes. "Yeah, yeah," he said, beckoning the dog over. "Bring it over, then."

With a glance at the door—Sully hadn't forgotten Frank's presence, oh no—Sully moseyed over and sat juuust out of reach. But long legs, long arms . . . Dale bent over and whisked the paper free.

> *There's not much time to find me—*
> *I'm planning on another spree.*

CHAPTER 3

I'm planning on another spree. . . .

Spree of *what?* When? *And why tell me?*

Dale gave himself a mental kick—*pay attention, you're working with the dog*—and turned his attention back to Sully, even if he could literally *feel* the note in his jeans pocket, prickly and burning and puzzling.

Okay, so he should probably be doing something else with his lunch time. Paperwork, maybe. Shopping for a new alarm clock on-line. Writing that E-mail to Aunt Cily. Making sure Sheri kept this note to herself, if she'd seen it . . . except that would mean revealing its existence to her if she hadn't.

But those things were all indoors with the construction and the noise and the bother . . . and even if they, too, had taken lunch, Dale was ready to be away from it.

Sully was ready to be away from it.

So Dale slipped Sully's show lead over that blocky little hound head and they did circles in the parking lot, practicing a nice free show gait without breaking out of the trot, and practicing the slower "down and back" for an invisible judge, glad for the looming dark monsoon cloud cover between them and the intense summer sun, and even daring to hope for a little rain.

After a quick free-stack or two, in which Sully set himself up in a square stance for examination by the same invisible judge and received much in the way of cookies for reward, Dale swapped out leashes, gulped water and offered the same, and

39

they played around with heeling work for a while. Nothing intense . . . not when they'd just done show ring stuff. Dale turned it into a game of *keep up with me no matter where I go and what I do* and somehow there was always a soft cookie tidbit waiting if Sully made it there. A few moments of that and they were both panting, and Sully's tongue lolled out with laughter as he pranced beside Dale in a perfect heel.

For an instant.

Then his nose went up and his tail stiffened and *sniffysniffy* off he went, heading for the pile of construction debris—the temporary dumpster, the discarded pallets holding discarded wallboard, the jagged broken two-by-fours and warped old kennel runs.

Except Dale didn't follow. Dale saw it coming and stood his ground, so Sully hit the end of the leash, having already forgotten he was on it—no room in the mind of a Beagle for such small details when the *sniffy* hit—he simply spun around and ended up looking at Dale in mournful surprise. His tail wilted; the wrinkles of great thought appeared.

sniffy! mine!

"How about you get back here on heel, while I think about it?" Because Dale *was* thinking about it—thinking about Sully's eagerness at obedience class, at his earlier interest in this pile . . . at the construction worker's words of caution.

Thinking about Laura's nephew, and how it might be a good thing at that to have a dog who could reliably scent out mice.

Which meant . . . being allowed to scent out mice. Learning when to do it and when not to do it.

"I mean it," he said to Sully, who had only continued to stare, bringing his wrinkles of great thought to the singular conclusion that Dale couldn't possibly have meant what he'd said. Dale pointed at heel position. "Right here. Heel."

woe. the sniffy. . . .

"Trust me, son." Dale pointed. Still full of disbelief, Sully oozed back over toward a heel position, sat at the halfway mark, and looked hopefully up at Dale, who said, "Get serious."

poop. heel.

"Oh, look!" Dale said, reaching into the treat bag at his hip. "Suddenly you get cookies!"

OH COOKIES!!

And after he'd dispensed that little jackpot, Dale kept Sully on heel for another moment and then released him. "Okay," he said, "Find it!"

Sully burst out in a short chop bark of excitement and plunged his nose to the ground, with no clue as to *find it* but every realization that he'd been released to do what he wanted anyway. Dale let him sniff the construction debris a few moments and then took them on a walk around the clinic perimeter, around the new boarder runs that were starting up today, down along the wood line where there were smells aplenty but not of the mousie sort . . . and then back to the construction, where he held Sully back just long enough to frustrate the dog and then again encouraged him to *find it* as he let the leash go to its full six-foot length.

"Hey!"

The alto shout was authoritative and accusatory, and Dale stiffened . . . possibly even jumped a little, but he wasn't quite copping to it. He turned, not without apprehension, and discovered himself the sole target of a short, stout woman full of march and efficiency. She marched herself right up to Dale. "You work here, right? Didn't I see you earlier today?"

He'd taken off his Dr. Dale lab coat, so the neat polo shirt and jeans of the day weren't going to give her any clues, just as her faded band T-shirt gave him little to go on—stretched to the max across the chest, snug around a well-padded torso that looked every bit as strong as the shout she'd aimed his way.

Worn leather gloves stuck out of her back pocket, and her arms and neck looked as though she'd forgotten sunscreen way too many days in a row. "Yeah, I saw you," she decided. "Cute dog, he yours?" And though Dale opened his mouth, she didn't wait for an answer to that, either. "Look, you know that Mountain Air guy?"

"The AC guys?" Well, and heating, too, but this time of year Dale thought about the air-conditioning. In fact, after the ring work, the heel romping, and their little walk, he was thinking really hard about air-conditioning. He scruffed his hair off his forehead and looked up at the glowering clouds. "Squeeze out some rain, why don't you?"

"What?" She looked startled, freckles all across her face opening up with her expression, as though hers was the only conversation she'd expected to have. "Rain. Right. Thing is, they were supposed to have that back area cleared out by now. You know anything about that? That one fellow . . . damn, I can't stand his kind. Doesn't get things done, can't be found when you need to know *when* he'll get things done. . . ."

And because Dale had so gladly left the daily construction details in Sheri's capable hands, he couldn't do anything more than shrug, as Sully tugged on the lead, rooting and snorting at the edges of the construction pile. "Sheri's the one to ask—the clinic receptionist. She knows pretty much everything that goes on around here."

The woman snorted. "The vets sure don't. Haven't seen hide nor hair of them. Typical. Too good to talk to the hired help. Probably old and snorty, anyway. So far it's just been that bossy Dru woman."

Dale made a startled noise, turned it into a cough. "I'm sure if you want to talk to the vets—"

"Doesn't matter so much—whoever'll get things moving back there. We can't pour foundation until that old duct work at the end is pulled, and I can't tell what's still attached to what, to move it myself."

"Well, you don't want to talk to the vets, then," Dale said. "They're shorthanded right now or something, all booked up with the summer load. Besides, it's always the people who keep things going who really know what's happening, right?"

She grinned. "Got that right."

"I'd stick with Dru." Dale took an unthinking step backward as Sully insisted on more lead, snorting mightily away at scent. "She gets things done."

"Yeah? Thanks. But that duct guy still needs a kick in the butt. John something. Or Ben."

Dale decided not to mention that the two names were nothing alike. In fact, even if he'd considered it he wouldn't have had a chance, for the woman's expression opened back out into startled and she said, "Didn't think a dog that size could fit under one of those pallets. That's what . . . four inches?"

Dale pulled a startled pivot to discover indeed, Sully had managed to worm his way beneath a pallet, his body turned partly sideways and his back end still splayed out behind, toes digging into the packed dirt, tail still sticking straight up, and all of his personal attributes fully displayed to the world.

"You must be one of those," the woman said, giving him a dismissive sideways look.

"One of those?" Dale repeated before he could stop himself. In truth, his mind was fully occupied in wondering whether Sully would come out from beneath the four-inch pallet as easily as he'd gone under it. How he'd managed entry was no big mystery—to judge from the snuffling noises, he'd used the vacuum effect of his mighty scent-hound nose.

"Sure," the woman said. "Identify with your dog, can't bear to have him neutered, better to let him be manly and run around producing little strays than to do the responsible thing—"

"Whoa!" Dale drew himself up tall, which in effect cut her off short. Cast assumed aspersions on his veterinarian self, okay, but on his Sully management? "He's still entire because he's showing in the breed ring, and he'll be entire until we're done with that. And even at that, he's just eighteen months, which isn't so much beyond the point that his growth plates have closed, so if I ever want to do agility with him then I wouldn't have neutered him much sooner than this anyway. Not to mention that I'll do his breeder the courtesy of checking before I do neuter him, in case she wants to breed to him. But I don't think she will; she has plenty of good dogs of her own. And *then* I'll neuter him."

"Geeze," she said, drawing back in affront. "I only meant—"

"Hey!" Dru poked her head out the side door, the one that led to Dale's office. "Dr. Dale! Car versus dog, on the way in! Sheri says *snap, snap!*"

Dale raised a hand and Dru did a chin lift of acknowledgment, disappearing back inside. "Hey, Sully. Gotta head back to work. Tell me you're not really stuck." He gave the leash an experimental tug. Sully's hind legs flexed and scrabbled and Sully grunted and squirmed and made a frustrated noise.

"You—?" the woman said. "But—"

Dale crouched by Sully, who had paused to take stock, and said, "Yup, me." He gave Sully a pat on the haunch and said, "Relax, son. Not unlike being born, I should think." And he did a quick test, moving Sully's leg's slightly to see that the dog had given himself up to Dale's hands. Finding acquiescence, he quickly flipped Sully all the way over on his side and slid him out from beneath the pallet. "See? Welcome to the world."

Sully squinted into the daylight, the sun sparking brightly from between two glowering sets of clouds. He sneezed, shook himself off, and looked up at Dale with his *let's do it again* face, tail wagging.

Dru reappeared. "Snap, snap!" Disappeared.

Sully tugged at his leash. *mouse. mine?*

"Later," Dale told him. "Gotta go."

"But—" the woman said, her confusion mixed with the very visible realization that she'd been talking to the man who wrote the checks.

Sully let his legs go out from under him in a tactic worthy of a two-year-old, stretching his nose toward the shallow pallet cave with the strength of his want. Dale scooped him up and told the woman, "Gotta go. Or, as we clueless snorty old vets with identity issues like to say. . . ."

"Oh, Gawd," she groaned, and hid her face in her hands.

Dale grinned, and said it anyway. *"Snip, snip!"*

He'd promised Sully they'd go back, and they did. With the construction debris as their guaranteed jackpot, he worked the game around the clinic grounds, using it as a reward for their obedience and ring work until the mere mention of the words *find it* sent Sully into quivering attention. He worked the woods and the torn-up back area of the clinic and even the indoor boarding area, and somewhere along the way he figured out that the sooner he heeled nicely, the sooner he got to his next sniffy hunt.

Not that they caught any mice. But Dale had a pretty good idea where to set the traps if he decided to clean the place up after the construction was done. And if he got skeptical looks when Dru and Sheri and Isaac and Brad and Jade eventually all figured out what he was up to—Dru in particular being pretty sure she already knew where to set a mouse trap if it became necessary—he also found himself thinking more about Laura's sick nephew and more about how he'd gotten sick and more about how his transplanted Midwestern self still had a lot to learn about living in this area.

And so he found himself, on Saturday morning, out on the oversized patio dog bed, hiding from the bright morning sun with the phone to his ear while Laura's cell phone rang. And rang.

Please, not the voice mail. It was nothing if not an invitation to babble incomprehensibly while never quite leaving the reason for the call.

No doubt she was at the hospital. . . . Saturday afternoon, and her Pine Country clinic hours were over. Unless she'd been called in to—

"Hello?" Laura's voice sounded breathless, and not a little frustrated.

"Want to clean sheds together?" Dale blurted.

A long pause, not the least undeserved. And then a cautious "Dale?"

"Oh. Right." He cleared his throat, leaning back on the dog bed. The dog himself was out in the main yard, wandering its fenced confines in search of stink beetles and horny toads. "I was just thinking. . . ."

"Sheds," she said. "Cleaning. Sure, if nothing . . ."—she took a breath—"goes wrong."

Dale had picked up on her habit of not referring to the boy by name—a Navajo custom that had lingered with her, and which she'd now deliberately revived out of respect to her cousin's stronger traditions. "How is he?"

"Still trying not to die," Laura said with a more normal asperity. But she sighed, and a moment into the following silence she said, "I'm sorry. I'm wrestling with frybread . . . I want her to have something familiar in case she comes home hungry."

"Sounds as though the frybread might be winning." But he said it with sympathy.

His reward was the smile in her voice. "There are still a couple rounds to go. I won't be able to break away until afternoon, though—it'll be pretty hot by then."

"Unless it rains," Dale said, heavy on the cheerful optimism. There were already clouds building up over the Peaks; maybe today would be the day. "Either way, we'll be inside. More or less. And if it's too hot . . . well, that's what the hose is for, right?"

"Well, hmm." She said it just like that, *well, hmm.* Giving it obvious thought.

"I've got the bleach," Dale said. "And a sprayer. And gloves. And quite possibly, a mouse detector."

"That's some significant sweet-talking," she informed him.

"Seriously," he said, suddenly glad she couldn't see him there on the dog bed, phone at his ear, losing a stare-down with the lizard peering down on him from the patio's three-quarter wall. Not a person to be taken seriously. "I don't know about your shed, but that little outbuilding of mine hasn't seen a cleaning since before I moved in. I tossed the weed whacker in there along with a shovel and the rake, and haven't been in there since."

"It's time," Laura agreed, an embarrassed tinge to her voice that told him she was thinking of her own shed.

"I'll come over, then," he said, daring to push it because they'd missed their dinner date after all—Laura had been at the hospital. "One o'clock." He heard the intake of breath that meant she was about to protest, and said, "Just call me if it doesn't work out, okay? I'm puzzling this morning."

"In fact," she informed him, "you're puzzling most of the time." But she laughed as she hung up.

"In the *puzzle room,*" Dale said to the severed connection. "The *puzzle room.*" But he knew she knew, and he grinned as he got to his feet and headed inside to the spare bedroom, where he'd already spread the new Neuschwanstein over his gi-ant raised puzzle table. New puzzle . . . still loaded with puzzle dust. He grabbed the water bottle, spritzed over the table, and settled in for some air-conditioned, puzzle-assisted meditation. It always worked.

Always.

Always.

Some old swing music in the background, Sully's tail trotting by the huge picture window on a clear mission of importance, ceiling fan lazily stirring the ceiling. . . .

Apparently not always.

He didn't see puzzle pieces. He saw Laura's expression when she'd told him about her nephew. Robert. He saw her struggling to deal with the concept of reaching out for help—a little confused by it, a little resentful . . . a little frightened. A lot reluctant.

An independent woman who had never learned that leaning on someone could make her stronger, not weaker.

Not that Dale had learned that lesson easily himself. Aunt Cily had taught him once when he was young and again when the clinic burned. And then, after helping him pick himself up and dust off the soot and ashes and grief, she'd helped him fly off across the country to start over. Stronger than he'd been, in a number of ways—because when he'd gotten here, he hadn't been afraid to reach out to the new people in his life.

Not even the ones who called him Mr. Dr. Dale with a smart-ass twinkle, or the ones who ran roughshod over his clinic edicts, or even Laura herself.

It only made him want to make things easier for her, which she hadn't asked him to do. And it made him want to hold her, but then again . . . nothing new about that.

And later that day he'd be there, but for now . . . he could only wrestle with wanting to be there.

Finally, he gave up on the puzzle. Building puzzles, hunting answers . . . they were all a way of driving forward to a solution.

He didn't have answers to those things in his past . . . he found it damned hard to give up on hunting them for the things in his present and hopefully in his future.

He headed for the den, where the laptop hummed away, already open to the E-mail program as a reminder that he owed Aunt Cily an E-mail. Or two. Or . . . yeah, or more.

Dear Aunt Cily. . . .

Everyone should have an Aunt Cily. Possibly not as a surrogate parent along with his Uncle Bud—who years ago had become just "Bud"—but simply to have an Aunt Cily. Cecilia, she was, and so possessed of common sense and motherly instinct and understanding that it was inevitable she be nicknamed Cily, and that she raise him as her own in her previously empty house when his parents had died in the early house fire. Inevitable, too, that he adore her . . . and miss her, and still turn to her for advice even if he never asked for it outright. Grown man and all that.

And yet he stared at the blinking cursor, fingers uninspired, words not flowing. He played with the touch pad, twiddling the cursor around the screen. Did he really want to tell her that he'd rearranged furniture at Laura's? Or that Sully had reasserted his mighty hunter's nature in obedience class? Or that the construction wasn't done yet . . . again?

"It all seemed interesting along the way," he said out loud, as if Sully was even there, or as if he'd have been listening if he was. And that seemed like a good excuse to open the patio sliding doors—but Sully must have been involved in something of great interest; he failed to appear. Dale made sure the outdoor water bucket was full, put a mental wish out to the universe that the something of great interest have nothing to do with anything dead and smelly, and returned inside to pull the laptop from the counter to the floor, where it plugged into a very short length of Internet cable. He sat cross-legged on a pad of orthopedic foam for aging pets, swore once more that he'd remember to buy a longer cable, and promised he'd write that E-mail *real soon now* as he fired up his browser to see what he didn't already know about hanta.

Transmissible by rodents. He knew that. He'd even known that the deer mouse was the most likely carrier, but no one took chances with any rodent. Besides, mouse poop was mouse poop. Dale never wanted to reach the point where he could tell which species of mouse pooped which poop.

He'd known it was caused by the *Sin Nombre* virus; he'd known that it was a rodent-human thing, and that various pets and other wildlife were out of the picture. He hadn't known there were strip blot tests to diagnose the thing, which made him wonder how the boy had gotten to the acute phase of the illness before anyone suspected. Days of aches and pains and fever and various other woes . . . but the aches had a pattern, hanging in the back and legs, and once the boy began having trouble breathing. . . .

They just hadn't been looking for it. Not in a year so dry, so hard on animal populations everywhere. There'd been one early death on the reservation near Tuba City, an older man who hadn't been able to fight the virus. And there hadn't been any since—

Oh, ho! Dale scrolled back up the list of URLs that Google had returned to him. Almost missed that one—a link to an archived article from the *Navajo Times*. There beside reservation political cartoons he didn't understand and doubted he ever would was a list of recent articles, and in that list was the headline:

Cameron Man Dies of Hanta

Informational gold mine! He learned about the averages—fifty people a year in the state, thirty to fifty percent mortality, depending on whether the big outbreak of '93 counted or not. And once it went pulmonary, it. . . .

It was bad.

The dog door flap heralded Sully's arrival with a hollow thwack of sound; he ambled into the den, following his nose, and sat down at Dale's knee.

me.

And Dale thought about that high mortality rate and decided that Laura didn't need to know right now.

me.

On the other hand, if you were going to die, it generally happened very quickly. And if they got the boy on ECMO—the heart-lung machine—right after he arrived. . . .

Laura would know that. But Dale couldn't ask without making her wonder why. He'd learned fast enough—he couldn't keep a secret from Laura. She was too smart, too perceptive . . . she damned well saw right through his feeble attempts to not be thinking about something, and once she asked him straight out. . . .

Well, he just told her.

me!

The dead Cameron man had been forty-five, in excellent shape, owned his own company, and his tearful relatives swore he hadn't been stirring up dust, cleaning outbuildings, or even spending much time at home. "Too busy," they said, with his successful business. A good husband, a good father . . . a family man setting an example for the reservation youth.

ME!

Sully's bid for attention exploded in a sudden bark, startling Sully as much as it did Dale. Dale's fingers skittered across the laptop touchpad, giving the browser so many commands at once that it locked up on him and then declared its urgent need to *end program*. Sully gave him a sheepish look . . . but not for long. *me.*

"It certainly is." Dale set the laptop aside to be miserable about itself and snatched Sully up with no warning, flipping him upside down in the cradle of his own crossed legs and mercilessly tickling him. Sully went "Wah-wah-wah!" in a cross between a whine and a protest, until Dale flipped him back upright with his legs scrabbling like a cartoon dog; as soon as his feet touched the ground he scooted away at top speed.

beagle ha! *i win!*

And at that, Dale rose to his feet, rubbed the carpet pattern from the back of his legs and the laptop print from his thighs, and grabbed up Sully's leashes—the show lead, for handling practice. The thin leather lead and lightweight chain collar for rally. And of course, the bag of treats to clip to the waist of his cutoff jeans.

Suddenly Sully was back, sitting alertly as if he hadn't just frapped off into silliness.

cookies. i think i'll eat them.

"Sorry," Dale said to Laura, as Sully sniffed wildly around the edges of Laura's shed, unconvinced that failure once meant failure twice. "I thought he'd be settled down. We trained before he came over to take the edge off, too. Ever since he got that first sniff of mouse at work—"

"In the clinic?" Laura stopped in mid-exodus with a storage bin from the shed, looking at him with nose wrinkled. She gave herself shade with an old ball cap with a faded logo, her braided hair threaded through the back. Dale had opted for his already battered straw cowboy hat, folded up narrow along the sides and pulled down in front. Ohio-born, like Dale.

"Outside," he told Laura, "in that pile of construction junk that might just be there forever. When the painters showed up, I thought there might be hope this project would eventually come to an end . . . but then the furnace guys chased them out before they were done." Not that Dale was sorry to see them go. Ladders everywhere, drop cloths and giant spackle and paint cans. And so far that was just the detail work. "But the work is getting there. And the new surgery closet—"

She gave him a sharp look, bending over to place the bin beside a stack of old flower pots. Dale lost his train of thought for a moment, watching this process. She said, "If you want it bigger, make it bigger."

"Actually, it's just the right size," he said, somewhat reverently—and then hastily pretended he'd been talking about the surgery closet, ever so grateful the words fit so well. "But it makes Dru's hair stand on end when I call it a closet, so I've gotten into the habit."

"Dru's hair stands on end regardless," Laura pointed out as she straightened, which was only the truth. "I think that's as far as we can go . . . anything more and we'll start stirring up dust. Take your mask and your mighty hand sprayer and see if you can't soak down everything in the front part of the shed, at least."

Dale pulled his carbon filter–lined mask up and then so-suavely whipped a bandana out of his back pocket and tied it over the mask. "It's more stylish," he said, perceiving from her raised eyebrow that explanation was needed. It was, in fact, simply more silly—and it had made her smile.

He ducked into the hot shed and held the sprayer low, soaking the shed dust with the bleach solution. In the corners, along the walls, and especially into the old bundle of scraps and paper and soft grass that had become visible as Laura removed the last of the storage tubs. *Mouse nest.* He'd certainly seen enough of them in rural Ohio to know. And heard enough of that sudden *rustlerustlerustle* to recognize a small rodent on the run, flushed from hiding by Dale's presence and heading for escape. "Oh *ho*," he said softly, double-checking along the sides of the shed until he found the tiniest of holes beneath the side of the old wooden structure. He soaked the area with bleach just because it seemed like a good idea, and backed out of the shed, just barely ducking enough to miss banging his head on the door lintel.

"Oh, ho?" Laura asked, stopped in the act of shaking out a new trash bag to receive the sodden shed sweepings. Or what would be sweepings if they weren't so wet they'd do better with the small flat-end shovel now leaning against the outside of the building.

Dale took a deep breath, still somewhat marveling that he could do so at all. Maybe it would pass this time, this asthma. Maybe it already was. He'd grown out of it once. . . .

Not this time, the doctors had said. He could draw that deep breath because he'd finally grown up in a different way, and started paying attention to the maintenance regimen they'd given him.

Still. Bright blue desert sky all around, monsoon clouds building up over the Peaks, horny toad basking in the sun over in the corner of this Xeriscaped yard, the hot high-altitude sun sizzling in the dry heat of the day . . . totally, inescapably beautiful. And good company to top it all off. She hadn't yet spoken of the boy, but Dale knew she would when she was ready.

"Oh, ho," he said, finally cued by her expression that it was time to come back to the conversation, "because I heard the scamper of little feet."

Laura reached for the shovel, which suddenly looked much more like a guillotine than it had just a moment earlier. "Still in there?"

From the back of the shed came a bark-squeak of stunned

joy, followed by a short scuffle. Sully came scrabbling around the corner at high speed, each leap a choppy unsuccessful *pounce* until coincidence happened to favor him and the fleeing mouse ended *pounce* under his *pounce* front paws.

Dale froze in disbelief. Laura laughed out loud. And Sully, after a flabbergasted double take, snatched the mouse up in his front teeth, shook it sharply, and flipped it up into the air, swallowing it on the way down.

Dale said, "Wuh!"

Laura said, "A mouser!"

Sully looked momentarily distressed, as if he'd had no intention of doing any of that, and his body had just gone and taken over.

And then, of course, he burped.

i think i ate it.

"Digest that well," Dale told Sully with mock sternness. "I don't want to see it again at three this morning."

"They think he'll be all right," Laura said abruptly, and looked just as surprised to have said it as Sully had looked about eating the mouse.

Dale felt the relief wash over him—not only for the boy's chances, but because Laura was, indeed, talking about it. "He's improving?"

"Not yet." She didn't look at him but almost at him, and he wondered if she truly didn't realize how much of her early life had stayed with her. She didn't assume on his space, she didn't point, she had a distinct style of listening—and if she didn't wait inside her vehicle upon arrival at his home, she did usually linger outside until he'd come to the door himself—a custom that didn't always translate effectively to an era of television and CD players.

And then, as if aware of his scrutiny, her gaze shifted directly to his and she said bluntly, "But he's not dead yet."

"That's good," Dale said, thinking about how most deaths occurred within very short order of the pulmonary phase, and that the boy truly had a chance to recover if he'd made it this long even if he was on heart-lung. And then he suddenly realized what he'd said, how it sounded out of the context of his own thoughts. "I mean, of course that's good. I was just thinking. . . ."

Laura gave him a look. He let the sentence fade away, and then realized, "You knew that."

"I knew that," she told him. "Now let's go clean out some mouse poop."

CHAPTER 4

The silence of the clinic surrounded Dale. Not late this morning, oh no. Not-late by design. He wanted the time to avoid the noise of construction, the scrutiny of his office manager . . . to stare at this note.

The first note had merely been baffling. But the second. . . .

His attention to it had been delayed by his concern for Laura and her nephew, the chaos of the remodeling . . . a difficult couple of days at the clinic. And now, seriously early on a Monday morning, the chaos would resume soon. No, not soon   *imminently.* All the weekend accidents and illnesses and walk-ins, inundating the morning. Sheri left room for it in the schedule, but "all at once" was the Monday motto. And the construction workers would arrive soon, and Dale half-expected to see the Wilsons today, grim with their final decision about their beloved old boy.

And still he had these notes.

> *Due to your expertise,*
> *This should be a breeze.*

Okay, innocuous enough. Annoying, with the implication that he should be doing something; annoying that it had been left anonymously on the doorstep, so to speak. But not hard to set aside in of itself, even for a puzzle-lover.

But none of that applied to the second note. On his desk. *In his office.* His very own turf, where only Sheri freely tread and even then she stopped to give a token knock if he was there, and knew she'd pay the Sully-petting toll.

There's not much time to find me—
I'm planning on another spree.

Not innocuous at all. A spree of *what?* Something that needed to be stopped, that seemed clear enough. But then why tell Dale about it all?

Taunting, that's what it was.

Fine. Taunting. Why *taunt* Dale about it? What was he expected to do? And why? And what would happen if he didn't?

"Ahhh," he grumbled, and tossed the notes back to the desk. Totally unsatisfactory. He was looking for revelations, not the *duh* effect. For something with a *wuh* effect.

Dru.

Dru had *wuh* to spare. Dru also had a good lot of common sense hidden under her abrasive nature, and had proven herself a reliable confidante when he'd had to call for help shortly after his arrival, out and about and in trouble without his inhaler— for Dale didn't talk about the fires or the asthma.

Laura knew; Sheri probably suspected. And Dru hadn't even asked. She'd brought his rescue inhaler and she'd snorted at his carelessness and she hadn't told a soul.

"You'll want to stay here," Dale told Sully. "I'm heading for the kennel."

Sully pretended not to care, and inspected the windowsill for dead flies. *busy.*

Dale wasn't convinced. He'd inspect the Sullybed for stolen goods when he returned.

He found Dru in the food room. There, metal shelves held a variety of specialty diets for their clients, and a decent kibble for their boarders. The hospital boarders had a too-small room to themselves, but the clinic also had a row of indoor/outdoor kennels for pets who needed more medical supervision than a standard boarding kennel could provide. Dru was the one who supervised these areas, eyeing each temporary resident with the same eagle eye she applied to her grandchildren and, Dale knew, occasionally to Dale himself.

"Mr. Dr. Dale!" Dru said, stacking dog bowls to dry by the side of the giant tub sink. "Well, if it isn't himself, taking time from his busy schedule to visit the lowly kennel. Say, isn't tomorrow surgery day?"

"I'm right there," he pointed out to her. "You'll never get to the scrotal remains before I do."

"I don't have to be first," she said. She pulled a clipboard from its hook on the wall, unmindful of the water she smeared across the laser-printed feeding and medications chart. "I just have to be smarter. Do I look worried?"

Dale waited as she double-checked the meals. The waiting itself must have alerted her; when she finished, she hung the clipboard up with a crisp smack and crossed her arms beneath a bosom that must have once been impressive. Grandmother many times over, waist and hips merged into one, that short bristled hair an unapologetic grey and a pack of cigarettes jammed unopened into the patch pocket at the hem of the scrub top she wore—that was classic Dru. When Dale had arrived that spring, the cigarettes were open and in frequent use, but Dru's oldest grandchild had recently sobbed her into quitting.

Somewhat warily—*what was I thinking?*—he asked, "You know about the notes?"

"Mr. Dr. Dale, honey, does Sheri know about the notes?"

"Point taken." So she *had* seen the second note . . . and if Sheri knew, everyone knew. "You have any ideas?"

"Who wrote 'em? Someone who thinks he's clever." She snorted her judgment of said cleverness. "But I don't think it's one of us."

"My *office*—"

"Hardly Fort Knox." Dru reached for the cigarettes, hesitated, and withdrew her hand. "It's one door past the bathroom. We send people down that way all the time. And that back hall door doesn't get locked like it should, what with this endless redecoration we've got going on."

Dale smacked his own forehead over the thought of the ongoing construction. "Why I ever thought this would be a good idea—"

"It *is* a good idea," Dru asserted in her *are you stupid* voice, which was basically her normal voice. "It just sucks."

"Your *grandchildren* kiss that mouth."

"So does your dog."

Dale shuddered at the logic, shook it off. "Listen," he said. "If you see anyone . . . or know of anyone. . . ."

Dru narrowed her eyes at him. "You're really worried."

He shrugged. "It's just a feeling."

She laughed shortly. "Right. Not worth a damned thing."

"Sarcasm will make your face fall off," Dale informed her. But he'd seen that flash of understanding—knew that she was on alert. Sheri might *think* she knew everything that went on here . . . but Dru was the one who saw the things no one else noticed, and who put together the pieces, and who didn't then necessarily think anyone else needed to know.

"Watch out for the painters," she told him. "That's who we got today. The duct guys ran off to do someone else's rush job, and Sheri got the painters back to deal with your little surgery closet and heaven forbid, that back hallway."

"Aurgh," Dale said. "I'd have left Sully at home if I'd known."

Dru gave him a knowing look. "Uh-huh," she said. "Now shoo. Some of us have to work."

Dale shooed. It was enough, after all—he'd set Dru's mind in motion. And from the hall—soon apparently to be festooned with ladders and buckets and painters—he could hear noises of occupancy from Sheri's corner of the world—rustling papers, the computer firing up with its beeps of complaint and warning, Sheri humming some unknown tune in a melodious voice she generally kept to herself and her son. He hummed along with her a moment, deciding to look forward to the day. It might be Monday Chaos, but Brad would be in at eleven to cover the lunch hours and they'd work through the afternoon together, pinch-hitting as necessary. It was a teamwork Dale enjoyed; if Brad was an uninspired vet, he was also utterly reliable, and didn't trip over his ego if it came time to consult.

He headed for the file cabinet to grab a scrub shirt, and found it gone. "I could have sworn—"

No, he hadn't. He'd been lazy and he'd left the clean shirt on top of a row of books on the back bookshelf. Right there, beside the dead spider plant he hadn't had the heart to upend out back. Right there in that empty spot.

He turned on his heel to target the Sullybed behind his desk, *mine.*

Well. That was why Sheri kept an extra clean one at her command center.

"He's just not eating right." The Shih-Tzu mix's owner gave the dog a concerned look, ably ignoring the two young children hanging off her arms.

Hanging, swinging, tugging. . . . Dale squelched the sudden impulse to snap a stern, "Sit! Stay!" at the boy and girl and glanced again at the dog's chart. Five pounds lost. Not that the little fellow hadn't needed it, but mystery weight loss was no good however you looked at it.

The Shih-Tzu mix looked back at him with big round soulful eyes, his undershot jaw barely visible through the abundance of archetypal Scruffy Dog facial hair. Dale followed his first impulse and gently lifted the dog's lips for a look at his teeth.

Ew, yuck. But that wasn't the impressive veterinary thing to say, so he cleared his throat and went back to the paperwork. "When was the last time he had a tooth cleaning?" The dog's name was right there—*Scoofball*—but Dale couldn't quite bring himself to use it.

Scoofball's owner blinked. "The last time . . . ? Is that something we need to do?" Her last words went vibrato as the boy used her arm for a bungee cord. The dog settled down on the exam table and put his chin on his paws, his eyes rolling to stay glued to Dale.

Dale gave the dog a pat. "It's the price we pay for the convenience of kibble," he said. "And your little fellow has a bad bite, which keeps his mouth dryer and throws off the balance of things in there; he's young for this kind of trouble. Here, look." He exposed the dog's teeth toward the back of its mouth, where the tartar and gum disease was graphically severe. "Can you imagine those teeth in your own mouth?"

"That's disgusting," she said.

"It is, isn't it?" he agreed cheerfully. "For now, I'd suggest soaking his kibble. But unless you schedule a cleaning, this is only going to get worse. Gums like these can lead to systemic issues, spreading infection to vulnerable spots in the body."

"He *does* have bad breath," she observed, transferring the girl to the same arm as the boy so she could tip the dog's face up to look at her.

"Once his teeth have been cleaned"—*and half of them removed*—"you can start a brushing regimen to prevent things from getting this bad in the future."

She gave him a most dubious look.

"Most dogs don't mind it," he assured her. "And we have some special products for problem mouths." He unwrapped his stethoscope from his neck. "Just let me check him out and make sure we're not missing anything, and Sheri will get you set up with an estimate and appointment for a cleaning."

So he listened to the dog's heart, and then was obliged to listen to various parts of the children, including their heads which he pronounced empty to their great giggles. They shrieked at the thermometer insertion; the dog only heaved a sigh. Dale imagined that after living with these two particular perpetual motion machines, a thermometer up the butt might not seem all that profound. As expected, the dog otherwise checked out normally, and before long he left owner, children, and dog to Sheri's firm guidance, hesitating at the counter to scribble a few additional notes in the dog's file. Off to his right, a drop cloth stretched down the hallway; a ladder blocked the hall by the exit, no doubt constituting some illegal fire hazard. An anonymous figure in white coveralls bent over an open can of spackle.

Dale resigned himself to working with the odors of paint and spackle and flipped Scoofball's chart closed as the family migrated for the air-lock door, looking more like an atom with vibrating electrons than a woman with children and dog.

And that's when the notes caught his eye. Both of them, up on Sheri's bulletin board.

"Sheri," he said. The growl in his voice took her by obvious surprise. It had taken him by surprise too, to tell the truth. "Taking things from my desk. Off-limits."

She blinked. "The more people know about those notes, the better chance we have of figuring them out—"

"I don't care if we figure them out." Blatant lie, but they were the words that came out of his mouth. "The notes are nothing, Sheri. I don't want to make them into *something*."

She looked at him a long moment, lips pursed, eyes narrowed. Trying to read through to the center of him. He didn't think she'd managed it but she eventually gave a short nod of agreement anyway. "All right," she said. "The notes are nothing." She plucked them down from the bulletin board and pushed them across the counter at him, somewhat the worse for wear after several sessions in his pockets. "But this don't mean I'm giving up my power."

He jammed the notes into his pocket one final time. "You *are* the power," he intoned in his best Movie Announcer Voice, very nearly inciting her to lose her stern cover and giggle. But her gaze fell on the schedule, and her expression changed so fast that he knew what was coming, no matter how reluctantly she said it.

"The Wilsons are in room two," she said. "They said they'd wait for you."

Dale swallowed against that sudden constriction in his throat. Right. He'd known it was coming. And it would be a mercy.

The phone gave a muted ring; Sheri picked it up and handed Dale the Wilson file at the same time—then held up her finger before he turned to go. When he looked back at her, she pointed at him. *For you,* that meant. And that he wouldn't want to wait for this one.

"Tell the Wilsons I'll be right with them," Dale said, and headed down the hall, treading cautiously on the uneven drop cloth. The sharp odor of spackle and paint permeated the air.

In the office, he found Sully in tight ball mode, having thoroughly incorporated the scrub shirt into his bed and working on combining the molecules of shirt and bed together. *mine.*

"Totally right, dude," Dale muttered at him. "Don't think I want it back." Casually, so casually, he opened the top corner desk drawer that held the overflowing bowl of dog food. Sully instantly translocated to stand in front of Dale, stacking himself in a show position just in case that might be what Dale wanted. He got a piece of kibble on principle, and then went into a *sit* at Dale's silent hand signal. *cookie.* And down. *cookie.* And sit again. *cookie, cookie.* All that while Dale reached for the phone, and then they were done. Sully knew there'd be no working for kibble as long as Dale's hand held the phone, but he gave the drawer a reluctant look and decided to hang around just in case.

"Hey, it's Dale," Dale told the phone, on the assumption that Sheri would have told him if he should have been wearing his company manners. But there was only silence on the phone, and he suddenly doubted that assumption, and then he thought to the threatening calls of that spring and was startled by the sudden tingle of tension of it—and then he heard an intake of breath that seemed so familiar he didn't think before saying, "Laura?"

"He's going to be okay." Yes, Laura. But her voice was odd . . . strained.

"Laura, are you—" Her words struck him, then. "That's great! But are you—"

And then he stopped, as it belatedly occurred to him that maybe she didn't want him to point out that she was crying in her relief. Quite obviously crying—and, it seemed, as taken by surprise by it as he was. So he said again, "That's great. How's Mary? Will he be staying at your place to recover? You need somewhere else to bunk?"

Good God. You and your mouth. No cookie.

But Laura laughed out loud. "And that," she said, "is why I called *you*."

"Because I always have absolutely no idea of the right thing to say?" Dale asked. That, too, was his mouth getting ahead of his brain. The only surprising thing was that he hadn't resigned himself to it by now.

"Something like that." And the tears were still in her voice, but so was a smile. "And no, I'm good. Once he's released, they'll stay with me for outpatient respiratory therapy until he's cleared to go home."

He resisted the temptation to point out that hers was a small house. "Good," he said. "I'm glad you called. I'm about to. . . ." He let his words trail off without truly realizing it, his thoughts going to the Wilsons and their dog.

But Laura had been there, done that. "I'm sorry," she said. "I hope it's an easy one."

"It's time," Dale said simply, and surprised himself with a sharp, dry little cough. Sully's ears flattened; he inched closer to Dale's leg and leaned.

Laura didn't say anything—but she didn't have to. "Damn," Dale said. "I guess the construction's got me closer to the limit than I thought. They're painting the hallway."

"You've done well to get this far without trouble," she pointed out. "Maybe I should have invited you to work at *my* clinic for the summer."

"Maybe you should have," Dale said, unable to keep the hangdog out of his voice. "Brad's coming in . . . and Sheri kept the schedule light for the Monday people."

"The Monday people will just have to wait until Tuesday?" Laura guessed.

Before Arizona, before Laura, he would have toughed out the paint fumes and then paid for it. Now. . . .

"Looks that way," he said, suddenly aware that yes, he had that tight burn in his chest . . . faint, like an undertone, but something he'd learned to heed. "After I take care of this one thing." He'd do paperwork; there was plenty of it waiting. He'd take Sully out for a slow walk. He'd work on the new puzzle. He'd. . . .

He had the feeling there was something going undone, something he ought to be thinking of but wasn't. But he shook it off, stifling another cough and stifling his faint unease at the same time. The Wilsons, and then he'd grab his paperwork and go.

As simple as that.

stinky. stinky intruders everywhere. stinky buckets everywhere. stinky equipment *everywhere.* in *my* place. mine.

i could just lift my—

no. dale doesn't like that. and dale made the bad cough. be good, dale. be good. i'll be very good too. even with that musky dusky intruder all the way *here in the office.* in my head i will bite! fierce!

my place.

my desk, my bed, my cookie drawer. my dale.

mine.

stay out.

CHAPTER 5

Dale spread office paperwork out on the bar-height counter dividing the kitchen and the living room, and wound his long legs around the legs of a slightly wobbly stool. He could have been in his den to work . . . *should* have been in his den. But here, indirect skylight sunlight made the fireplace flagstone bright, turned the cathedral ceiling light and airy. Here, it didn't quite feel as much like work.

Or maybe that was because, heh heh, he hadn't actually started the work. Instead, he'd finally turned his attention back to that long-delayed E-mail for patient Aunt Cily. Amazing how the thing he'd been procrastinating suddenly became easy when he now had other things begging for priority procrastination.

Dear Aunt Cily,

Some things are universal. Deer mice, for instance. Except out here they carry hanta, and Laura's nephew has somehow paid the price for that—even though his mother swears he had no reason to be in contact with them, and her older brother had cleaned their outbuildings only weeks before the boy got sick. It's one of those unanswered questions. I hate those.

I will now pause so you can counsel me to patience and remind me I can't resolve everything and no, we might never know who set fire to the clinic. (And you think I don't listen.) Anyway, I helped Laura get her house ready for her cousin, who came in off the reservation to stay here while her son is in the hospital. It's been touch and go but now it looks as though he'll recover.

Sully says hello, by the way. No, really—he's right here in my lap and hjleiplknll.esz—

Gone now. The lap thing wasn't working out very well.

So I've cleaned out my shed . . . I made myself welcome at Laura's to clean her shed, too. She was humoring me, I think—but we did clear out a mouse. I don't know what kind. Sully ate it.

And yes, I'm fine. Taking care, taking meds, breathing deep. And Sully is fine. He's doing better with his classes than he thinks he is, and has decided he likes showing off in the breed ring. I get the feeling that a couple of months from now he's going to surprise himself by suddenly taking all that new obedience learning for granted. Until then, we're at least providing the class with entertainment. The trick will be waiting to put him in a trial until *after* he reaches that point, and not while he's still flipping back and forth between genius and dork.

I'm glad Laura called me to help with the whole furniture moving thing. Not because I'm big on moving furniture, but. . . .

You know.

And that hadn't taken nearly as long as he'd hoped. He suddenly wasn't exactly sure why he'd even been putting it off. Guy genes, he decided and, thus absolved via cop-out, moved the computer over to the short Internet cable so he could send the E-mail and finally turned to the paperwork. He pulled it from his messenger bag briefcase in one big clump, spreading it over the counter. At least some of it should have come home with him the Friday before, but no-oo . . . he'd been thinking about the potential of turning the cold hose on Laura over shed-cleaning in the hot Saturday afternoon, not about office paperwork.

Sully, aptly sensing the impending tedium level, made for the dog door in the bedroom, *flip-flap* and away to freedom and bug-sniffing. Dale squelched idle wistfulness—maybe he, too, could escape through the dog door—and spread the paperwork slightly, hunting the easiest starting point. Signatures, that would do it. He'd hunt sticky notes, Sheri's fluorescent reminders to *sign here*. There had to be some, there among the bills and decisions and lab reports and recent research and his own notes reminding him to read up on the latest vaccination discussions and there, in the middle of it all, an unfamiliar sheet of half-size yellow legal paper.

> *How unimpressive . . .*
> *You're clearly not getting the message.*
> *Take a glance around*
> *There are things to be found.*

And his stomach got that hard, cold feeling and his fingers tightened on the paper and he said, "What the f—" except he didn't finish because he had, after all, just been writing E-mail to Aunt Cily and he knew better than to use that language in front of her.

But still.

He froze that way for a long moment, his mind racing back to his office and who had access—*anyone who wanted it*—and when they'd had access—*all damned day*—and then went straying off to calculate when the note had been placed by its geological placement in the stack of papers.

Except if the note had ever been on the top, he'd have seen it. Whoever left it had stuck it smack in the middle, just as he'd found it; it could have happened on Friday or it could have happened five minutes before he'd left the clinic.

On sudden impulse, he went back to the messenger bag—black, blocky, indestructible, and possessed of more accessory pockets than any man should ever need—and he emptied it. All of it. Never mind that the contents spilled over the sides of the counter, or that Sully immediately returned from the yard, trotting smartly into the big open room with his curiosity set to full speed ahead, tail flagged.

"Mine," Dale told him shortly, pawing through the various pens, adaptors, chargers, paperclips, and old notes. The premium for the Prescott show . . . he set that aside for entry. An interesting rock he'd picked up two weeks ago. A weirdly misshapen cat molar, saved in a pill bottle because it had seemed interesting enough at the time.

Nothing else out of place. Nothing missing. No one, he thought, had been in the messenger bag. It had come from his desk—from the pile of things on his desk.

He took a closer look at the paper. Half-sized lined yellow paper with perforations at the top. Beyond common. The words were so carefully transcribed as to be drawn rather than written—not anyone's normal, recognizable handwriting.

And the words themselves. . . .

He put the paper aside. He let his gaze wander and he thought about that instant grip of dread and wondered if it was because the notes were truly threatening or just because they represented something he hadn't been able to resolve.

An insult, a little derision . . . a warning. Coupled with that last note . . . *Threatening*. Definitely.

Dale cleared the counter and pulled the other notes out of his back pocket one last time. Wrinkled, worn . . . torn along the edges. He suddenly wished he'd been more careful with them all along.

He just hadn't known, when he'd gotten that first oddball

note, that there would be three of them.

He lined them up and stared at them, then walked around the counter and looked at them from the other side—a puzzle-building habit that did him absolutely no good in this context. In the background, the *flip-flap* of the dog door suggested that Sully had again given up on getting entertainment from the human. Just as well. Dale didn't see it happening.

Three notes. Three different kinds of paper. The yellow third note, the faint pink second sticky note with the stickum long worn off, and the first note, white, square paper smudged where it had been stuck in the door. Dale took a closer look at the back of the sticky note. Animal hair was stuck copiously to the top strip of stickum—which actually ran across the bottom, because the paper had been oriented upside down at use.

Never intended to stick it anywhere, then. Just grabbed it. Not well-planned, then, these notes. Or not meant to look it.

One thing was clear enough: whoever had written the notes expected something of Dale.

There's not much time to find me.

Time before what? The spree? A spree of what?

A spree of something, Dale decided, that he didn't want to see happen.

But if the note-writer wanted to do it, why would he chivvy Dale about finding him? Presumably stopping him?

"Aurgh!" Dale said—and, not quite satisfied, said it again, growlier. *"Aurgh!"*

The grumbling sound made him cough, short and dry . . . the kind of thing he once had done as a matter of course, but that was now rare enough to be worthy of notice. In fact, even though he'd used Big Blue upon arrival home, that tight undertone of not-quite-enough air wasn't yet gone, and neither was the cough. And that meant. . . .

Dale snarled silently at the notes and at life in general. *That*

means acting all of my thirty-something years and facing reality.
He'd taken what he could of the dust and disruption at the
clinic; he'd pretended it wasn't a problem for as long as he
could.

Before he could change his mind, he picked up the phone
and auto-dialed the clinic, stalking over to the window to stare
at the gorgeous view without seeing a bit of it. Glare at it, more
likely. "Sheri," he said, and didn't make any effort to hide his
growly mood, "I'm out for the week. Half days next week . . .
we'll see how that goes."

"You did better than we thought you would," Sheri said, full
of understanding condolence.

"You—" That stopped him short—but only for a moment.
Because, right. As though Sheri had never looked in Dale's
desk . . . never run across Big Blue II. As though she weren't
the sort to look it up if she didn't recognize a basic albuterol
rescue inhaler. As though she weren't the sort to tell everyone
in the clinic . . . and then, apparently, to have significant
conversations about it with regards to the impact of the
construction. All without the curious looks and knowing glances
that should have given her—should have given them *all*—away.

Sheri read the silence with pinpoint accuracy. "Oops."

"Damn," Dale said. "You're good."

"I *am* good." She took instant advantage of the gap in any
indignation he might muster. "Don't you forget it."

"Then you won't have any trouble applying that to the
rescheduling this will involve," Dale said, cheerfully enough so
she'd know he'd gotten her.

"Damn," she muttered. "You're good, too."

"And Sheri," he hesitated, heading for more serious. "If you
see any more of those notes . . . I want to know about it. Don't
put them up on that board of yours, don't show them to Isaac
and Jade and Brad and Dru and—"

Sheri broke in, and the wary in her voice was just what Dale had wanted to hear. "You got another one?"

"Someone's playing games," he said. "And I'm not at all sure it's *nothing* anymore."

CHAPTER 6

Dale spent the night, on and off, staring at the ceiling. Woken by coughing, kept awake by thinking. An old pattern, recently abandoned.

It made him realize how content he'd found himself here. How disgruntled Note Number Three had made him. And how disgruntled he was at being disgruntled.

Enough to reach out for official help, however reluctantly. Not trying to pretend it wasn't a problem, not at this point.

The night of ceiling inspection also made him realize that Sully had reached the snoring stage of Beaglehood.

"You," he said, pointing at Sully in the parking lot outside both the RoundUp Café and the vet clinic, a manila envelope tucked under his arm, his mouth ready for orange juice and donuts, heavy on the donuts. "Snoring strips."

But Sully knew enough to ignore such nonsensical human utterings. He wandered the end of his leash, distance-sniffing the dried weeds around the base of the single parking lot light.

"Hey!" Sheri yelled from the clinic in the adjoining lot, sticking her head out the door. "What're you doing, being on time for once? You're supposed to be sick."

"No," Dale said, not quite as loudly, "I'm trying *not* to get sick. Different thing. Just keep the construction over there, and I'll do my thing over here. On time, *as usual.*"

"You'd best skedaddle." Sheri checked her watch. "Those clients see you over there, they're gonna tromp over and ask you to look at Fido on the spot. Get it, on the *spot?*"

"Okay, *now* I'm sick." And as Sheri grinned her triumph, Dale did indeed skedaddle—but into the space between the café and the clinic, giving Sully a few more morning moments to himself.

Run by the Yazzie family, the café was much more than its name implied. Deli, coffee shop, morning donuts and bagels. All day long, manned by either Terry or his wife or one of his teenaged children—and just occasionally by the ten-year-old— the deli served West Winona. That meant they caught people commuting into Flagstaff in the morning, commuting out of Flagstaff in the afternoon, and had a monopoly on those in West Winona during the day. Terry had been a silent but present support during the sabotage inflicted on the clinic, and had just as quietly stepped in to help when Dale, Sully, and Laura had undergone a drive-by macing along the road frontage. Dale figured the Yazzies had his business for life.

As it happened, they'd picked up another steady customer along the way—Deputy Rena Wells. First responder to Dale's discovery of a body only days after his arrival here, she'd now become a familiar face—one Dale hoped to see when he went inside. Because if you're gonna ask for help . . . might as well go all the way.

Here on the outside, Sully's tail stiffened in delight at the bounty between the buildings, quivering ever so slightly. There in the dry weeds—one maturing but tiny tumbleweed, some Rocky Mountain Bee Plant that didn't have a chance, and a scattering of tiny desert dandelions—scuttled a tell-tale blot of gleaming darkness. Sully focused his entire being on the black carapace, leaning into the leash and waiting for just the right moment to—

leap!

The offended stink beetle lifted its rump into firing position, and Dale found sudden reason to walk the other direction. "Oh, look!" he exclaimed in theatrical tones. "Look over here! Let's get it!" Sully bounded to Dale's side, ears in eager investigation mode.

"Never mind," Dale told him, scuffing in the weedy patch where the asphalt had crumbled. "Just a stick."

stick. mine. Sully acquired the stick, tucked it gently into his mouth, and looked up at Dale, ready to go.

"Okay," Dale told him. "No drooling, though." And they headed for the café, breezing past the door sign that said *No Dogs Allowed* with *except for Sully* scrawled in a ten-year-old hand beneath. "Waiting for Rena," he informed Terry, and then dropped the exact change for a doughnut and an orange juice on the counter.

Terry was already reaching for the single-serving orange juice bottle. "Give her five minutes," he suggested.

Good, enough time to eat the confectioners'-sugar-covered goodie he'd just snagged. He took a plastic chair, slapping the manila envelope down on the table. As usual, his legs were just that much too long, knees not quite sure where to go. Sully sat beside him and dropped the stick to regard it sadly, as though he couldn't remember just why it had been wonderful in the first place. Then he transferred his attention to the donut.

"Not gonna happen," Dale told him, unflinching before that practiced gaze. "You should just have a seat and wait it out." But he didn't take his time, unwilling to be caught with his hands or mouth full when Rena arrived, if Rena arrived.

But life was good to him this morning. He was licking the last of the sugar from his fingers when she pulled the door open, bells chiming at the swing of it.

Her face lit up into a smile—an angular face with freckles more obvious than they'd been at the beginning of the summer, her lanky efficiency making arrival at his table a quick one.

"Hey, Dale," she said by way of greeting. "You're not in work mode." Question sat in those words, for Dale didn't hit the RoundUp on his days off. And given the cutoff carpenter's jeans he wore and the T-shirt with printed muddy dog tracks up over his shoulder and down the other side, there was no question how she'd surmised he wasn't working.

"Looking for you," he said simply.

She grinned broadly. "Hey, really?" She pulled out a chair and sat down across from him. "Usual, Terry—on my tab? Man, I don't see how you can chow down on that stuff and stay trim."

Dale gave his stomach a poke to double-check. "Metabolism," he said. "My dad was like that. I don't know—"

Don't know if he would have stayed that way; didn't know if or when the metabolism clock would stop being on his side and switch over to slow mode. His father hadn't lived long enough for anyone to know, nor his mother. "And sit-ups," he added, making no attempt to finish what he'd started.

She snorted. "I do my share of those."

"You stay pretty fit, I'd imagine," Dale said, because it seemed the thing to say and because he couldn't quite get what she was driving at . . . or for. With her rangy build and lean-unto-scant figure, he couldn't imagine that she couldn't sneak herself a donut now and then.

But the comment seemed to satisfy her. She ran an unnecessary hand back to her ponytail and said, "What's up, then?"

The manila envelope sat beside his elbow; he pushed it over to her. "Thought you'd know the right desk for these."

Fleeting disappointment crossed her face. Then she gave her ponytail a last tug and said matter-of-factly, "What're you into now?"

"Me? Nothing. More like the other way around, I think. Maybe." He watched as she pulled out the three notes, each one in a baggie. "The first two got a lot of handling. The third went straight into the baggie, but it was jammed in with my papers when I found it . . . not exactly untouched."

"Hey," Terry said, bringing Rena's coffee over—something fancy that Dale wouldn't recognize if he had the menu shoved under his nose. "You and that nose for trouble at work again?"

Dale winced. "Don't even say it."

Rena glanced at the notes in turn, swapping them out as she noticed Dale had marked the baggie corners with numbers. Her wide mouth tightened; she grew still with reluctance. It wasn't the reaction Dale had expected. Maybe laughter, along the lines of *there he goes again.* Maybe concern, if she saw the warning laced throughout them as he did. Maybe a shrug. But not tense reluctance. "What is it?"

She looked relieved that he'd asked. "You have to understand." She shuffled the notes together and tucked them back into the envelope. "The way things happened this spring . . . it was a little embarrassing. To all the local LEOs—I mean, law enforcement agencies."

For a moment Dale didn't understand. Then he blurted, "But that was just chance!"

Terry raised an eyebrow at him. "Now you're playing dumb," he said. "Chance is when a safe falls on your head. What happened this spring . . . that was because you listened."

Terry, it seemed, might be more observant than he generally let on. Dale let his point slide on past. "It was chance that we found that body . . . that we got involved in the first place." After that . . . maybe not so much. Not once the clinic sabotage began.

"Dale, it doesn't matter." For once Rena didn't have any of the undertones he couldn't seem to read. "Things worked out the way they worked out. You caught the eco-killers and none of the people who ought to have caught them were close. On the surface, everyone's grateful. But if I take these notes in . . . that is, there's not enough to them. I think—" She stopped, and if she didn't quite squirm in her seat, the look on her face did it for her.

Dale got it. "You think they'll be looking for an excuse to take me less than seriously, and these notes will provide that."

She sat back, relief on her face.

Dale found himself so surprised at the petty nature of the situation that he wasn't sure how to feel. He had to close his eyes, and then he found it—the nugget of annoyance, the little hard spot of anger. He looked at Rena, and his voice was tight enough to make Terry and Rena exchange a glance. "What about you? Do you see what I see in those notes? Or do you think I'm just full of myself after this spring?"

She touched the envelope. "I don't like them." And then shrugged. "But it's subtle, Dale. Real subtle. There are threats here, all right . . . but nothing to be done about them, exactly."

"Oh," he said. "No, I know that. But I didn't know if this was just me, or if this guy's dropping notes all over town. I figured . . . I'm not the right person to have the big picture view."

That startled her a little; got her attention. As if maybe she, too, had expected him to think as the others did—a little bit full of himself. "Listen," he said, and then bit down to get frustration out of his voice. "You have the notes. If you hear of something else like this going down, you'll know who to give them to. For now . . . just hang on to them."

"You made copies," she said, and there was a little suspicion in her voice. As if she knew he couldn't let go of it so easily.

Well, dammit, she was right. He couldn't. And come to that it *had* been him who'd followed his nose—and Sully's nose—to the eco-murderers. "Yes," he said, without apology. "I have copies."

She quite suddenly released her tension, sipping her coffee, and gave a little nod. "Sounds like a good way to go. They may be nothing, you know . . . some groupie who wants your attention."

"*Groupie.*" Dale made a face.

Rena grinned at him. "All part of the deal."

"It wasn't a *deal*," Dale grumbled. It had been someone targeting his clinic because of something he'd done. It had just been a miscalculation on their part.

"Gotta get into work," Rena said, pushing her chair back with her usual gusto. "Come by again some morning, Dale. We can share a donut."

"You're buying," Dale said, only belatedly realizing he'd pretty much made it a date.

Rena's grin widened and she sauntered out into the early morning heat. Dale frowned after her. "I'm not sure what exactly happened there, but it wasn't what I thought would happen."

He hadn't expected a response, but Terry laughed. "What happened is exactly what she wanted to happen. That woman has a mighty thing for you."

Dale stared. Just stared.

"What do you think brings in half my late afternoon crowd, *Mr. Dr. Dale?*" Terry's broad face got even broader with his grin.

Dale couldn't help his wary squint of response.

Still grinning, Terry was. "What happens almost every afternoon before you go home? Right before you get in the car?"

Still wary, too. "I hose down Sully so the car won't seem so hot."

Terry nodded wisely, indicating the side of the clinic, visible through the huge plate glass window beside Dale. "Right there at the spigot. Tall man, short dog."

Horror made his swig of orange juice go down hard. "Good

God. They're looking at my—"

Terry nodded again, but the wise demeanor had changed to something less repressible. "Ah, the tips are good on those days."

Dale opened his mouth . . . closed it. Opened it. . . .

Closed it. "Dammit." And then, "If I weren't in shock, I'd have something clever to say about this." As it was, he just sank down in the chair some. Sully took it as an invitation and propped up on Dale's thigh, his nose just clearing the table and inhaling hard enough to stir the crumbs. "Not gonna happen," Dale grumbled. "And you can forget about those hosings. Home isn't that far away."

"Oh, no, man." Terry looked properly horrified now. "Give me at least another month to get them hooked on my coffee!"

"Monsoon clouds mean it's not as hot in the car as it was before," Dale noted.

"Sully's got privileges in here," Terry noted.

"Ah, crap," Dale said.

"Just pretend I never said anything."

Dale swallowed the rest of the orange juice in a long series of gulps. "I'll work on it," he said. But he had the feeling he'd never put his back to the diner again.

A week off to breathe. A week off while Laura was anything but—working, hosting her cousin, visiting her nephew in the hospital. A week off while everyone else stayed plenty busy, summer in full swing.

Dale took an impromptu drive to the red rocks of Sedona, pondered the two hours to the Grand Canyon. He took Sully along the forest trails, working his focus exercises in the distracting, scentful environment. They heeled sideways and halted and walked backwards and worked stays with Abert's squirrels frisking in the background, and a few days of that worked wonders for Sully's understanding of the phrase "we're working now." Of course, they also walked fallen logs, jumped from rock to rock together, and lay back in the pine needles to view the towering Ponderosas from beneath. They hid out during the hot mid-day hours, and Dale caught up with his paperwork, finished the current Neuschwanstein puzzle, and sent Laura a photo of it in E-mail. He sent in his entry for the Prescott dog show, and in a fit of utter insanity, included one day's entry in rally obedience.

And he twiddled his thumbs.

By the end of the week, he was entirely twiddled out. His chest was clear; he hadn't woken coughing in darkness since that first night. Laura's E-mails had been short and sporadic, and he had the feeling he wouldn't see her for the nearby puppy match that weekend. The puppy misnomer aside, the match was an informal opportunity to practice trial manners in a faux trial situation, and he planned a day-of-match entry with Sully.

And there had been no further notes. Not mixed in with the paperwork he'd picked up on Thursday; not delivered to the clinic in any manner that Sheri had discerned. The painters were nearly done with the main office work and the tilers had stepped in. Dale offered them a bonus if they would work over the weekend, giving him a solid floor and mostly dried tile glue by the time he started half days the next week.

"Definitely ready for work," he told Sully, sitting on the top of the patio's tall adobe back wall to watch the eastern sunset as the day cooled. He'd been astonished to discover that here in the Southwestern sky, the sunsets painted reflected bands of coral, turquoise, and deepest inky blue along the eastern horizon. Unless, of course, the clouds had moved in—then reflected sunlight-washed tumultuous pink clouds against a bruised and darkening sky. Tonight, flickers of dry lightning moved through the clouds, and Dale thought it a shame when Sully moved into the patio area and triggered the motion light behind him. *Gotta remember to turn that off.*

He twisted to find Sully on the flagstone, looking up at Dale on the five-foot wall, tail wagging tentatively. Dale succumbed to impulse. He did a backwards sit-up down the length of the adobe wall, inverted right at Sully's level. Already maybe not such a good idea, but Sully danced with delight, his body curling into its happiest comma as he snuffled Dale's ears. Dale rumpled him, hanging like a bat and his lower legs already tingling with compressed nerves. "Getting out of this could be bad, buddy."

Sully didn't care. *mine!*

Maybe if he just let go. . . .

But Sully bayed alarm right in his ear, bounding away toward the patio entrance with noise that quickly changed to a greeting of excitement and then silenced into little escaping yodels of glee. Within moments, Laura appeared over top the low northern section of the patio wall, leaning on her elbows to regard Dale. "I almost grabbed your ankles," she admitted. "But I thought that wouldn't turn out well for either of us."

"Well," Dale said, trying for some small dignity. "You do manage to catch me at my best."

Her smile, from his upside-down vantage, took him by surprise—the genuine amusement edged with something wry. She said, "Maybe this is why I come here. Maybe there's something delightful in finding you upside-down for Sully Dog's benefit."

"You think?" The notion surprised him. And with the blood rushing to his head and his legs falling asleep, he was about done with upside-down; he extended his arms down until they took his weight, and pushed away from the wall to flip over a handstand and back to his feet. "That worked out better than I expected," he admitted, joining her at the wall from his side. "And please don't tell me I was supposed to be expecting you and somehow forgot."

She shook her head. "I took a chance. The lights were on, so when you didn't answer the door. . . . The side gate's unlocked, and I know you spend a lot of time out here."

Ah, to be predictable. But he did love it out here. The enclosed patio butted up to the house, half covered by roof overhang and half open air; the height of the walls varied, with the tallest at the back, the second tallest to the north, and the lowest to the south—no particular reason, as far as Dale could tell, except that the tall back wall offered both shade and privacy. A cheap grill tucked into the corner; it could have been cleaner, and scorch marks on the picnic table attested to its use. Outside the north wall, against the house, a coiled hose stood by, ready to deal with the grill if things got out of hand. Sully's big dog bed usually sat just beneath the overhang; Dale dragged it out for his own benefit if he was stargazing. And inside a storage nook with the door propped open, Sully's dog flap to the bedroom was perfectly buffered from the seasonal winds. Perfect little space for man and dog. "I'm still getting over the total luxury of dusk without mosquitoes."

"They're here," she noted, but had to admit, "Mostly in the valley. All the irrigation."

Dale wrinkled his nose. "Still not getting the part where people move to the desert and try to make it green."

Laura made a brief face of agreement and stretched, rubbing the small of her back. "I might as well admit it . . . I came by to borrow you again. I should be able to move that desk by myself, but . . . just one of those days."

"Tough at the clinic?" He'd certainly been there, done that.

But Laura frowned, shaking her head ever so slightly. "Just worn out." She rubbed her forehead, a gesture that spoke volumes to Dale. He stopped himself from reaching out to push her hair from her face. Black and thick and getting longer . . . as if he had a chance of keeping his hands off it if she wore it down. Good thing she had it clipped back now.

Belatedly, her words got through to him. "Wait a minute. Things are getting better, right? Hanta is fast to come on, fast to get out of that critical stage. Your nephew—"

"Renal complications," Laura said, and the words sounded as though she'd forced them out. "Back in ICU. Mary wondered if the desk might not fit into the bedroom. I'm not sure if she'd like to use it or if she's worried about being in my way, but anything I can do to make things easier for her. . . ."

"Hey," Dale said. "I'm going stir-crazy here at home. Please, please, *please*—can I come over and move your desk?"

That got a genuine grin. She said, "No wonder I—" and then stopped, as if surprised at her own words. Quickly, she added, "Please, please, please . . . *would* you?"

"Just let me check a mirror," Dale said. "There's no telling what I've got in my hair after *that.* Come on in. I'll grab my keys and follow you over." Not far from here, Laura's place. Her Cosnino community was just big enough for its own post office and its own exit off I-40, but the back way from Dale's Cinder Hills area was shorter and prettier to boot, even in the dark.

Laura accepted the invitation, threading the entry where two patio walls briefly ran parallel to one another, and once they reached the full pool of that back door motion light, she looked up, bit her lip on amusement, and said, "Spider webs."

"Gah." Dale scrubbed his hand over his head, through his hair. "No telling what Sheri could do with *that.*"

"Let's not tell her," Laura suggested. And then, to the small wrinkle-faced dog poised on the edge of indecision, "You coming, Sully? I've just fed the snake—you're safe."

yes! me! me!

"He thinks that's a manly sound," Dale told her, holding the door open. "Can't bring myself to tell him that manly dogs don't squeak like that."

Laura looked him straight in the eye. "Joy of life," she said, "is about as manly as it gets."

Me? Dale somehow managed not to squeak.

~~Barely.~~

CHAPTER 7

The desk wasn't hard to move. The desk was, in fact, a relief to move—after a week of making busy, Dale was finally making useful. "Anything else?" he asked, and tried not to sound too eager.

Laura smiled nonetheless. "If you can think of a way to smuggle Sully in to see my nephew, that would be useful."

"I thought about the whole therapy dog thing," Dale admitted. "Problem is, if he sounds off, the whole hospital would know it. I'm thinking it would only take once."

"There's something to that." Laura tipped her head back, rubbing the small of her back, and sighed.

"You look tired," Dale said—and then realized that it wasn't such a graceful observation, and added, "I mean—"

Laura gave a small laugh. "It's okay. I *am* tired. I guess the worry is wearing me out. I can't imagine how my cousin. . . ." She let that trail off.

"Long-term guest, also not so easy," Dale noted, figuring she wouldn't say it out loud no matter how true it was. Not that Mary looked to be high maintenance. There was hardly any sign of her here, only a big canvas tote leaning against the neatly made bed. A stick emerged from within, but the rest was hidden in the belly of the bag.

Laura saw him looking. "It's a spindle," she said. "Mary weaves. Of course, her loom wouldn't fit in the pickup, so she's spinning some backlog." She tipped the bag open for him, revealing neat clumps of carded grey wool. "The old way," she said. "She even cards it."

Dale gave the wall hanging a second look—rectangular, woven in earthy stripes of rust and brown and wide grey, with brown and pink squash blossoms lined up in the grey areas. "Did she—?"

Laura gave him a startled look, still massaging her back. "That's a Crystal rug," she said. "Mary weaves in Two Grey Hills. They're actually not all that divergent compared to some of the other styles, but Crystal uses vegetable dyes and Mary's work uses all natural wool colors." She stopped, her eyes roaming the wool weaving with affection, and then admitted, "There's more to it than that, but I think I see your eyes glazing over."

"Just for that," Dale said, "I'm going to get a stack of books, and the next possible opportunity I'll spout off all sorts of shallow, memorized trivia."

Laura laughed, but as she tucked the spinning bag closed again, she quickly grew pensive. "She usually takes it with her to the hospital. To have forgotten it. . . ."

Dale got it quickly enough. Mary must be beside herself. "Have you seen him?"

Laura gave an absent shake of her head, which surprised him; she'd been going nightly as far as he knew. She caught his gaze, eyes of darkest brown surrounded by fatigue. "I just wasn't up to it," she said. "I should probably do the smart thing—what you did, cut back on work until this situation eases up a little."

And Dale frowned, and looked at her again. A searching look, not caring that she noticed. It was more than tired eyes; her face was drawn, skin tighter than usual so her cheeks showed more of her Navajo heritage, the broad planes more evident. Tendrils of hair at her forehead looked damp and clingy.

Without thinking, Dale reached out to her, touching her

temple with the backs of his fingers. *Warm.* "Hey."

Laura closed her eyes and took a deep breath and stepped back. "I'm all right."

Dale probably should have backed down—should have given her the space she needed so badly, so self-sufficient she didn't even know how to belong to her own family. But that would have been for himself—to make things easy, to make himself more likeable. It wouldn't have been for her. "It won't do your cousin or her son any good if you wear yourself into a ditch."

"That," Laura said with a little snort, "was the worst mixed metaphor I've heard in a long time. In ever."

He gave her a look. *I am not to be distracted.* "Got a thermometer around here? How about a nice local clinic?"

"Closed at this hour," Laura said. "And I am *not* going to the ER for a fever."

"And muscle aches," Dale noted. "And anything else I should know about? Or should I just go look up a list of hanta symptoms?"

The words were out of his mouth before he even thought them through; he and Laura regarded each other with something akin to mutual surprise, and then Laura gave another little snort. A tired sound. "Knowing you," she said, "you already have. So you know as well as I do that early hanta presents like any old virus—just as it did with Robert. Diagnosis depends on environmental factors as much as symptoms. And *you're* the one who went inside my shed to chase the mouse dust." She shook her head. "If I have something, I picked it up at the hospital. All those germy sick people. . . ."

She was right again. Of course she was right. And she was righter yet when she added, "Hanta just isn't that prevalent, even without the environmental factors. We haven't had a significant outbreak since they identified the Sin Nombre virus in '93. It would be easy to think differently—your first summer here, and already you know someone who has it—"

"I know, I know." Dale scrubbed his hands over his face, trying to shake the little chill the conversation had given him. Because she was right; he'd done the research, right there on his living-room floor. There generally weren't more than fifty cases of hanta a year in all of Arizona, and all of those people had obvious environmental factors. "I just . . . it just struck me. I don't want anything to happen to—" and then, because he was basically a big fat chicken and he'd gotten this far by respecting Laura's emotional boundaries, he changed gears to something more practical and said, "Sick is sick. You need to take some time—"

He'd lost track of Sully. He'd gotten immersed in concern for Laura, and he'd lost track of the world's nosiest dog. But the world's nosiest dog abruptly made his presence known in the adjacent room, his triumphant chop bark for *treed* ringing out so loudly that Dale and Laura both jumped; the windows rattled. And the cry rang out again . . . and again . . . and—

mighty me! mighty! treedtreedtreed!

"Aurgh." Dale smacked his forehead with the palm of his hand in a deliberately dramatic gesture, then held up a finger—one that said *I'll be right back and we're not through with this conversation yet.*

Laura shrugged, and likewise pointed at the kitchen. *You can find me there.*

"And this," Dale muttered to himself as he headed for Sully's noise, "is why you're *not* a therapy dog."

He'd entered the adjacent room before he realized he hadn't been here before. A bedroom.

Laura's bedroom. Her private space. He stopped short, realizing that his big sneakered feet were on an exquisite Navajo rug, that two other rugs hung on the wall and one covered the cedar chest at the foot of her bed—curling wrought iron at the head and foot board, echoed in the light fixtures and curtain rods. Simple loose weave panels hung at the sides of the windows, with closed wooden blinds creating privacy. The bedspread was a nubby cream-colored weave, and if she'd ever had closet doors she'd removed them and replaced them with hanging panels of the same material.

The overhead light abruptly flicked on, surprising him with how long he'd stood here in the semi-darkness, soaking in the ambience of the room even as Sully stood on his hind legs to press his nose to the blinds, knocking them askew and bawling away. Laura came up behind Sully, tapping him smartly on the head; he only bawled louder in anticipation of being pulled off his find, whatever it was. Bigger than a stink beetle, smaller than an elephant, still a mystery.

Dale finally came alive and swooped in to remove him, twisting to avoid Sully's paddling and righteously resisting legs; eventually he flipped the dog upside down, startling him to silence. "You done? And what was that all about?"

"Good question," Laura said. She pulled the blinds up to reveal an air conditioner damp from Sully's nose. "I keep this thing on in the day, mostly . . . just enough so this room doesn't hold the heat. Southern exposure." Her toasty complexion had paled—as if the commotion had been the last straw, as if she'd better sit down right this moment or she would just plain fall down.

One-handed, Sully still tucked beneath one arm, Dale dumped a neat pile of clothes off the nearest chair—wrought iron, like everything else—and slid it in behind her. "Sit," he suggested, tugging the chair cushion into place. "Because I think otherwise you're going to—"

"Fall," Laura agreed faintly, and sat hard, with none of her usual self-possession. "Maybe you're right. It's time to take it easy. But if I've got something, I don't want Mary—"

"Stay with me," Dale blurted, and winced. But he thought about it again as he gently set Sully down, and nodded. "Okay, that was kind of startling, but it's not a bad idea. Mary can't afford to get sick right now. The alternative would be to dump her out to a motel."

"No!" Laura said, and then winced just as he had—for totally different reasons. She closed her eyes, put a hand to her head, and took a deep, even, and determined breath. "That's not going to happen."

"Then pack a bag, leave her a note, and come back with me. I've got a spare room, you know that. I'll behave myself. I can't swear to Sully, though."

Sully, standing between them, was the perfect picture of personal conundrum. His lip had stuck to one tooth, leaving it in crooked face malfunction. Wrinkles appeared on his forehead; he stood perfectly square as if by design and stared at the window, his tail wilting a third of the way up its length. Thinking mode, all right.

Never really a good thing.

want! The decision was made as quickly as that, and with much purpose Sully bounced back to the window, propped his front feet on the wall, and jammed his nose against the air-conditioner louvers to inhale scent with jet engine force. When he drew back, it was only to give the louvers that same wrinkle-headed stare—but this time his tail was straight out and quivering, and this time Dale saw it coming; he swooped Sully away before the noise could start. "I'm going to crate Sully in the Forester. I'll grab you some aspirin on the way back, if you'll tell me where to find it. And we'll go to my place. In the morning, if you want, we'll hit up a clinic."

"Dale—"

"*Laura.*" He tucked Sully over his hip and said, "Just give this one to me. It's my big chance to make comfort food and stoke up the virtual fireplace and let Sully earn his keep as a hot water bottle."

Her smile was half-hearted, but he grabbed the implied assent and ran with it. "Let me get him crated. I'll be right back. We'll lock this place up tight, leave a note for Mary, and have you feeling better before you know it."

CHAPTER 8

Sully took his banishment to the small SUV in good graces, especially once Dale produced a pressed rawhide chew, rumpled his ears, and told him he was a good kid. He was in vigorous chew by the time Dale made it to the front passenger seat, hastily clearing out a modest accumulation of fast-food wrappers and old used-up water bottles. He jammed it all in a plastic grocery bag—also conveniently drifting around the passenger foot well—and headed back to the house, hoping he hadn't given her time to change her mind.

And yet. . . .

Too many questions unanswered. Dale had been good; he'd been patient. And he'd about reached his limit. As he tossed the garbage in the big bin by the side of the house, he found his attention focusing not on the front entry, but along the side of the house. The south side of the house, and the window that had so entranced Sully.

For Sully's enthusiasm didn't make him *wrong*. He'd smelled something in that air conditioner—and access to the air conditioner was here, on the outside.

Dale fished in his pockets, found his car keys and the little mini LED light on the key ring, and stepped around the side of the house, crunching on the gravel and hoping the soft clumps of plants he stepped on were weeds and not cultivated Xeriscaping. The air conditioner loomed large at the side of the house, a black blot dully illuminated by the light filtering out from the disturbed slats of the blinds. If Laura heard him out here, there was no sign of it—no peeking at the edge of the blinds, no movement from within. Dale played the thin light of the LED flash card over the blocky apparatus, feeling a little bit silly and yet not the least deterred.

And *huh*. The unit's cover wasn't lined up properly, evident even in this iffy light; it only took a moment to see the dark blot of a hole where a screw should have been but wasn't. He crouched low over the gravel beneath, playing the light back and forth, looking for a glint in its eerie blue gleam . . . expecting nothing and doing it anyway.

And there. The glint. His fingers fumbled it at first, and then he pulled it up and rolled it into his hand. *The screw.* Well, the spring and fall winds of this area tended to work all kinds of mischief.

Sully, however, did not turn his brains inside out for a fallen screw. Dale tucked the thing away in the watch pocket of his jeans and returned to the air conditioner, concern for Laura niggling at the back of his mind . . . he needed to get her tucked into bed, drinking tea, being waited on as necessary. *Sick was sick,* he'd said. It didn't have to be kidney failure to need tending.

More or less the lesson he'd had to learn for himself, and darned ironic that he was now applying it to the person who had been so instrumental in his own education—

Dale froze. "Oh, crap," he said out loud, words biting into the otherwise silent dark air. There, along the bottom . . . where the cover was the most skewed from the missing screw. A tuft of dried grass. Nothing, really—certainly nothing he would have recognized if he hadn't just been on a shed-cleaning spree. He gripped the edge of the cover, pulling it away just enough so the focused little LED light could shine within.

Just enough to see it was indeed a little nest—a ball of dried grasses, tiny twigs, and a few scraps of material.

He sat back on his heels. What were the chances? That there was a mouse nest in Laura's air conditioner? That she would get sick with a stray summer virus at the same time her air conditioner was blowing across that mouse nest into her very bedroom?

It might not even be a deer mouse, Kinsall. It could be a harvest mouse. Or a vole of some sort. And if it *were* a deer mouse, who's to say it wasn't a healthy one? There were plenty of those around. Plain old healthy mice. And this wasn't even a bad year for—

And yet here he sat outside Laura's bedroom window with his heart pounding and his gut instinct cranked so tight he couldn't, for the moment, quite take a breath. He muttered, "Aw, hell," and gave into it, abandoning the air conditioner and the nest it hosted, jogging back around the house over the uneven stones; Sully gave a single cautious woof of concern from the SUV. Dale reached the front door and strode through Laura's house as though he owned it, already arguing with her in his head. *Hospital. I'm wrong, I pay for it.* A simple test, that's all it would take, and then she could say *I told you so.* In fact, he would be delighted to hear her say it.

And so he started even before he reached the bedroom door. "Laura—"

She wasn't in the chair.

He found her quickly enough, stretched out on the bed and looking remarkably small for a person of such quiet firm presence.

No, not stretched out on the bed. Crumpled. As though she'd gotten that far and just no further.

"Hey," Dale said, and if he didn't rush to her side it was only through an extreme application of casual. He did crouch by the bed, as close to eye level as he was going to get, and he did reach out to tuck a bit of hair behind her ear, even if it was totally unnecessary and totally cliché. And yeah, she was warm. *Fevered.* He observed her for a few moments, using his clinician's eye—the one that could see her breathing was too fast, and found the slight furrowing of her brow easy enough to read. He had just that long to be observant and objective, and then his heart started thudding again. He touched her shoulder. "Hey."

She frowned, opening her eyes to look at him sideways. "I didn't mean to fall sleep," she said. A hand made its way, somewhat uncertainly, to her head. Her eyes drifted closed. "Headache."

"Yeah," he said. "I'll just bet. Look, I found a mouse nest in your air conditioner." Or maybe not, but he was pretty sure. "I know it's far-fetched and I know it's a pain in the ass and that you don't feel good and you'd rather be tucked in bed somewhere, but I just have this feeling—"

Her eyes flew open again, focusing with startling clarity on his. "What?"

"Let me take you to the hospital," he said. "They've got tests. It won't take long. If I'm wrong, you can be back at my place getting waited on hand and foot and—"

"Yes," she said, and closed her eyes.

It scared him more than anything else.

Dale slipped his arms under her knees, under her shoulders, and he settled her into place and stood. She didn't protest that, either, but rested her head against his shoulder in a trusting fashion. The day before he would have given anything to experience that sensation; right now it terrified him. He carried her out to the Forester with careful steps, fumbled through getting the vehicle's door open, and somehow slid her into the seat without fuss or stumble. As he belted her in, he said, "I'll go lock up the house and bring you the keys." Then he closed the door on her.

He used the walk to the house to take deep breaths—"Don't Panic" was a fine motto in real life as well as in his beloved *Hitchhiker's Guide to the Galaxy*—and then swooped through the house to gather her keys, her purse, and a shawl he thought she might use if the ER disgorged them far into the cool high-desert night.

And then he closed the tailgate, tucked himself in behind the wheel, and met her gaze with a crooked grin. "Come morning, I'm probably going to feel all kinds of fool," he told her. "But it's a risk I'll take."

"Gosh," she murmured with just a hint of faux wide-eyed naiveté. "That's just about the sweetest thing anyone's ever said to me."

Dale snorted, cranking the ignition. "Then I'd say we're both in trouble."

He prepared himself for a fight at the Flagstaff Medical Center emergency department, with twenty-five minutes of tense, silent driving and only Sully's continued contentment with his pressed rawhide as background music. But he carried Laura into the waiting room just as he'd carried her out of her house, and he said, "Mice in the air conditioner. Headache, body aches, and she just started tachypnea," by which he meant he could feel the frighteningly rapid rise and fall of her chest against his arms—and they took her away and left him looking at his empty hands, unexpectedly bereft.

For a few moments he sat in the big square waiting room, taking up a corner of the endless padded bench that lined the wall. But his legs stuck out in the way and Friday night in the ER was no better than Monday morning at the clinic—except that Dale's patients weren't usually there as a result of abusing alcohol, and half of these people were accompanied by a bored-looking police officer.

I must be crazy.

Off in the other corner, a young mother tried to comfort her flushed and miserable baby; nearest to Dale, two young women whispered furiously about the family member on whose behalf they'd come here, and their voices held annoyance rather than concern. On his other side, a scruffy middle-aged man curled up in a ball and groaned to himself.

I'm never going to live this down.

Sheri is going to hear about this and I'm never going to—

Oh, hell. I hope she does hear about it. I hope I'm so wrong that I never *hear the end of it.*

Dale stared at his toes for a while, trying to make himself smaller. Then he paced off to the side, casting glances at the unappealing packaged sandwiches in the vending machine and almost willing to eat one just for something to do. He went out to walk Sully and make sure he had the windows cracked enough to let in the cool nighttime air.

Damned well better *be wrong.*

Upon his return to the waiting room, Dale found an anonymous young man in scrubs calling Laura's name. He hesitated, hovering near the vending machines, when the young man spotted him and beckoned. "You," he said. "You're the only one out here who fits the description she gave."

"Tall, needs a haircut?" Dale guessed.

"Something like that," the young man said, and suppressed a smile that made Dale wonder. "Come with me."

"She's okay?"

The nurse—now identifiable as such from his name tag—frowned. "You're on her list of contacts . . . but give it a moment, and she can tell you herself." They moved briskly through a wide hallway made narrow with beds and stretchers, one side a long nurse's station and the other a line of curtain-rooms, and turned down another hall—Dale was already lost—and then to an enclosed room with several patient bays within. And there was Laura at the end, pale in a thin patient gown, her belongings sitting at the end of the bed in a giant plastic bag with her name on them and the usual number of tubes and needles attached to her body.

Another nurse, frizzy and blond of hair and freckled of complexion, fussed at the IV bag, injecting the contents of a syringe into the bag through the bottom port and then adjusting the drip. "There you go," she said. "Just to get you started." She glanced over at Dale and her eyes widened. "Ooh," she said, and gave Laura's shoulder a pat. "You didn't say."

But Laura didn't respond, just caught and kept Dale's gaze with a dark silence he couldn't read, and the nurse patted her shoulder again and said, "I'll be back to check on you. Don't worry if you feel a little rush when that stuff hits your system. All part of the deal."

But when she left, Laura at first still said nothing. Dale moved closer to the bed, reaching for her hand and thinking better of it; he rested his own on the bed's raised railing and opened his mouth, hunting for words, when he suddenly realized that her eyes were glistening with unshed tears.

It stopped him long enough for her to say, her voice both hard and miserable, "You were right."

He knew then that the tears were anger; he felt a flush of the same, thoroughly mixed with the sudden cold feeling in his stomach. "F—" he said, cutting himself off just in time. "Sorry. I mean—"

"I know what you mean," she said, and closed her eyes, swallowed once, and came back to the conversation as quietly strong as ever. He didn't find the look totally compatible with the nasal oxygen cannula, or the tubes taped to her arms or the

101

bright hospital bracelets, one orange and one red, that looked big on her wrists. But she didn't give him a chance to comment on it. "Thank you," she said. "If it wasn't for you. . . ."

"You'd have figured it out."

"Maybe. Or maybe I would have ended up with bacterial pneumonia sepsis or gone straight to hanta pulmonary syndrome—over the weekend, with Mary too involved with her son to even wonder why she wasn't seeing me."

"No," Dale said simply, and left it at that. "They tested for it, then?"

"Western blot," she said. "They've started antibiotics against the sepsis and just gave me dobutamine—standard procedure vasodilator, should help with all the kidney issues and hypoxia." Even on the oxygen, she sounded short of breath; her chest rose and fell far too rapidly. "They'll probably have to intubate, you know that."

"I know," he said. "Want me to feed your snake while you're doing that?"

She suppressed a smile. "He's good for a week. But my cell phone is in my purse. I can't use it here, but . . . Mary's cell number is programmed in as number eight. She's not used to checking messages yet—she only got it to help deal with her son's illness—but when she gets home and I'm not there, she'll probably look. If you could leave a message . . . if you wouldn't mind answering her questions . . . make sure that she gets checked. . . ."

"Sure," Dale said, trying not to sound too eager—something to do for her, something he *could* do.

"While you're at it . . . you might as well take my things. The purse doesn't need to be here . . . and I guess I won't be using my street clothes for a while."

"How about I trade them for pj's . . . ?"

She looked away. "I don't know when I'll need them."

"Then they'll be here waiting," he said firmly. And then, into the long silence between them, he said, "Laura. You'll be okay. This rates high on the suckage meter, but it's nothing you can't beat. Especially if you let yourself not do it alone."

She shot him a look of pure ire. He didn't care a bit. He took it in to himself, memorized it, instantly treasured it, and gave her blithe smile in return. "That's not going to work, either. Get used to having bedside company. I may even smuggle Sully in." But the thought made him frown. "I'll have to rig up a Cone of Silence, of course. Anything for you."

"Now you're just getting sappy," she said, and crossed her arms as defiantly as she could given the extra accouterments they'd gained.

Dale grinned. "Yeah."

Small hospital, small parking lot. Dale made the call to Mary right outside the doors, then headed out to the Forester in the cool nighttime air, greeting Sully absently as he opened the driver's door and tossed Laura's things inside—and then suddenly ended up leaning against the frame, just plain needing a moment. The rawhide was either gone or had lost its charm; Sully moved restlessly within the crate and essayed a short, mournful yodel of want.

strangeness. woe.

"I know, buddy," Dale said, just as woefully—but already thinking ahead. They'd be home for the night, but damned if he didn't plan to be right back here in the morning, armed with books to read out loud, Laura's most suitable pair of pajamas, her very own toothbrush and toothpaste . . . and whatever else struck his fancy as useful.

Inside the Forester, an unfamiliar ring tone caught Dale's attention, so surprising that he froze several important seconds before diving for the bag of Laura's things. "Mary," he said, barely checking her caller ID. "This is Dale."

There was a pause, but with enough of an intake of breath that Dale knew she was still there . . . just struggling. Finally she said, "I'm sorry. I hoped—"

"Yeah," he said. "Me too. Listen, I'm in the back by the emergency entrance—you still on the grounds?"

"Front lot across the street," she said. "Wait for me."

And that he did, glad for those moments to take his own deep breaths, a brief break between handling things when he could push down the simmering panic. *And she's been doing this for over a week. Nearly two.* At the sight of a slow-moving truck coming in from the west side of the lot, Dale walked to the tailgate and stood there; it was enough. Mary pulled up behind his vehicle, blocking the aisle as though she was right at home here.

Probably was.

"Hey," she said, her voice even softer than Laura's quiet tones. *"T'ááláhádi áhoot' háádóó t'óó tsék'eh áhooníít."* She got out of her truck but stayed there by the open door, her warm brown skin turned strikingly sallow in the cab light, her round face drawn with worry and fatigue. Her hair, long and longer, trailed back over the seat from the tie at the nape of her neck.

"Laura does that," Dale said wistfully. "Phrases like that. I think she remembers more than she thinks she does about her time with you."

"Home is what we are," Mary said simply. "Whether we know it or not. What happened?"

"Her place isn't safe right now," Dale said. "There's a mouse nest in the bedroom air conditioner."

Mary absorbed that bit of absurdity with remarkable aplomb. "She keeps that door closed. It's the only room that heats up the way it does."

"Lucky for you, I'd say." They both gave the implication a moment's thought, and Dale added, "We can get the house cleaned. But until then, it's not safe for you to stay there. I don't even know if I closed that door on the way out. I doubt it. I was carrying—well, I had my hands full."

"How did you even know?" Mary asked. A broad question . . . how did he know to look for the nest? How did he know to rush Laura here and have her tested?

Dale answered them all in the most basic way, giving her truths he might have skimped with someone else. Almost anyone else, but Laura and his aunt. "I followed a feeling."

"Ah," she said, and nodded. "She said you were strong like that."

Nonplused on an evening when he was too tired to work it through, Dale skipped ahead. "Listen, you're welcome to stay at my place. It's a guy house, but there's plenty of room. I've got to get some of Laura's things; we can go together and close that door, do a quick in and out."

"Before I knew I would stay with Laura, I called around," Mary said. "My cousin's friend has a little motel on 66. Run down, you know, but I don't need much right now."

Dale hesitated, uncertain how hard to push. In the end he left it alone. "If you change your mind," he said. "But do you mind if we trail you home? I've got Air-Aid masks in the back seat . . . left over from cleaning sheds. They don't look like much, but they're supposed to be good against hanta. Anthrax, too, if it comes to that."

"I think the hanta is enough." Mary shook her head. "My son and my cousin . . . what are the odds?"

Dale didn't have an answer to that, but she didn't wait for one. "Follow me out," she said. "I'll pick out some of her personal things and save you the trouble of going through her private drawers."

Whoa. He hadn't even thought of that. Mary nodded at the look on his face, and climbed back into the truck, pulling up just far enough so he could get out, then leading the way out through a series of dizzying back street shortcuts Dale couldn't replicate if he tried.

At Laura's house he silently handed her a mask and they went through the house as quickly as possible, closing up the bedroom after Mary emerged with a small overnight bag. He carried the modest suitcase while she grabbed the wool tote, and they closed the house up—which is how it would stay, until Dale could get a cleanup team out to do their thing. They parted ways, two tired people made heavy with worry—although when he got home, Dale took no chances on forgetting his evening maintenance inhaler dose. Not when Laura was counting on him.

Then he dragged the porch Sullybed out under the stars, shook out the sleeping bag, and settled in to watch the stars, letting them clear his mind until he could sleep.

Sometime in the middle of the night, he crawled back inside and made it as far as the couch, feet sprawling off the end, cushy fringed pillow jammed beneath his head. Far too early, the sun splashed in the tall picture window and into his eyes . . . but he was already awake. With Sully curled up in a dog ball on his stomach, taking advantage of Couch Rules to share warmth through the chilly night, Dale lingered there . . . but once he could no longer turn his eyes away from the sun, he deposited the dog gently on the floor. Sully shook off and stalked away toward the dog door, offended.

And because Dale couldn't stop himself, he said, "Want a cookie?"

Sully reversed course with alacrity, bounding up to present himself in a barely restrained sit, brown eyes expectant. Dale grabbed a tiny biscuit from the always-open cookie jar on the kitchen half-wall and put Sully through his paces—sit to show stack to down—and offered up the cookie. Sully left for the dog door at a trot, his mission remembered but his offended mood long gone.

Not a bad way to live. Maybe Dale should come back as a dog in his next life.

Until then, he'd deal with this one. That meant a shower, and then, in a weird cognitive disconnect, housecleaning—a quick vacuum in the traffic areas and Sully's favorite shedding spots, a few moments in the bathroom, more than a few moments with the dishes.

Because he'd meant what he'd said to Laura. She'd need a place to recuperate. There was no way he'd let her go home alone.

He discovered he was scrubbing the bottom out of an innocent pot and made himself take a breath and get back to reality. There was no *letting* Laura do anything. He'd just hope he could convince her—that the doctors would be on his side. And if he could, and if they were, then it'd take several days of cleaning to make this place suitable.

Drying his hands from sink duty and slathering on unscented hand lotion—a lesson learned early in his transition to this climate—Dale moved on to the Sully situation. Although Sully would be happier waiting in the Forester, there was no way he'd sit out the heat of a summer's day. And Dale could shut the dog door and leave Sully in the yard—plenty of shade beneath the patio, plenty of water in the silly oversized tub . . . but then, too, it would be a long and unpredictable day, completely out of their usual pattern.

He hit the garage, lugging out the oversized wire crate that puppy Sully had occupied in the Ohio clinic office—one of the few items to survive the fire in usable condition, even though

Dale had thought he'd never be able to bring himself to use it again.

Amazing how priorities shift. By now Sully was back inside, watching with intense curiosity and wrinkles of deep thought. Dale assembled the black wire crate, flipped the door open, stuffed the living-room Sullybed inside, and then gently pushed Sully out the dog door. When Sully poked his head right back in, undeterred, Dale had already shoved the crate into place— right up against the dog door. Coming inside would give Sully the indoor space he was used to—but only a crate's worth of it.

Sully frowned, ears long—but only for a moment. Then, his assessment made, he fell to serious scratching and rearranging of the bedding. Clearly Dale hadn't gotten it quite right.

"Have at it," Dale told him. "See if you can clean up that patio while you're at it, will you?"

busy.

Dear Aunt Cily,

You're not going to believe this. No, really. I don't believe it, and I'm here. Because Laura is in the hospital with hanta.

No. I'm not kidding.

What're the odds? That's what her cousin said last night. First Laura's nephew sucked up some hanta badness a couple hours north of here, and yesterday I found—well, Sully found—a nest in Laura's bedroom air conditioner. She was already sick. I took her to ER and that was that. Hanta.

No, don't start worrying. I was only in the bedroom for a moment—and get that knowing look off your mother-aunt face—! I was *in the bedroom* because Sully helped himself to a sniff fest, which was the part where he found the nest. Or pointed at it, anyway. I found it outside when

I went to. . . .

Never mind. It's not really that complicated. Laura is in the hospital and I wanted to let you know I'll be hard to reach for now. It's your own fault. You made a pretty big impression on a sickly kid, all that reading by my bedside. I figure I'll pass it on down the line.

I hope things are well with you and Bud. I'm fine, yes, I'm taking care of myself. Sully is fine, too. In a couple of weeks we head for another show. Plus rally this time. One of us is training the other but I'm not sure which.

Love, Dale

PS: Sully says BIG BARK! to you but then again he's never had a *little* bark to work with. . . .

PPS: Hey! Sully *is* a real grandchild. (See, I can hear you thinking that, too.)

CHAPTER 9

Earth Woman, send the rain,
  The rain, kind and gentle—
  That all may be happiness before me,
  That all may be happiness behind me,
  That all may be happiness round about me. . . .

Dale caught movement in the doorway and lowered his book to find Mary hovering in the half-open doorway, her short, stout stature already recognizable to him at a limited glance. "Hey."

"Ya'at eeh," she said, and it took him a moment to recognize the greeting he'd before only read. By then she was nodding at the bed where Laura slept, surrounded by boxy metal equipment with digital readouts and soft beeping—and not-so-soft beeping—and the harsh, mechanical sound of the ventilator that breathed for her, pushing as much oxygen as possible into fluid-filled lungs.

Even with the curtain liners drawn over the window, the harsh summer sun filled the room with light, leaving no room for shadows or illusions.

Dale said softly, "You know, I'm a vet. I do surgery. I have my own fancy machines. You'd think . . . you'd think this wouldn't be so hard."

Mary shook her head. "This, you never get used to."

Dale gestured at the other chair in the room, pulling his pointing finger at the last moment. "Have a seat?" Not bad, as comfort went; clearly the hospital was prepared for long-term visitors as well as long-term patients.

"Can't," she said. "My son is waiting for his new comic book. I left it out in the car . . . thought I'd stop by here on the way back."

Right. Robert was in the west section of the hospital—across the street. But Dale didn't point that out. He was glad enough for the company—for not being quite alone in this room with its very sick occupant. "How is he?"

Her smile was faint but still somehow added a buoyancy to the room. "He's passing water. The doctors think—" She stopped suddenly, looking at the book he held. "That was Navajo," she said. "Translated prayer."

Dale checked the book. "To Navajo Mountain," he said. "I won't even try to say the name of it—that would embarrass us both." He hesitated, looking down at the book—one man's description of a journey through Navajo lands. "I know I don't get this . . . that I *can't* get it. But I thought. . . ."

"You had a feeling," Mary said for him.

He shifted uncomfortably. "Call it an impulse. I thought it might reach her, there. Wherever she is."

"You know . . . ," Mary said, and now it was she who looked uncertain, as though she might not even go on.

"Please," Dale said. He set the book aside—there with the poetry collection he'd brought and right beside his battered old favorite, what he liked to think of as biological science fiction.

"There are medicine men who come here. They don't interfere with Biligaana medicine, but they. . . ." She gestured, making a circle of her fingers. "They look at the whole. The spiritual person. Certain things that white medicine doesn't."

Dale looked at Laura. Her chest rose abruptly with each forced inhalation; the tube going down her throat jerked ever so slightly. Her arms lay quietly outside the worn, nubby blankets.

"God," he said suddenly. "I'm so glad this won't last long. Not this part of it, anyway."

"One way or the other," Mary murmured. She took a slow breath, one of thoughtfulness. "She hasn't been with the family for a long time, but she is still born for Red Running into the Water People." She looked at Dale and said, "I could make this decision, but she's in your world now."

She—what? What was that supposed to mean? Was he supposed to delve that for cultural layers of meaning, or—

"You tell me," she said. "What would she want?"

He knew what she'd want, all right, but also what she'd never ask for. Well, she didn't have to. "Yes."

"It won't be a whole ceremony," she warned him. "Those take days. And it'll be a private thing. . . ."

"I assumed," he said.

Mary's small, darkly amused little smile was subtle, but he'd come to see the Laura in her, and he recognized it. "Some do the opposite."

"You thought I'd take advantage of the situation to peek inside another culture?" he said, keeping the volume of surprise out of his voice only because Laura was, after all, sleeping nearby.

"Not really. But—"

"Some do," he finished for her.

Mary smiled, a real smile this time. She looked at Laura and said, "She isn't without family here." And then she left.

Dale picked up the novel, careful with the worn binding, his fingers running over the familiar pages. He moved the chair closer to the bed—right there beside it, so he could put a hand beside her arm if he wanted. And though he thought he'd been quiet, that the steady mechanics of the ventilator had covered the sound of the chair moving, Laura's eyes cracked open. They hesitated that way, and Dale could almost feel her confusion—

her attempts to sort out this strange world of sounds and stringent smells and intrusive tubes and the sickness within. "Hey," he said softly, and her eyes opened wider, looking at him in a way that told him she wasn't quite focusing.

A nurse came in, smiled briefly at Dale, and set about playing with IVs, putting up a new bag and injecting it with the contents of a syringe, then injecting the contents of another syringe directly into the IV line. He didn't ask; he didn't want to talk about Laura as though she weren't there, and besides, he already knew. A bolus of vasodilators, along with a slower drip— all to keep the blood flowing to her heart, brain, and kidneys as her circulatory system tried to shut down . . . the same process that had filled her lungs with fluid.

There was no fix for hanta, no treatment . . . just support measures the medical community had learned to apply early and hard.

The nurse looked down at Laura and said firmly, "You're doing very well. You certainly have a devoted fan."

Laura's gaze switched back to Dale; he waggled his fingers at her. She tried to say something; with her voice and lips obscured by the ventilator tube, he had no idea what it might be. After a moment, a tear rolled out of the corner of her eye and down to the pillow.

Dale smiled. He recognized that tear. Not despair, not fear, but anger and frustration. He grew so bold as to wipe his thumb over the track it had left. "Give it a day," he told her. "You can tell me then." And he leaned back in the chair and lifted the thick, battered paperback. *"The sign was rain-smeared and had never been overly straight. . . ."*

CHAPTER 10

"Well?" Sheri demanded.

Monday morning and Sheri was loud in every way. The bold flower print slacks, one size too small on her large-and-flaunt-it frame; an orange and blue shirt, broad horizontal stripes that defied the eye. Her hair towered behind her head, slicked and sprayed to helmet properties and adorned with a spray of rhinestones. Her lipstick matched the orange of her shirt; so did her nails.

She stayed up late over weekend nights planning these outfits, Dale was sure of it. Mondays were always a day of sartorial splendor.

"Well?" She tried it again, notching up the volume. Dale wasn't unaware of the eavesdroppers—Dru from the entrance to the kennel, Isaac from inside the procedures room, Jade from one of the exam rooms. Brad would be here later, still picking up the lion's share of the work while Dale avoided construction dust. "I hope she's doing better than you. You look terrible."

He probably did. He didn't care. Just as he'd missed the weekend's puppy match and didn't care, had failed to do his laundry and didn't care . . . had a huge big grin plastered all over his face, a big sappy one about which Sheri would tease him for months and he didn't care a bit. "She's off the ventilator this morning," he said around that grin.

He hadn't planned ahead for a public service announcement, but he should have realized how fast the word would spread . . .

and that his people would care. The collective sigh of relief was, in fact, quite audible. Sully, crabby and out of sorts after two days of Dale's crate-and-dog-door-and-abandonment arrangement, gave the sound a suspicious look and growled deep in his throat, then gave it up.

woe. give me cookies. give me pets. make me special.

Dale did, in fact, scoop him up, absently rumpling his ears until he found the spot that made Sully give up his sulk and switch to dog-purring. "She'll get over it pretty fast, now, they say."

"Think it had anything to do with that medicine man?" Sheri said, and now that her worries were assuaged, she switched to gossip-tabloid mode. She plucked the bag of donut holes from the counter where Dale had just set them—Terry's donation to the clinic when he'd heard the news moments earlier. "I'll just ready these up in a nice bowl."

How had she even known about prayers said over Laura—? No, never mind. He didn't want to know. "Save some for me— I'm not eating until after surgery. And I'm not going to answer that. It was a private thing." And yes, Laura had been different afterward. She hadn't yanked out the ventilator and danced down the hall, but her eyes had been brighter; her body more relaxed. The frustration was gone; there had been no more tears. *In beauty may I walk; All day long may I walk. . . .* He had read those words to her, and felt this time that she absorbed them. As if she found it easier to accept his help.

"Damn," Sheri said, but there was no feeling behind it. "Well, if we're not gonna get any juicy details, you might as well get some work done around here before you *leave early.* Some of us got to work all day. Some of us worked all last week, too. Go put that neglected little dog away and find yourself a patient."

"Yes'm," Dale said, because she amused him just enough, thinking she'd hidden her concern and relief. He headed down the hall with Sully, anticipating a goodly pile of mail and paperwork, and stopped short at the door to his office. "Whoa."

"Didn't I mention?" she said airily, the wheels to her chair squeaking as she rolled in that direction from within her own domain. "They did your office last week."

"No kidding," Dale said, unaccountably dazed by the change. He'd known it was coming . . . heck, he'd picked out the furniture and paint and new shelves and blinds and even the short, nubby Berber-like carpet. He just hadn't anticipated the combined effect of it all. His rickety desk was now a solid black-topped creation with organizers on top, set into the back corner so he'd be facing out, sitting in a new black chair—a big-and-tall-sized chair. The blinds were a significant improvement simply because they worked, but the charcoal color looked sleek against cool white walls—freshly painted at that. And the carpet . . . a short loop, easy to maintain and plenty sturdy, but the padding made it a pleasure to walk on.

"Whoa," he said again, and set Sully down to hunt out the Sullybed while he checked out the new shelves, light fixtures, and the squeakless roll of the chair. Sully didn't make it as far as his bed. He dropped to the carpet and rolled ecstatically, freely offering up the scent of Beagle.

Sheri couldn't help herself. She came up behind him. "*Well?*" she asked once more, but this time her voice held suppressed excitement—a child at Christmas, giving a gift. No doubt she'd supervised putting the office back together.

"Whoa," he repeated once more, except this time he did it in his Keanu Reeves voice, and Sheri giggled.

She bumped past him to enter the office, heading for the blinds to demo them. "Look!" she said. "They work!"

"Be a shame to pay for new blinds that didn't," he told her, but he couldn't help but admire their smooth efficiency. Sunlight fell across Sully, who stopped rolling to blink at the dust motes he'd stirred up.

"And look at this," she said, gesturing at his new shelves—books lined up as they'd been on the old shelves, but much straighter—and then at the organizers. "And there's a new computer in the procedures room, and you just better keep yourselves updated after each appointment, and in here it's nothing but nice, neat—" She stopped, frowning at the desk. "Now what—" And then she hushed up quickly, as though she wished she hadn't spoken in the first place, and stepped back. "Think I hear my phone ringing—"

But Dale had seen it. Stirred by the faint breeze of her Vanna White gesture, it slipped across the slick new surface of the desk and into his field of view.

Another note.

"No," said Sheri, and now she hovered as though she might clap her hand over it and make it disappear. However lightly she'd taken the things before, his reaction to the last one had made an impact. "We don't even need to look at this. It's just meanness. And my Tremayne could write better poetry."

Dale couldn't argue that last bit. But he made it across the office in two long strides anyway, widening Sheri's eyes as he beat her to the note.

"Damn," she said. "I forgot about"—she gestured, out of words for once—"those."

"Legs," Dale said, sliding the note across the desk and flipping it over. "I keep them tucked away for emergencies." He had Sully's attention, too—anything worth doing that fast was worth investigation.

"You look, you gotta share," she told him, inching closer—but not quite close enough to see the note. He'd made an impression, all right. "What's it say?"

He shifted so she could see it.

Survivors are few
With slackers like you.

"Holy crap," Sheri said.

Dale didn't respond. For a moment, he *couldn't* respond. His throat tightened down in anger and horror and his jaw tightened, muscles twitching.

Laura.

He knew it, in that moment, without any doubt at all. And though the absurdity of it, the sensible *you must be kidding* of it, came flooding in almost too fast to separate the two reactions, he hung onto that horror. He listened to it.

"That's a threat," Sheri pointed out. "That's exactly what that is, a threat."

"No." Dale had to fight to keep his hand from closing around the note, crumpling it into uselessness. He shouldn't even have touched it at all. Now, carefully, he placed it back on the desk. There'd be a plastic bag in the break room. "That's not a threat," he told her. "It's a confession."

CHAPTER 11

Sheri followed him back down the hall, past the waiting room and procedures room, taking a sharp left toward the area of continuing construction, in front of which sat the stairs; she followed him latched on, and her demanding tones had worry in them, too. "How do you figure, a confession?"

"Put it together with the other notes," Dale said over his shoulder. Taunting and implications and promises. Expectations. "Whoever wrote that note wanted something from me . . . he didn't get it. Now he's making sure I can't ignore him any longer."

"You're not making sense—"

Dale spun around at the foot of the stairs; Sheri didn't quite stop soon enough, so the one ferocious step he took was enough to bring them closer than either had intended. "*Laura*, that's what. The son of a bitch got to Laura. And that's as far as he's—"

And this time he was the one who stopped, because Sheri looked up at him—head tilted back, not giving an inch of space—in complete bewilderment. "Laura has *hanta*, Dr. Dale. Some damned mouse got into her air conditioner. There ain't no way to *make* that happen."

And a very sensible comment it was.

"It's just coincidence—" Sheri started, but her gaze tracked off to something behind him and Dale turned around to see one of the painters heading for the exit—the little guy, his movement on the furtive side of casual, and even so very nearly hid-

119

den by the piles of gear and supplies jammed in at this end of the building.

Of course. "Idiot," Dale growled, meaning himself. *Of course, the construction workers.* "Hey—wait!"

The painter scuttled through the door and not even long legs did Dale any good in navigating the overstuffed hallway—he tripped, he recovered, he lunged for the closing door—

"Dr. Dale!" Sheri cried after him—but it wasn't enough to cover the sound of a big diesel truck chugging out of the construction area behind the clinic and accelerating up the steeply inclined drive to the four-lane.

Dale slammed the flat of his hand against the closed door and whirled around to set his back to it, full of glower. "Who *else,*" he said. "Who else has had unlimited access to this place? To my office?"

"Me?" Sheri suggested, strikingly tentative compared to her norm. "Dru? Any of us? Just about any client? We don't exactly keep that room a secret."

"He *ran,*" Dale snarled. *If only I'd been a little smarter, a little faster. . . .* "No reason for that, unless he was up to something."

"Yeah, like maybe he saw the look on your face," she snorted, much more like herself. "Maybe he's skimming paint off the top." Dale shot her a look and she drew herself back up into fully indomitable Sheri-mode. "No, no, you *must* be right. That pathetic little poop-log of a painter writes bad poetry, and has it in for you, and he's the Hanta Santa to boot."

The Hanta Santa.

Now that you put it that way. . . . But Dale didn't say it out loud. He remembered that gut feeling of horror and he clung to it. He *tried* to cling to it. . . .

From beyond the waiting room came the sound of knocking.

"And no wonder." Sheri pointed at her watch—a gaudy thing on a pink fluorescent band. "It's five minutes past the first appointment. You're only here half a day—you'd best get through them all. And wipe that glowering broody hero look off your face. If we got an old lady here you're gonna scare the crap out of her, and if we got a young one she's just gonna fall in love. But don't worry. If she does, I'll be sure to tell her you're crazy."

smells. everywhere, smells. and new things. gotta roll. not as good as dale hair, but gotta roll. scratchy itchy roll.

nose stings. stinky walls, stinky everything.

where's my bed?

where's my food?

can't smell the important things. the people here. too many people here, can't tell who. can't tell when.

that's not right!

beagle woe!

CHAPTER 12

And so there Dale was. Trying to hang on to that certainty, even just the memory of certainty. Waiting on the industrial side of the Flagstaff tracks, past the alluring consumer opportunities of the giant warehouse store, the hardware store, and the nursery, and sitting in the County Sheriff's office. Or rather, the parking lot, where he still pretty much stuck out like a sore thumb.

He had one of those, too. Not all of the day's patients had been happy to see him.

Dale sat sideways in the driver's seat, stretching his legs out. The raised tailgate let the hot afternoon air stir through the car. He'd already walked Sully in the shade of some thoughtfully planted trees still too young to do much good, and refilled the water bottle attached to the side of the crate. The steady grinding noise in the background meant Sully had accepted the offering of a super-durable nylon bone and hadn't yet noticed it was getting close to dinner.

Dale hoped he didn't notice for quite a while. He'd intended to leave Sully at home and fed when he went to visit Laura, but the day hadn't turned out as expected. Not since the moment he'd seen that note.

The grinding stopped. A short, querulous yodel took its place. *feed me?*

So much for the not noticing. Well, Dale had a handful of kibble somewhere in the vehicle. Just a matter of finding it, which he'd been too sapped by the heat to attempt before now.

Not to mention feeling sorry for his throbbing thumb.

feed me?

"Yeah, yeah." He leaned back to check the glove compartment, but that would have been too easy. Likewise a glance into the back seat footwells, crowded as they were by having the seats flipped down. Sully circled inside the wire crate, toenails scuffing and bone forgotten. *feeding me.*

Not there. Not stuck in various nooks and crannies, not in the obvious places. Dale finally gave it up . . . he was going to have to get out and reverse himself, stretching over the driver's seat to grope beneath the passenger seat. Stretching. . . .

"Hey there," Rena Wells said to his butt.

"Just what I've been waiting for," he muttered. But he'd snagged the baggie of kibble, and brought it out with him, turning to find Rena watching with a certain avid interest.

He was going to get Terry for this. He would have been happy in his blissful ignorance, oh yes he would have. "Hey, Rena," he said, so casually, as he ducked around back to dump the kibble on Sully's crate tray, giving him a free-for-all type of dinner. A kibble hunt. "I was hoping to see you here."

"Figured you might be waiting," she said, though a faint disappointment crossed her face before the all-business expression took its place. "I don't really have anything to tell you . . . I haven't heard a thing that relates to your notes."

"That's not why I'm here," he said, and then doubled back on himself. "Well, it is, actually, but—hold on a sec." He dropped the baggie on the passenger seat, wiped his hands on the seat of his jeans, and reached up to the dash for another baggie—that one thing he knew exactly how to find. The note. "Another one."

Reluctantly, she took it. Uniformed officers filtered through the rest of the parking lot; low comments reached Dale's ears, nothing audible. Rena glanced at them, scowled, and then read the note and scowled again. "This is getting a little more serious."

"I thought so." He didn't mention the hanta. If Sheri, who normally leaped to join in any absurdity, any bizarre conspiracy silliness, had given him *that look* in response to the Hanta Santa, Dale didn't think Rena would react any better. At this point, he just wanted the notes taken seriously.

Another low comment in the background, followed by laughter. A rude kind of laughter. A *laughing at* kind of laughter.

"Hey," he said suddenly. "You're taking crap just for talking to me."

Rena shrugged, still looking at the note. "No one tells me who to spend time with." She looked up quickly, her words coming just as fast. "Not that we're actually *spending time* together, but—"

"I get it," Dale said. "I appreciate it. I didn't realize. . . ." He looked over the tops of the cars, the backs of the high pickup truck beds. Off-duty folk, disappearing into their cars—but not without a final look and gesture in his direction. "You said something, but I didn't realize. . . ."

"They felt stupid," Rena said. "They should have figured out the killings before you did. And you know what? They're right. They should have." She raised her voice. "I'd have a lot more respect for them if they owned up to it like *grown-ups.*" She snorted. "Manly men."

Dale stifled a wry grin, but not quite successfully enough; she caught it, and social horror crossed her face. "I mean, no offense. Some of them are even women. But you know what I mean."

Maybe he even did. But he didn't think he was going to admit it. "What do you think?"

"I don't like the looks of it," she said. "I'm going to talk to someone tomorrow. Anything going on that worries you? Pranks, like last spring?"

Dale bit his tongue on the words *Hanta Santa.* "I'm keeping my eyes open," he said. "But things have been a little crazy lately."

"Yeah," she said sympathetically. "Laura."

He quite suddenly liked her a whole lot more. "She's off the vent," he heard himself saying. "I'm headed over that way now. But honestly, I don't think I'd notice if anything odd went on right now."

She nodded, and it hit him then how true his words were. He wouldn't notice. The Hanta Santa could come trouping through with a sleigh pulled by deer mice and *he wouldn't notice.*

If Dale was right, if Laura's illness had been no coincidence, if the notes were as much a threat as he thought they were . . . then the Hanta Santa might not be done. And the next time, Dale might not be paying quite enough attention. The next time, he might be too late.

And so he almost opened his mouth to say something . . . and then he saw Rena wince at the last lingering laughter on the other side of the small parking lot, and he thought of how fast the phrase *Hanta Santa* would spread through the entire local law enforcement community, and he thought *how can I possibly be right?* So he cleared his throat on those intended words and instead said, "Thanks for asking."

She nodded again, although she hadn't actually asked. "Do your best to keep that eye out. And . . . tell Laura feel better soon."

Those things, he could fervently promise.

"She's still very ill," the nurse said, casting a leery eye on Dale's duffel bag. A spur-of-the-moment duffel bag. The Forester: a vehicle of many resources.

"Yes," Dale said, quite solemn. "All those tubes and beeping things, the way that blood pressure cuff thing does its thing every fifteen minutes, the funny pale color of her face—"

The nurse rolled her eyes, having encountered Dale's occasionally inexplicable sense of humor already. "Be good," she warned him.

Dale waggled his eyebrows and walked backwards toward Laura's room at the same time, and just happened to give the wiggling duffel a bump so it stayed on his back, out of sight. He waited until something else caught the nurse's attention—not a long wait in this busy hospital—and then turned so he could slip silently inside Laura's room—still in critical care, but possibly to be moved tomorrow. *Out of critical care. Yes!* He eased the door closed.

She was asleep. All the tubes, all the machines, the funny color of her face . . . but no ventilator. Hanta took its best shot, a hard shot, but it didn't linger. Dale tugged the duffel around, patting it when it made a muffled noise, and unzipped it in slow motion, as silently as possible. Not a twitch from Laura.

Her breathing still came fast and a little shallow, and he didn't even want to think what her lungs sounded like . . . but he wasn't here with his stethoscope. Ohh, no. He was, in fact, here with his incredible face-licking dog.

As the front half of Sully emerged from the duffel, Dale's hand hovered above his muzzle, poised to close should the oddity of things inspire a bark. He bent near the bed, aiming his missile of unconditional affection, and knew exactly when Sully saw Laura—when he smelled her and recognized her amidst the oddities. His tail beat furiously inside the duffel. Dale grinned, unable to stifle what was undoubtedly an immature glee.

They moved close enough so Sully's whiskers stirred Laura's hair—loose and strewn across the pillow, starting to acquire that lived-in look. Dale whispered, "Git 'er, Sully, git 'er."

Sully's tail revved up, thwacking the canvas until finally all that energy had to come out somewhere; he made a little *wooo* and commenced to lick. After a moment, Laura stirred. And then she smiled, eyes still closed, a sleepy, tired smile. Dale withdrew his secret weapon just enough to stop the licking but not the sniffing or the tail, and Laura cracked her eyes open. Her voice was little more than a whisper. "They're gonna be so mad at you."

"I'm tough. I can take it." It was worth it, anyway, to see the smile.

"You're not tougher than these nurses," Laura promised him.

"Let's pretend I am. Just for now." Dale slipped the duffel strap off his shoulder as Laura patted the bed, moving her arm aside as much as the tubes and her obvious weakness allowed. He snuggled Sully, duffel and all, up against her side, and sat gingerly on the edge of the bed to make sure the arrangement stayed stable. Laura rubbed Sully's ears—a little clumsy, not with any vigor—and Sully set to washing her hand.

mine.

"As if," Dale told him, but gave him a pat through the duffel. "I earn points for this," he told Laura. "Braving the nurses, taking the stairs so we wouldn't get outed in the elevator. . . ."

"Uh-huh," she said, unimpressed. Her hand stilled; she looked up at him. "I guess I get to make it, huh?"

Dale shrugged. "If you were gonna go, odds are you'd be gone."

She suppressed a sudden weak snort, not very successfully. "Oh my God," she said. "Don't you have a silver tongue."

"Standard operating procedure," he said. "Wait till I tell you about the Hanta Santa."

She laughed outright and then coughed from it, and coughed some more, while Sully's ears tented in concern and his forehead wrinkled.

woe.

127

"It's not the same thing," Dale told him. "She'll be okay." Wouldn't she? She still had the nasal oxygen cannula, but he wondered about a full mask or inhalation therapy or—

She finally took a deep breath—then glanced at them and almost burst into laughter again, stopping herself only by clapping a hand over her nose and mouth. "Oh," she said in a strangled voice, from behind her hand. "You two . . . your expressions. . . ." She shook her head, helpless to continue, and concentrated on her breathing, but her eyes still sparked with humor.

Dale looked at Sully and Sully looked at Dale, and Dale finally said, "Oh, right. Mock my concern."

Laura settled against the pillow. "Your own fault," she said, but her voice wasn't as strong as it had been, and Dale knew she was already tiring. He dumped Sully out of the duffel and directed him to curl up at the foot of the bed, where he covered the dog with one of Laura's light blankets. It would protect them from a cursory glance. . . .

Maybe.

He pulled the chair over to her bedside and said, "I got another note."

Her eyebrows raised; she opened her mouth. He got his fingers there in time, though, hovering just over her lips. "Rest a few more moments. I'll tell you everything."

She searched his eyes for a moment; he wasn't sure what she was looking for. But she gave the faintest of nods and he sat back. "I'm an idiot," he said for starters, and almost broke her silence right then and there, but subsided. He hardly liked that any better; he would rather have been at the receiving end of a dry, sly remark than see the exhaustion pulling at her. But he said none of that; he merely continued. "It should have been obvious . . . all those construction workers . . . who else has that access? Other than the staff, I mean, and it's not like any of them would bother to rhyme a note. They'd just put something in my food."

That got a smile. Good. He said, "So I figure it was one of them. The way that painter ran this morning? He was strange from the start, but I figured he was just, well, *strange*. There's enough of that going around here. But now I think he was being strange at *me*. Anyway, he ran."

And now she gave him a very cross look, an impatient one. He grinned. "Feeling a little better?" Something inside him relaxed; he put one foot up against her bed rail. "Here's what you want. It said, 'Survivors are few, with slackers like you.' "

Her eyes widened.

"Yeah," he agreed. "So I would have been here earlier, but I gave the note to Rena. It kinda looks like I didn't make any friends with the Staties this spring, though. Or probably the Flagstaff cops, when it comes to that. But she's on our side—"

Laura didn't stop herself this time. "*Your* side."

"Same thing," Dale said firmly. "She's going to turn the notes in tomorrow." He hoped she didn't take too much grief from it. But that final note . . . even a begrudging soul should be able to see it was a threat. Not even necessarily to Dale. "Here's the thing," he said. "I was thinking . . . okay, it's a little hard to swallow, but. . . ."

She might be sick, but she still wasn't slow. "You're dancing, Dale."

He sunk a little lower in his chair, which pushed his knee a little higher. Not dignified. "When I saw that note . . . I know, I know . . . I just suddenly thought . . . your illness isn't an accident. That note wasn't a threat . . . it was a *gloat*. I know, I *know*—" He cut her off, as her expression finished working its way through astonished and into reaction—into response. "Hanta needs mouse excretions to spread. Gotta have the poop. It's not like anthrax . . . it's not bio-terrorist material. I'm just telling you my reaction. Unfortunately, I reacted in front of Sheri, so. . . ."

"Hanta Santa," Laura said, pretty much a perfect summary.

Dale let his head tip back against the upper edge of the chair cushion, and not gently. "I'm doomed," he groaned.

"For a while," Laura agreed. She tucked hair behind her ear. "Status quo at that place, don't you think? I have to tell you, Dale . . . no one ever hangs dog testicles from my rearview mirror."

"I didn't—" No, of course he hadn't told her. But the culprits obviously had. "I have a plan," he informed her.

"Beside the point. If it's not that, it'll be something else. It might as well be these notes and the Hanta Santa. And you might as well follow your instincts."

"I—what?" He lifted his head, made a show of clearing his ear. "What?"

"You know," she said, clearly changing the subject—except he doubted it would be just that. "You were right. To have Mary's friend come in. It helped. I don't know if it helped the disease, but it helped *me*. So you can laugh at the whole Hanta Santa thing, but . . . don't lose that ability to follow your nose."

"Sully's nose," Dale murmured.

She didn't back off. "That, too. It's how you got me here in time for them to get ahead of this thing—and you know as well as I that getting ahead of this thing makes all the difference in the world. In my life."

Huh. "You didn't think that way not so long ago." Like, when Dale met her. "Common sense. Things are what they are. Etcetera."

Laura shrugged. "We change," she said. And then, pointedly, "*You* did."

CHAPTER 13

"Mr. Dr. Dale. . . ." There was Dru, leaning in the doorway of Dale's office, her scrub top rucked up over her jeans to be particularly shapeless, short grey hair looking particularly brushy. And Dale wasn't used to the reluctance in her voice.

He swiveled around in his comfy new Big 'n' Tall chair so she could see the phone at his ear, and held up a finger. "Look, he's one of your men, and I'd like to—"

Blah blah blah since he bothered you he won't be back. . . .

"That's not the point. I need to get some information about him."

Blah blah blah privileged.

"I've got concerns about things that happened while he was working here. He *ran*—" Dale's hand tightened around the phone. If anyone knew something about these notes, it was the painter who'd run. He sure as heck knew something about *something.* Hence the running.

Blah blah blah you chased *him.*

"He ran first," Dale said, and rolled his eyes at the sound of that.

"Pretty pathetic," Dru told him, in obvious agreement.

Blah blah blah If you have evidence of wrongdoing, call the police. Meanwhile he won't return to your clinic as we finish the job.

Yeah, well. That was about what he'd expected. He'd just *hoped.* And he hadn't given up; he'd just tucked that little loose end away—because if he had to, he *would* tell Rena about it.

But not until she wasn't fighting bad attitude on her end. He had other things to do, first. He mumbled a few polite words and hung up the phone.

Dru held up a dead mouse for his attention, dangling not from the tail but one limp hind leg. "This yours?"

He hastened to retrieve it. "I told you I'd get those!"

"So fire me," she said, following him down the hall and into the procedures room, where he donned gloves and a mask to handle the little creature. No messing around; he had to get its blood drawn and cooled.

"You really sending those samples to Stanford?" She gave him her most skeptical eyebrow.

"Surprisingly cheap," he told her, ignoring the eyebrow. Well, not the shipping. But that's why he was doing it in batches. And it had been surprising and even a little alarming how quickly he'd gathered samples. Who knew they'd had so many mice around the clinic? The edges of the property had become Sully's hunting ground; Dale set traps and little live traps; he hunted nests and cleaned them out. Here, at home . . . at Laura's. If Laura's hanta had been only coincidence, then there had to be a local population carrying the disease.

So far he hadn't found it. But then, he'd only been at this a couple of days, and had yet to receive the results from his second batch of little victims. Not long, now. The test took a matter of moments, once the Stanford comparative medicine people got started.

And they used E-mail.

"Dale," Dru started again, dropping the Doctor and the Mister, and getting his attention that way. "You don't think you're going a little bit overboard?"

He looked over at her, surprised at the wrinkles of concern nestled in with the wrinkles of just plain oldness. "Obsessed, you mean?"

"That's one word for it." She crossed her arms, a tad of the usual attitude creeping in; her fingers twitched in the direction of the unopened cigarettes in her sleeve. "Mice everywhere. Traps waiting to snap someone's toes off. And you're still on half days on next week's schedule."

"I wouldn't be, if construction hadn't stopped dead at the beginning of the week," Dale said. "You'd be the first to have words at me if I didn't stay away from the dust."

"True," she admitted. "No point in being an idiot. But you're worrisome. Tell me you don't really believe this Hanta Santa stuff. Stop poking that damn dead mouse with a needle and look at me, and tell me you don't really believe."

Dale's heart sank, rather unexpectedly. He hadn't realized that he'd counted on Dru, of all people, to withhold judgment.

But he cleared his throat, and he pushed back that twinge. "The place has fewer mice than it did," he said. "What's the problem?"

"The problem is that you're *worrying* us. And we don't like it. *I* don't like it."

Dale did put down the syringe, and leaned back against the counter to regard her, propping his hip against hard composite counter top. "What I'm doing," he said, his voice gone a little flat, "is trying to *disprove* the Hanta Santa. If I can find the disease in the mice around Laura's place. . . ."

"Oh, *pfft*," she said. "If that's *all* you were doing, we wouldn't be trapping around the clinic."

He couldn't help his startled look. "You have a problem with knowing that we're in the clear? Knowing for *sure?*"

"No," Dru said, tapping her sleeve. The cigarettes were mighty close. Her fingers twitched and withdrew. "But I don't think that's all you're doing, and neither does anyone else. You're really looking for the Santa—and you ought to just be spending more time at the hospital."

"They've got Laura in therapy half the time," Dale said, glad for ready words to fill in over that still-sunk feeling from Dru's defection. "She's busier than I am." *And I want this* done *by the time she's released.* No more Santa. No more notes. Just Laura, feeling safe and welcome at his place. He took a deep breath. "Thing is, Dru, I don't need anyone's blessing. I'm doing this thing. And I don't want to hear about it again, unless you happen to come up with words of unmitigated and admiring support for my persistence in the face of generalized mockery." He caught her eye; his voice went flat again. Deeper. "I mean it, Dru. End of discussion."

"*Well.*" Dru stood tall—which wasn't very, as she was probably already an inch shorter than she'd once been—and gathered her dignity and her expression. "I guess *that's* clear enough."

For an instant he wondered if he'd gone too far.

For an instant.

And then as Dru marched noisily out of the room, she hesitated to call loudly out into the waiting area and Sheri's command center. "Hey, Sheri! He's in a *mood.* You'd better hide the new Anta-say and the mouse-deer."

"Deer *mouse,*" Dale muttered, but was just as glad that no one heard him. There was, it seemed, no such thing as going *too far* when it came to his staff.

Sully shifted around the office, air-scenting . . . not quite finding whatever he thought he was looking for. Dale raised a leg so Sully could check under the desk, and grabbed a donut hole from the sadly depleted bowl there, mentally adding sit-ups to the evening tally. Terry had taken to saving day-olds for them; quite possibly too much of a good thing.

He popped it in his mouth, closed his eyes in appreciation, and let it melt there a while. *Nah.* No such thing as too much of a good thing.

In the background, something made a deep and ominous clanking noise that echoed through the clinic via the new ducts, setting off a round of barking from patients and boarders alike. A muffled curse; a short argument. The lights briefly cut out.

"It's all right," Dale said to the office air. "I'm done for the day. And Laura's about to call." On the cell, but Dale didn't want to be caught on the road in not-answering mode.

Sully ignored it all, casting about the office for the elusive scent and baffled by all the new-things smells. New carpet, new furniture, new paint, new blinds . . . none of which had been properly broken in and Sullified yet. He'd given up on moving around and stood in the middle of the office, his tail forgotten and wilting at half-mast, his nose in the air. He spared a quick glance at Dale. *find!*

"Don't look at me, son. I can barely tell which laundry is clean and which is—" The cell phone saved him from that revelation; he grabbed it. "Breathe on!"

"Hello to you too." Laura's amusement came through so clearly to him he wasn't sure how he'd ever thought it understated. And whoa, she sounded strong. She sounded *good*.

"Sounds like they pumped you full of air, all right." *Oh, crap.* "Okay, wait, that was a lot more rude than I meant it to be."

"Uh-huh," she said. "I think my afternoon entertainment might just be listening to you dig your way out of it."

"How about I just skip straight to door number two?" Dale asked. The desperate in his voice showed through, but upon reflection he thought that maybe wasn't a bad thing. The lights went out again; in the background, Sheri said something sharp and strongly suggestive.

The fun had gone out of the ongoing construction, it seemed. His fault, probably. He'd turned it serious and strange, and even the Hanta Santa cutouts couldn't save it.

"I heard that," Laura said. "Good thing it's your lunch hour there. Who's covering?"

Emergency walk-ins, she meant. "Brad," he said. "And just for the record, I had a salad before I sat down with these donut holes. So, door number two—you have a chance to talk to your cousin?"

Laura laughed, and then coughed, and then said, "So this is what it's like to be you. No offense, but you can have it."

"I'd say it's yours for a while yet. But no permanent damage, right?"

"They don't expect it. And yes, I did. She says you're welcome to take a look around, set all the traps you want. She left her keys with me, said she'd call her neighbors."

Dale didn't respond right away, thinking that one through.

"So they won't take you out with a baseball bat," Laura reminded him gently. "It's a close community, Dale. You're going to stand out if you go poking around, permission or no."

"Would they?" he asked, startled. "Baseball bat?"

Another laugh. "Not likely. But you could count on an uncomfortable conversation with tribal police."

Hmm. The Hanta Santa theory would be a hard sell if the community was acting watchdog. Not that he *had* an actual Hanta Santa theory. Just some vague arm waving that precluded random factors and included human intent. "I'll go out this afternoon," he decided. It would mean for a very late night, and boy would morning come early. . . .

But the sooner he resolved things, if only in his own mind, the sooner the clinic renovations would again become the biggest challenge of his life. The sooner he could put all his energy into getting Laura well again.

Or at least as much energy as she would allow. And then, he knew—deep down, he knew—he'd have to back off, give her space. Let her reassure herself that she was still whole unto herself.

"I'll probably be sleeping when you come by for the keys," Laura admitted. "Those respiratory therapy guys have way too much fun." Then she hesitated, long enough so Dale plucked another donut hole from the bowl, turning it over in his fingers. Sully gave up on whatever impossible thing he'd been trying to scent down and bounced to attention, riveted to Dale's hand. *mine!*

Dale raised a warning finger at him with that very hand as Laura finally brought herself to ask, "No more notes?"

"No." Dale couldn't keep the disappointment from his voice. Well, that was just stupid. It wasn't not as if he *wanted* more of the things, was it?

"Dale!" Laura seemed to think the same. And Sully couldn't have cared less about that warning finger; his eyes were riveted to Dale's hand; his nose was riveted to Dale's hand.

"It's just—" he said, uncomfortable and on the spot and full of blurt, "It's just if I had another one, maybe I'd understand—"

"Or not," Laura said, as an atypical whine burst its way out of Sully, surprising them both but hardly deterring Sully; he followed every minute movement of Dale's hand and now that the first whine had broken the noise barrier, soft little yodels of *want* commenced in its wake.

"Or not," Dale admitted, half his attention on Sully's oddball self, half on the words he hadn't really wanted to say. Time to fill his mouth and go think about just how right Sheri and Dru might be when it came to pointing the finger at obsessed.

It was Sully who stopped him. Sully who followed his hand so avidly that he stood on his hind legs with front legs dangling in Beagle-meerkat pose, his expression so full of passionate *want* and *disbelief* and *ohplease ohplease* that Dale thought twice, that he actually *looked* at the small round object he was about to pop into his mouth, inches from target and *"Yeaghh!"* And his fingers spasmed closed on that thing once so beloved of the young mixed breed he'd neutered the morning before, and it pinched right out from between them to fly across the room, bounce off the opposite wall, and skip over the carpet.

mine! Sully gave a short squeak-bark of delight and pounced, missed, pounce-pounce-pounced across the room until one of those pounces ended just as it had with Laura's shed mouse, *pounce-flip-gulp!*

And Laura said, "Dale? *Dale?*"

And Dale said faintly, "It's okay. Sully caught a . . . mouse. Thing. A mouse-thing. And ate it."

From down the hall at Sheri's command center, he was certain he heard an insane cackle of triumph.

Dear Aunt Cily—

Oh. My. *God.* Why didn't you ever warn me that this is the way women think? I'm never eating donut holes again. Ever. And if they think I was kidding about that tea. . . .

Listen . . . could you just remind me one more time . . . just because I got the answers once, doesn't mean I'm going to get them this time? Or that anyone will? Or that there are even answers to get . . . ?

No, never mind. I just can't stop myself. We both know it. Say hi to Bud, will you? And don't think I didn't notice that sly little line you dropped about heading into Columbus for a couple of simple little tests. They do *simple little tests* right there in the local hospital. Nice try, though.

Sully would say hi, but his mouth is full.

Love, Dale

CHAPTER 14

Dale picked up some Cold Stone Creamery ice cream for Laura, and left it tucked away in a small cooler filled with ice and marked *urine sample* so it wouldn't disappear while Laura slept. He scooped the keys off the tray table beside her hospital bed, kissed her forehead, and lingered long enough to note her hair was freshly washed and her face had something of its usual quiet strength even as she slept, and felt much better as he headed out to his latest obsessive investigation. *Sleep in beauty,* he thought at her and hoped it wasn't too irreverent, and headed on out.

Laura's cousin lived on the reservation—not quite at the Four Corners heart of it where Utah time and reservation time and Arizona time zones all mixed in to make watches in general completely irrelevant, but the southern Arizona section between Cameron and Tuba City. Route 89 headed north past the pines, past the lava fields of Sunset Crater, and then down past the flats and ancient stone homes of Wupatki, the summer heat of the lower altitudes beating against the Forester while Sully mumbled dream thoughts to himself in the back crate. Dale felt as though he was driving from one world into another as the Painted Desert sketched in the distant east side of the two-lane highway and hogans dotted the side of the road.

Not to mention the hand-painted signs proclaiming the existence of dinosaur tracks, bones, eggs, and, for good measure, cheap Indian jewelry.

Mary lived just north of Cameron in a small community near the Little Colorado, one full of stark rock landscapes. She'd left a sketched map with the keys, which was just as well; these dirt roads weren't on any state map. And although the vast landscape allowed him to see the clusters of homes, they weren't quite in the proximity to be what Dale would have called neighborhoods.

Small homes, modest homes, half of them with traditional hogans to the side, a small corral for a horse with a lean-to for shade and various outbuildings . . . not much living off the land to be done in this arid place. Mary taught school in Cameron, Dale knew that much. And to judge by her map, this was her turn-off, here to this sturdy little double-wide trailer sunk permanently into place, her nearest neighbor not all that far away after all. It gave him some odd comfort to think she wasn't quite that alone out here—and then as he pulled to a stop outside the trailer, taking the spot Mary's own vehicle would normally use, he had to remind himself again that he was seeing things through his own limited Ohio farmboy eyes.

"Well, *still*," he said out loud, as Sully yawned loudly and, as they just sat there, ran one paw slowly and deliberately down the crate wires, claws ticking across metal. "We're waiting," Dale told him. "We're being polite." Not that anyone would come out to greet them, because there was, after all, no one here. But he could remind himself of the cultural rules here just the same.

After a moment he cut the engine, jammed his battered straw cowboy hat over dark hair that otherwise soaked up the sun, and went around the back to flip up the tailgate. From there he spent a few moments adjusting to the wash of overwhelming heat while stretching his legs and Sully's legs, walking around the house and sizing up the situation. Neat, tidy . . . landscaping of natural rock and sparse cactus, with no vegetation to speak of around the house, the scruffy desert equivalent of weeds cropping up around the homemade shed behind.

Beyond that, the ground grew rugged and raw, climbing weathered sandstone and unstable rocks, reds and ochres and browns creating a foothold for the stout miniature mesa that grew up behind it. A jutting finger of rocky ground crept down between Mary's yard and her neighbor's; to judge by the map, behind them lay nothing but the untamed earth cracks and plateaus of the area lining the Little Colorado gorge.

Of course there were mice here. And coyotes, and lizards, and snakes, and whatever else could eke out a living from this land. And though he'd brought live traps, he'd been uncertain of those logistics from the start.

"It's not like we're going to drive out here every day or so and check them," he told Sully, crouched beside the dog to eye a squiggle in the dust that could only be lizard trail. Sully gave it a disinterested sniff, turned away. Not a snake dog, not a lizard dog. Not into reptiles, apparently. "So how about we look for nests?"

Sully gave a brief wag of his upright tail, certain he'd been invited to a game but not yet quite sure just what the game might be.

"C'mon," Dale told him, picking the same phrase he'd used since he'd first started trapping mice. "Let's find it!"

find it! find it! beagle woo! i bound! i leap! dustydusty musty sniff!

sniff here! sniff there! Sniff everything!

i pant. hose me off, dale, hose me . . . *shakeshakeshake!*

nothing there. boring. under the shed, dry scale-thing, stingy-dry musty. beagle *sneeze!* boring. under the house . . . bugs! bugs!

no bugs? woe.

dale, leave the big noisy cold machine. nothing there this time. dale, over here! dale, smell this! dale, this other place! daledaledale!

bawh! dale, *bawh!* at you! dale, leave that and . . .

oh fine. i'll do it myself.

Sully had shown no interest in the old window air conditioner jutting out of the back of the house—and no one else in the house had gotten sick, including Robert's older brother, now staying with relatives—but Dale couldn't stop himself from shining a flashlight around in the fan and coils, checking the screws, and in general hunting for signs of occupancy. He had every intention of letting himself in to check the boy's room next—vents, ceiling panels, whatever he could see without leaving any sign he'd been there at all—but Sully had other ideas.

Sully, bored and panting and his sleek black back already dry from the quick hosing Dale had given him, definitely had other ideas.

He air-scented his way down the flagstone path leading away from the house to the shed; he tugged gently on the leash attached to his martingale collar until it slid out from beneath Dale's foot, officially freeing him to wander. For by Sully rules, if Dale was going to leash him, then turning loose the leash meant turning loose the Sully.

And Dale, distracted, didn't realize it until a moment too late. Until several moments too late.

Until he heard the far-too-faint and all-too-triumphant *bawh* of Beagle-on-scent.

Wuh!

Dale dropped the flashlight; he dropped the Leatherman he'd had at the ready; he smacked his head into the air conditioner as he jerked to attention and just as quickly scrambled to his feet. *Stupid, stupid, stupid. . . .*

But Sully wasn't far and the noise of him hadn't moved, and Dale's instant panic faded to anticipated embarrassment as he loped cross-country toward the neighbor's house, one hand on the water bottle at his hip to keep it from bouncing. *Sorry, he got loose . . . sorry, he really is loud, isn't he? Sorry, didn't mean to intrude . . . a friend of your neighbor's . . . Gosh, sorry, I hope you weren't fond of that part of your house foundation. . . .*

By the time he reached the neighbor's property, a good quarter mile away over rough ground and roaster-oven hot even in the late afternoon, Sully's cries had grown more muffled if no less insistent. Not necessarily a good thing. *Do* not *be digging your way into someone's house,* Dale thought sternly at the dog. But he didn't waste breath shouting for Sully, knowing it would only add to the noise level and while everyone else might hear it, Sully certainly wouldn't.

But no one else had appeared in the yard; no one else had appeared anywhere. These folks might consider themselves neighbors, but quite evidently, no one was home. Surely no one could have failed to respond to Sully's siren call.

"Bawh!" That muffled sound led him past the rock-lined driveway, the railroad ties that defined an area otherwise identical to the rest of the caliche yard for parking. And there it was, another shed, newer than Mary's, practically fresh from the lumber yard and built to last. Sturdy four-by-four posts in the corners, solid three-quarter-inch plywood over tidy sixteen-inch stud spacing, recently painted and every solid detail in place, including the honkin' big lock on the door. Around to the side, he found Sully.

Or rather, he found Sully's butt.

The butt stuck up in the air in the least dignified possible fashion, tail presenting itself in tempting handle configuration while Sully's head and shoulders disappeared into a hole beneath the side of the shed, his body jerking with the force of the muffled *bawhs* he released into the space beneath.

Dale pondered the tail, the tempting tail, his hand closing in the air above it; he gave a reluctant shake of his head, and instead nudged Sully's haunch with his sneakered toe.

Sully withdrew his head just long enough for a triumphant look of victory *mineminemine* and Dale spluttered his planned admonishment out into laughter at that dusty face with happy brown eyes behind suddenly greyed eyebrows, whiskers, and muzzle, nose still wet and shiny black. Then it was gone again, back into the hole with tail a-wagging and front paws going back to work.

Oh, no—enough of *that*. Dale had enough reverse engineering to do, with nothing more than his hands and feet for tools, the fine dust of Sully's efforts already disbursed out over the caliche ground. With a quick snatch and no warning, he popped Sully out of the hole, forestalling the expected protest by flipping him out into the air slightly on the other end of the swing, an indulgent dad with his toddler child except in this case it just happened to make Sully's eyes bug out and interrupt his *mineminemine* long enough for Dale's presence to make an impact. Dale caught him, wiped his face with the hem of his T-shirt—so much for stopping anywhere nice for dinner on the way home— and set him firmly on the ground, leash in hand. "Now," he said. "*Stay*. And what's the deal?"

Sully made big eyeballs at the shed, big oh-I-want-to-break-this-stay eyeballs, but he was too hot to hold the tension and gave up, breaking into a big lolling pant.

Dale poured water into his hand and considered the shed while Sully lapped and waited for more, lapped and waited for more. He'd told Sully to *find it*, hadn't he? And while his first impulse was to write such tricks off to Sully's irrepressible curiosity, the truth was. . . .

Sully didn't care about snakes and lizards, he was distractable on stink beetles, and he was unfamiliar with anything larger than a really fat mouse. And only the mice had gotten this level of response from him—the hell or high water, world could fall down around him unnoticed kind of response.

Maybe Mary's wasn't the place to look for Robert's hanta after all.

"What's a nosy vet to do?" Dale muttered out loud, hands propped at the pockets of his jeans, hat jammed back on his head, and scowl firmly in place as he contemplated the shed.

Sully, in a stay position in the shade of said shed, glanced sadly at the hole he'd started, and which Dale had refilled the best he could. *woe. want.*

"You just leave it." But Dale knew he looked at the shed with much the same expression. He gave Sully the Meaningful Finger of Doom and left him to walk around the shed, circling it for the first time.

And ah. Who knew? Here in the back, a louvered air vent. Taller than eye level for most . . . not taller than eye level for Dale on his tiptoes, especially not Dale on his tiptoes if he dragged that rock over this way. That he did, and if he wobbled a little on his tiptoes on the rock, there wasn't anyone to see.

And if he muttered profound things under his breath as he peered into the shed, his flashlight shoved up against the vent beside his face to shine interrupted light into dim recesses of the little building, well . . . there wasn't anyone to hear.

Except, of course, for Sully, who took it as a release from his *stay* even though he knew better, and thus came around the corner of the building in a guilty slink.

But Dale's eyes and Dale's thoughts were too full of what he'd seen—what he'd *thought* he'd seen. . . .

A clean, neat shed. Preternaturally neat, in fact. One stout narrow work surface along the side, some unidentifiable structures too close to the vent wall for Dale to identify. Boxes along the other side, neatly labeled, leaving an aisle just comfortably big enough in which to maneuver. Nothing truly easy enough to see, with the vent louvers and the marginal lighting.

But Dale knew a respirator mask when he saw one. Much more significant than the Air-Aid mask he'd been wearing to clean sheds . . . this one was a three-piece gizmo that the *Dr. Who* special effects team would have been glad to slap on a guest star to create an alien visage. High-tech and impressive . . . it didn't fit with anything else he'd seen in this entire community.

Except maybe the fine, shredded grasses, horsehair and leaves, double-bagged on the bench beside it and extra-long biotech clean-room gloves neatly placed beside that. Several wire cages, either recently occupied or ready for imminent occupation, complete with inverted water bottles, feeding cups, shredded bedding and the ubiquitous toilet paper tube hidey hole.

Dale turned away from the shed, removed himself from the rock . . . only long enough to sit on it, as uncomfortable as that was, knees sticking up high and awkward, seatbones grinding into stone. Sully slunk right up beside him. *pet me.*

And Dale did. He took that moment to argue with himself—that he couldn't have seen things clearly enough through the vent, that he was jumping to conclusions even though he hadn't literally thought past that first punch-in-the-gut reaction yet—and he rubbed behind Sully's ears until Sully forgot he had legs and ended up in the dusty dry ground on his back, legs dangling and entire undercarriage presented for scratching.

"Because, yeah," Dale said suddenly. "This is where I want to be if the guy who lives here comes home. Even if I'm so totally wrong."

But he didn't think he was so totally wrong. He didn't

understand it—he couldn't even *begin* to understand it, why one man would have all the pieces that fit his vague obsession. *Yes, Sheri, there really* is *a Hanta Santa.*

He had answers. He was certain of it.

He sat with that a moment. *He had answers.*

He knew who'd written the notes. He knew who'd spread the hanta. And yet it suddenly didn't seem to be enough. It didn't fill the spot in him that had been looking.

He still didn't know the all-important *why* of it—why did this man write notes to Dale? Who *was* he? Had he targeted Laura only to prove a point, or was this somehow tangled up in Laura's family? And he suddenly realized his stomach had tightened; his throat had tightened. He discovered his teeth grinding together, and very deliberately relaxed his jaw.

No. It wasn't over yet.

He stood, returned the rock to its original position at what could be called the edge of the yard, and headed back to Mary's place, trailed by a dejected Sully and his dusty leash.

Sully might have looked back over his shoulder once, a longingly possessive glance at the shed . . . but not for long. He trotted to make up the ground he'd lost, and touched Dale's hand as Dale bent to scoop up the abandoned tools by Mary's air conditioner, and then sat in Dale's shade at the Forester, happy to gulp water from his collapsible fabric bowl while Dale dug his cell phone from the front passenger seat of the car, checked his watch—nearly five p.m.—and placed a call. Barely . . . a one-bar reception, and lucky at that.

Not to Rena, because he knew better. This wasn't something he could tell Rena, not until he had every possible fact. And not to Laura . . . he wanted more, before he told Laura. It would mean too much to Laura right now. And not to the clinic, because Sheri would have plenty of fun with her Hanta Santa riff later on. Way too much fun.

But to the person he was perhaps least comfortable calling out of the blue.

"Hello?" Mary said, and he knew from her surprised and somewhat cautious voice that she'd seen his caller ID, hadn't expected his call and wasn't sure she wanted to know why he was calling, given that he'd been out to her place. Was still here, but she couldn't know that.

"Hey . . . I'm not interrupting anything?" *Like another crisis with Robert. . . .*

"We're at Laura's," she said. "About to have a dinner in which all vegetables will be eaten." A dramatic groan in the background.

"He's there?" Dale couldn't stop his surprise.

"Yes." Her smile came through in that single word, her initial wariness forgotten for the moment. "We have daily visits to FMC for a while."

"That's—" Dale started, and fumbled, unable to think of words that were quite cool enough. "That's great!" Definitely not up to the moment. "Laura knows?"

"She might," Mary said. "I woke her. It depends on whether she remembers. But she sounds better. And now you're going to tell me whether you think it was a coincidence that these two people in my family who live so far apart became sick together?"

"Wow," Dale said. "Way to get to the point. And I guess I am. The thing is . . . no, I don't think it was coincidence. But I don't know just why it wasn't coincidence."

A short silence. "I don't know you very well," Mary told him, "so I hope you'll forgive me if I say that doesn't make a lot of sense."

He laughed. At his feet, Sully lifted his dirt-caked face in inquiry, just in case this was one of those times when a laughing moment led to food. "You wouldn't be the first to point that out lately. Listen, can I ask about your neighbor—what his name is? Do you know him well?"

"Not as well as he'd like," Mary said, some of the same quiet dryness that Dale heard so often in Laura. "He's been there a little over a year, which isn't long as things go out there. His name is John Benally. He's been a good neighbor."

"Very neat," Dale observed, while the name triggered a vague memory, something he couldn't quite put together. "Keeps things up."

"Yes." She hesitated, more out of distraction on her end than deep thought; he heard rustling as she handled something in the kitchen, and water ran in the background. "He's been helpful when we needed. He's been kind to Robert."

"I wondered if your son ever visited his shed. He might not want to say," Dale added, guessing that the shed would be off-limits to anyone other than the owner, never mind young boys who might poke around and get sick and lead nosy veterinarians back to peer through the slats of the vent—and therefore any young boys who might have gone visiting would have been breaking the rules.

Mary shifted the phone away from her mouth and asked, a short quiet phrase in softly musical Navajo. Dale didn't have to speak the language to hear the denial in young Robert's voice—or the insistence in Mary's reply. He had, after all, grown up with Aunt Cily. By the time Mary returned to the phone, Dale already knew the answer, just not the details. "He says there's a key under a rock off the back porch."

"Does he remember anything of what he saw?"

She'd already asked him that one, it seemed. "Cages," she said, bemused—it was clearly too late for parental disapproval, and she didn't bother. "They were up too high for him to see inside, although reading between the words makes me think he tried pretty hard."

Dale could just imagine. Little boy, stolen moments in a neighbor's mystery shed, the faint scurry of rodent feet firing childish curiosity. . . .

Firing adult curiosity, if it came to that. *John Benally.* Where the heck had he heard—? He gazed over at the neighbor's house. From here, the shed was hidden behind the house, but he could see it clearly enough in his mind's eye. He cleared his throat. "He, um, happen to remember which rock has the key?" Because it wasn't like there weren't plenty of them. It wasn't like the entire surrounding landscape wasn't rock of one sort or another, striped and layered and jutting and dramatic, filling the big western landscape and stretching out beneath the big western sky.

"You don't think—" She stopped, shaken—understanding all the implications quite clearly. They weren't talking about accidental hanta, caught in a dusty old outbuilding. They were talking about a shed built to harbor the disease, and the man who would do such a thing living right next door to her. A man who then wrote Dale notes, and invaded Laura's home to infect her as well. "Surely you don't think—"

It made no sense whatsoever, and yet . . . here they were. Dale swallowed hard, feeling Mary's fear over the phone, mired for the moment in his own. "I don't know what to think," he told her. "I'm going to get it untangled, one way or the other. That's all I can say for sure." He cleared his throat. "But a key would help."

Mary gave a little laugh. Very little. "The rock with the lizard, he said, which may be a thing that only makes sense to little boys. But—"

Yeah. *But.* If this is where Robert got hanta, maybe Dale shouldn't go anywhere near it. And if this *did* have anything to do with Laura's hanta, maybe he shouldn't go bumbling around the evidence. *Not that anyone will be looking closely enough to find it.* "I'm not sure I'm going to go in," he told Mary. "But if I can get a better look, I can know if it's worth *someone* going in."

Mary hesitated; dishes clanked slightly in the background. The homey sound of a meal being made at Laura's place, without Laura. "If you're calling from my place, don't count on getting a connection again, especially if you need it in a hurry," she said finally. And then, leaving Dale faintly startled and faintly pleased, she added, "And don't get me in trouble with my cousin. Stay safe."

"Hey," he said to Sully upon hanging up. "That's a *good* thing. Aunt Cily always told me . . . she only got that upset because she *cared.* It's got to be the same thing, right?"

hot. feed me. pet me. do something me!

"How about I crate you here in the shade while I go hunt a rock with a lizard?" But first Dale grabbed a towel from the back, because aside from not panicking, *Hitchhiker's* had also taught him never to go anywhere without a towel, and Sully had reinforced that lesson tenfold. A careful blot of water from one of the ever-present gallons tucked up beside the wire crate and Dale had the doggy equivalent of a spit-bath, wiping around those squinty, watering eyes until Sully squirmed away like a little boy under the attentions of a great-aunt. Then, while Sully was still smarting under the insult, he popped the dog up into the crate, latched the door, and said, "I'll be right back!"

Back out into the sun, and glad for the lengthening shadows. Even if John Benally had a long work day, he'd be back soon enough, and Dale didn't waste any time looking for a lizard rock. He didn't waste any time finding it, either. Benally's back patio was a collection of rough-set flagstone lined with local rock, a random scattering of which had been painted with simple charm—lizard, snake, cactus, roadrunner. . . .

But Dale checked under all the lizard rocks, and found nothing. And he checked all the other painted rocks, and found nothing. Frustrated but persistent, a warning clock ticking in his mind and sweat sticking his shirt to his back and trickling down behind his knees, he checked the lizard rocks again . . . and found beneath one of them an odd worn spot that didn't fit the bottom of the rock.

Where the key had *been*.

Face it. The guy was no idiot. He'd built a sturdy shed; he'd locked it up tight. And he'd moved the key once he realized his neighbor's son had been poking around.

"If I was you," Dale muttered out loud, "I'd be taking further steps to cover my tracks right now."

Or not. Why should John Benally have any concerns? A little boy had gotten sick; Laura had gotten sick. Notes had been written. No one had put it all together; even Dale didn't truly understand what was going on. And he knew, in his suddenly knotted stomach, that even if he'd had all the pieces, Benally still had little to fear.

Well, he imagined himself saying to a straight-faced tribal cop, *I got some notes, and my dog got sniffy on mice, and my friend got hanta, and I came trespassing on Benally's land and discovered he was in the nefarious occupation of raising mice.*

Raising mice. It was to gasp. For all Dale knew, Benally, too, had himself a snake.

Except he *did* know. There, in that gut feeling, where it counted. Where it hit home before he started over-thinking it all.

He straightened the rock, settling it back into its original spot . . . and thought again.

If he couldn't get to this man head on, if he couldn't see him in cuffs and behind bars and paying for what he'd done, maybe he could still give him something to think about. The equivalent of his own note, sent in return. Crouching there, the sun beating on his back and the battered straw cowboy hat shading his eyes, he squinted at the shed, imagining that door open, any suspect contents bagged and burned. *Okay, maybe not quite.* But he looked back down at the lizard rock . . . and he very deliberately rolled it over again, baring its underbelly to the sun and exposing the place where the key had been.

Give the man something to think about. It might throw him off. Slow him down.

Until Dale could catch up.

CHAPTER 15

Dale hit the office early the next day, desperately hoping to wrap his head around normality. Obedience class that evening, right after a visit to Laura, and after a partial day at the—

Who am I kidding.

His head was full of what he'd seen the day before, and—when he slipped into the office after circling the clinic with Sully in an empty-handed *find it* patrol, he discovered the place festooned with paint gear—drop cloths and interior scaffolding and ladders and—

Sully stopped short, righteously wary.

"Yeah," Dale said. "Me too."

But he was determined—just a little normalcy, please, even with John Benally looming in the background bigger than the season's monsoon clouds—and he took them down the hall to his office, where he tore the latest Hanta Santa from his office door and absently tossed it into the trash. Sully ran after it and stuck his entire head into the wastebasket, convinced, as he had been since the office redecoration had supplied this new container, that if it wasn't meant to be his, it wouldn't be so perfectly Beagle-height.

Dale thought maybe he had a point. Dale thought maybe he'd replace the wastebasket, even if this one did match the blinds and the carpet ever so perfectly.

After a perfunctory sweep for unwelcome notes—a new morning routine that had kept his office neater than in his entire previous career—Dale did a quick Sully patrol of the interior clinic and then headed upstairs to the break room, where a little rummaging netted him the garbage gold he'd been unable to hunt under Sheri's eagle eye. He tucked away his booty, made several mugs of morning Irish tea, and had them waiting on the counter when Sheri, Dru, and Isaac arrived a few moments later.

"Now this is more like it," Sheri said. "Are you back, then? Done with all the silliness?"

"Home, sweet home," Dale said. He glanced around the hallway. "Well, almost."

Sheri dismissed the mess with a wave of her hand. "They're as good as done. Just cleaning up today, that's all."

"Believe that when I see it," Dru snorted.

"I'll be in the back," Isaac said, wisely choosing to stay out of it.

Or trying to, because Dru snagged his arm with two iron pincher fingers as he passed by. "Come out to the expansion," she said. "I think we'll be ready to transfer the patient boarding tomorrow or the next day. Let's make sure we've got what we need."

Isaac looked back at Dale, hangdog eyes full of *rescue me.* But Dale nodded. "Good idea," he said. "Let's start looking ahead." And to Sheri, "What's on the schedule today?"

Sheri looked at him squint-eyed, as if the regular old Mr. Dr. Dale was a little too good to be true. The background noise had already started up—rumbling trucks arriving in the lot and pulling behind the building, the back hall door opening and closing, men moving and muttering among the leftover mess in that area and stirring the air so the still-fresh paint fumes wafted through the waiting room.

Dale ignored it all, and Sheri slowly pushed the schedule across the counter at him. "Allergies," she said. "Limp. Puppy shots. Eye gunk. Old dog-itis. Guinea pig going bald. Bunny claws." She tapped the neatly printed sheet. "That last one's for Isaac, but you're gonna want to see it. That bunny means business." She squinted again, patently hunting his expression for signs of strangeness, for any quirk of expression that might tie him to the Hanta Santa.

"Those are nice earrings," he said, admiring the giant orange disks. "I didn't know you could get them to match eye shadow like that."

Sheri slapped a hand down on the schedule, nostrils flaring. *"All right, then!"* The squint had become a glare. "Who are you, and what have you done with our Mr. Dr. Dale?"

He shrugged. "Just having a day, Sheri. Got things to do, places to be, dog to train, house to get ready . . . it's what you wanted, isn't it?"

She subsided, sitting back into her chair so hard it squeaked. "Well, yeah," she said, but it sounded distinctly sullen.

"Cool. I'll be in the office. Buzz me when our first appointment arrives—let's try to get ahead of things today. And don't worry about booking me into the afternoon. Paint fumes aren't great, but it's better than dust. It's about time I geared back into the schedule."

"Okay," she said faintly. She slipped something out of the hidden nook at her elbow—a cardstock cutout that flashed red and to Dale's now-practiced eye shouted *Santa*—and bent it around itself several times, casually dropping it in the trash.

Glory be.

Good thing he'd done his clinic patrol with Sully *before* she'd arrived. Dale hid his smile and headed to his office with the tea, put Sully through a few quick obedience exercises, and, unable to quite stomach the donut holes sitting perkily on his desk, pulled an orange from his desk.

"Oh," Sheri said, ignoring the intercom system and why

bother when her voice carried that well anyway? "I forgot. It's Frank N's weigh-in day and here they come."

Hank and Frank? How could she *forget*—? Dale pointed at the Sullybed. "Hide," he said, taking on the dramatic tones of a man at war. "Hide while you still can!" Sully gave him a blank stare—definitely not playing the straight man for Dale today— but a moment later, the familiar *grr-grr-GRRF!* filtered through the window from the parking lot, and Sully dove for the security of the bed, ensconced behind the desk and out of casual view, human and football terrier alike.

"Smart boy," Dale muttered, and thought hopeful leash thoughts as he headed out of the office. Technically, Hank could weigh the dog, report the results to Sheri, and head on out again without Dale's involvement, but realistically . . . that wasn't gonna happen.

And then Sheri said, "Hey! Watch where you're going with that ladder, we got clients in here—"

And Hank said, "Oh! Heh heh! I didn't realize there'd be painters—"

And Frank N said, "Yipe!" Which was pretty much a first as far as Dale knew, and inspired him to come from the office at some speed.

There in the junction of the hall and the waiting room, Hank and Frank and their leash had somehow tangled around the world's shortest monobrow painter and his ladder, with Sheri already heading out from behind the L-shaped counter with her setting-things-straight face on, a look only a fool would fail to quail before. And she might even have done it, deftly putting herself between the horizontally held ladder and Frank, with the painter on the other side, untangling the leash with practiced skill, had not the painter looked up from his already compromised situation and seen Dale.

Seen Dale stalking down the hall.

The monobrow painter who'd left notes, who'd been called off this job, who wasn't even supposed to be on the property any longer.

Dale lengthened already long strides.

The painter made a break for it. With a panicked glance at Sheri, at Hank—clueless, still going, "Heh heh heh, he just doesn't have the hang of that leash"—the painter pivoted in the middle of the ladder just as Dale came within the end of it and—

Thwack!

—Slapped Dale against the wall, a giant flyswatter at work. Sheri said, "Hey!" and Hank said, "Heh heh—wha—?" and Frank said, "Grr!" in the most unconvincingly possible fashion, his cover blown, and the painter muttered something under his breath and made another break for it.

And Sheri said, "Uh-*UH*," and Sheri said, "Not to *my* Dr. Dale, you don't!" and just as Dale was crawling back up the wall to regain his feet, the ladder went—

Thwack!

—and slapped him against the wall, and Sheri said, "Oops."

After a moment, Dale opened his eyes.

He found himself underneath the hovering ladder, which was still against the wall; he found, at the midpoint of the ladder, that Sheri had stopped the painter's flight by the simple and expedient measure of flattening herself against the metal rungs opposite him.

Pinned. Pinned like a butterfly on display.

Hank scooped up the portly terrier, and unclipped the lead—no doubt the better part of discretion, since the rest of the leash still resided somewhere between Sheri, the ladder, and the painter. "Heh heh," he said, most uncertainly. "Did I come at a bad time?"

"Not at all," Sheri said, flashing him a beatific smile through gritted teeth. "Help yourself to the scale. Use a hot dog or two or three to get him to stay on it, if you need to."

Hank brightened. "Yeah!" he said. "Hey, you need help there?"

"No," Dale said, even as the painter said, "Yes! Call for help! Call anyone! Don't leave me here with these people!"

Dale found his feet, rubbed an aching rib, stuck his finger through a tear in his shirt. He got a glimpse of Sully—of half of Sully's face, just enough to peer out of the office—but it was short and sweet. Sully retreated. *Hide. Hide while you can.* "As I recall," Dale told the painter, walking the length of the ladder to stand behind Sheri and lean on the wall, a casual arm that completed the man's capture, "you weren't supposed to be *here* at all."

"I'm *not*," the painter said, desperation doing odd things to his features; the brow became especially scary, and Sheri gave him a look that he'd have paid closer attention to if he'd been smart. "I'm just grabbing a few things the guys were supposed to have dropped off at another site last night. It's not my fault!"

Yeah, but that never worked for Dale, either.

"You want I should lean on him?" Sheri asked, sounding a little too eager after he'd ignored her look.

The painter's eyes bugged out in supplication and protest. "Aw, come on!"

"Suddenly you've got the holiday spirit?" Dale asked her, affecting surprise.

She scowled. "That's different. He whacked you with a ladder! I'm gonna let him get away with that?"

"Well, no, of course not." Dale could be reasonable, too. In the background, Hank plunked Frank on the large, flat floor scale and cajoled him to stay put long enough so he could straighten and read the numbers. It would take a while, Dale decided, and leaned a little closer to the man. "John Benally," he said.

The painter's alarmed expression fell away, leaving utter blankness. "What?"

Okay, start closer to the beginning. "You've been leaving notes."

And the painter hesitated, which was all Sheri needed. "Get it?" she said, pushing her weight against the ladder. "*Lean* on you?"

Aurgh. Dale wanted to rest his forehead against the wall—it was so close and inviting, and his ribs really did hurt. But the painter's eyes were bugging out, so he pretended he was still in control, and he said, "I won't get answers if he can't breathe, Sheri."

She considered it, easing back slightly. "Yeah, maybe. But he doesn't have to breathe *all the time*, does he?"

"Are you listening to this?" The painter cried to Hank, albeit with much less volume than he probably intended.

"Oh, okay, then," Hank said to Frank. "Just one little piece of hot dog. That's a good boy."

"That would be a *no*," Sheri informed the painter.

"Notes," Dale said.

"Just the one," the painter snapped, barely letting Dale finish. "He asked me, I did it. Big deal, okay?"

"Enough so you ran."

"You *chased* me."

"*You—*" Dale stopped himself, closed his eyes, took a breath. No point in going there.

"You want . . . ?" Sheri asked, letting the sentence trail away with no question as to its meaning.

"Not just yet." The note thing had been a guess . . . the painter had been guilty over something, had known *something*, and yet he wasn't John Benally—not a drop of Navajo blood in that body—and he wasn't so involved that he'd been afraid to show up here and grab the ladder that now held him trapped. "Tell me about John Benally."

The man shrugged—as much as he was able, with his hands still wrapped around the ladder and his body pressed firmly against the wall. "Can't, much. He's a duct man. He didn't make any friends here . . . he walked off the job a week or so ago. Why do you think it all took so long?"

"What, contractors gotta have a reason?" Sheri looked genuinely surprised.

But Dale was only half paying attention. Benally had *been here*. Had *worked here*. And so Dale had been right, too, about who'd had access to his office. Not just paranoid after all. Not just a head full of the Hanta Santa . . . or out-of-his-head-worried over Laura.

He'd been here, but he'd left—right about the time Laura got sick. Playing it safe, cutting down his exposure to Dale.

Unless he'd intended to plant another nest . . . and was literally cutting down his exposure to hanta.

The thought must have done something to his face, to his jaw—to judge from the way it suddenly ached. And to judge from the painter's reaction. "Listen, I'm telling you what I know. He wasn't with them long and now he's gone. He had an attitude or something. He asked me to leave a note, I didn't have any problem with that. I didn't think it was a big deal until you chased me—"

"You *ran!*" Okay, so he couldn't help himself. Not with his mind whirling around the realization that Benally had indeed been here and that he'd since left, and all the implications that came with it. Like could there be a coincidence that big, Laura's cousin's neighbor, working here and turning Hanta Santa? *No.* Surely not. But if not, what came first? Where the hell did this story start, and where had Dale come into it?

161

More importantly, perhaps . . . how would this story end, in a town full of cops looking to make Dale the butt of every joke they could find?

Another deep breath. First step, getting past this moment. The second. . . .

Have a little faith, Dale. So far, following the impossible had led him to the answers. And if his tools were oddball, he still knew how to use them. "I'm kind of surprised, Sheri," he said, pushing away from the wall. She gave him a *who, me?* look and he added, "This is the kind of thing you usually know about. I mean, knowing everything, having all the power. Sounds like you missed out on some good gossip with this Benally guy."

"No!" she said, but she didn't look him in the eye. "That doesn't count. That's contractor stuff."

Dale shrugged.

"I'm serious!" She glared at him.

"Okay." Dale gave it a quick moment of thought. "Maybe Hank knows. Or can find out."

Sheri's eyes widened, then narrowed in warning; she glanced behind them to assess Hank's attention level, finding him fully engaged at the scales. "You leave him out of it! I can handle this!"

Uh-huh.

"I mean it," she warned him, as Hank made a satisfied noise and scooped the dog off the scale, ignoring its growl of response. Dale held up his hands in surrender as Hank joined them.

"There we go!" Hank said, shifting Frank under his arm to the tune of more *grff-grff-grrr.* "That didn't take too many little hot-dog pieces after all, not really. And he's only gone up half a pound!"

"Most of it right there on the spot," Sheri said.

"Hey, what about me?" the painter demanded. "I've got places to go, you know!"

"I need your name." Dale switched gears almost effortlessly at this point. And besides, there was nothing to be done about the fact that Hank was soaking up this good gossip material like a paper towel commercial.

"Why?"

Back to being belligerent, was he? But Sheri didn't hesitate; she *leaned*. And the painter knuckled. "Wyatt! Wyatt Snelt! Geeze! I should report you!"

"Probably a good idea," Dale said. "I have a friend in the Staties, her name is Rena. She's fed up with me right now, too. You go to her, and you tell her about Benally while you're at it." Because hey, it couldn't hurt, could it? Really?

"Never mind," Wyatt Snelt muttered. "Just let me *go.*"

"Sure," Sheri said. "I'm busy, anyway. You think I don't have anything better to do? I figure you've learned your lesson, anyway."

Behind them, the outer air-lock door opened; the inner door opened in short order. Hank clutched tighter to Frank and said under his breath, "Probably oughta get my leash back before he sees whoever that is. . . ."

In walked a woman with a badly scarred plastic carry crate, bunny-sized. Angry clawing and thumping noises came from within, distracting her until she was well within the doorway; she stopped quite suddenly short when she did glance up. "Oh," she said, and blinked. "Should I reschedule?"

"Not at all." Sheri pushed away from the ladder, brushed her hands off against one another, and briskly resumed her throne in the power seat, turning toward the closed doors of the procedures room to call in her best company voice, "Isaac! The bunny is here!"

Isaac's muffled reply was, mercifully, not intelligible. And the painter staggered into his freedom, threw a resentful look at Dale, and headed down the client room hallway. Hank fumbled at the leash still tangled in the ladder, following right along. Dale wasn't entirely sure they'd see him again.

But he had other things to think about. Like how perfunctory his Find It rounds had been this morning, and how Benally had been here but cleared out, and the implications of that defection. Rats fleeing a sinking ship . . . Santa fleeing his impending hanta. . . .

"I'll be starting a little late this morning," he told Sheri, as if the previous moments hadn't happened at all. "Sully needs a quick walk."

Sheri looked up from the computer and the bunny's records, her fingers instantly stilling on the keyboard. "A walk? Now?"

Isaac appeared from the back room; he was heavily aproned and gloved, and at his most polite as he took possession of the shuddering, thumping crate. The woman sighed in resignation and sat in the waiting area, hands neatly folded in her lap. Awaiting the carnage, Dale would have said.

But Sheri was not to be distracted. "You just got here. Don't tell me you didn't walk him before I came in."

"He needs another one."

"You said you wanted to start early."

"I won't be long."

"You made tea. You pretended to be normal."

Dale shrugged. "What's more normal than a guy taking his Beagle for a walk?"

She narrowed her eyes. "You're going hanta hunting!"

Dale headed down the hallway. "Won't be long," he said over his shoulder.

He could have sworn she muttered, "That's more like it."

He smiled.

CHAPTER 16

Monsoon clouds glowered over the Peaks, grumbling and mumbling but offering no break from the heat, and nothing more than token spits of rain. Mindful of their impending trip downtown, Dale hauled Sully's new crate cool pad out to the spigot at the side of the clinic, filling it and burping the air out until it seemed he had the right balance, then tucking it inside the crate as he opened the Forester to cool before they headed out to see Laura. Today, he'd find a spot in the shaded parking garage and leave Sully with the back hatch locked partly open with a Ventlock, enthroned on the cool pad with his own personal crate fan.

Add that to the dousing he was about to get, and the dog would probably be more comfortable than Dale, stuck out in the car or not. *I have crossed the pampered pet line,* he decided, and then decided that he didn't care.

"Hey," Brad said, hesitating at the counter with patient chart in hand as Dale breezed back inside to nab Sully, waving at the client who sat with her mournful stitched and bandaged dog, an Elizabethan collar completing its misery. Brad rubbed the back of his neck. "Thanks for staying later today."

From the sound of it, he was just in time—a squeaky toy was in dire need of rescue in his office. "Least I could do, after the late start we got this morning." No wonder Brad looked so tired—they were down a vet, they were under construction, Dale had been keeping short hours after a week off, and they were in the middle of the summertime rush. "Listen, things should be getting back to normal soon. I'll be full hours next week, and Laura will be out of the hospital—"

"Amazing." Brad shook his head. Nothing outstanding about Brad, not in his dishwater blond appearance or his personal presentation or his work. But he was steady, he was devoted to his family, and his utter failure to succumb to flights of fancy kept the clinic from floating right off into rarified air.

Or so it seemed to Dale sometimes.

"I can't believe you caught the hanta so fast," Brad was saying. "You may well have saved her life. Who knows how long it would have taken them to test for it, without any of the risk factors present."

"Big risk factor present," Dale said. "Me."

Brad's weary contemplation turned to surprise, his eyebrows getting lost in a limp forelock washed to the side. "You really think those notes? I thought the whole Hanta Santa thing was Sheri's idea."

From behind the counter, Sheri—deep in transferring charges from chart to billing program—snorted expressively but said nothing.

Dale said, "It's getting harder to shrug off."

"Yeah," Sheri said. "And who is this John Benally character, anyway? Because my superpowers are having to work mighty hard on him, I can tell you that much."

No information yet, in other words. No good gossip from any source.

"A man who raises mice," Dale told her. "And makes sure he isn't exposed to them along the way."

She stopped typing. She pulled her fingers from the keyboard. She looked at him, her expression giving way from habitual overconfidence to uncertainty.

"Yeah," he said. "So I'd kinda like to find out more about him."

The confidence came rushing back. "I got more sources," she told him, and went back to work.

"Point is," Dale said, watching Brad work through the implications and decide to leave it alone for now, "you've done a great job these past couple of weeks, and I really appreciate it. We'll get someone else on board here as soon as we can, and get you a break." He'd dropped the ball on that, sent Laura's Albuquerque friend a quick note explaining the circumstances . . . but it was time to get his act together.

"That'd be great." Brad smiled, gathered his folder, and went off to the new painted and furnished treatment room to greet his next patient. For a moment, the guilt weighed heavily. The time off—*to protect your lungs*—and now that the construction was wrapping up, the time spent at the hospital—*family leave time*—and once again, it seemed as though the things in Dale's life had landed right here in the clinic, on the shoulders of the people he cared about.

Get over it, said a voice in his head that sounded suspiciously like Dru. *The world doesn't revolve around you, Dale Kinsall,* added another voice that sounded suspiciously like his Aunt Cily. He stopped, closed his eyes, shook his head.

"What?" Sheri asked, sounding suspicious.

"Double-dose of mother-voices." Dale gave an exaggerated shudder. Never mind that the voices were right.

"Ah." Sheri nodded wisely. "The inner bitch-slap."

"I'm *not* telling Aunt Cily you said that." He gave her a double take, narrowed his eyes, loomed over the counter slightly. "That was a trap. You said that on *purpose* so I'd—"

"Be serious." Sheri flipped over one chart, turned to the next. "I'm busy here, can't you see that? I don't have no time to be thinking up traps for you. Say hi to your Aunt Cily, next time you talk to her."

Dear Aunt Cily—

Just stealing a moment here at the office—I'm about to run out to the hospital. Laura's doing really well. I'd say she's blowing her respiratory therapists away, but then you'd have to come all the way out here to give me *that look*. I think they'll release her very soon now, and she's either given in to my campaign to convalesce at my place or she's decided to quietly do things her own way. I'll find out soon enough.

The construction's almost done. They're just cleaning up, and I'll be back to full days the moment they stop stirring up the dust.

Sheri says hi.

Sully sends silly little kisses and would like more cookies, please.

And thanks for the reality check. You don't have to understand that. Just nod and take credit for it.

Love, Dale

PS: Yes, I've noticed that you haven't said anything about those tests in Columbus. Whenever you're ready. . . .

Sully trotted out of the clinic in I-own-the-world mode, tail jaunty, nose lifted to scent the air, gait free and reaching. The moment Dale turned for the spigot end of the clinic, he transformed.

woe. hose.

"It's hot. You're going to be in the car."

woe. hose. let's go this other way.

But Dale was unmoved. His mind on the visit with Laura, on his hopes of finding her feeling well and ever closer to leaving the hospital, he led the skulking Sully around to the spigot and walked his hand down the leash as Sully cannily spiraled away from the hose sprayer—only until the first stream of water hit, at which point he stopped, hunched up like a little canine Eeyore, and squinched his eyes shut to just let it happen.

Dale made it merciful, soaking him down as quickly as possible, bending to cool Sully's chest and undercarriage and then replacing the sprayer on the hose rest as he cranked the spigot down.

Sully offered up his ritual shake, liberally spattering Dale's jeans. *oh. not so bad.*

"I told you."

Another shake, a little shimmy . . . a silly little bark. *wooo! feels goood!*

"Yeah, yeah. You think this time you'll remember that when it comes to tomorrow?" But as Sully cast out to the end of the leash, air-scenting toward the RoundUp Café, Dale knew it would never happen. Come the next time, they'd go through the whole slinking ritual all over again. . . .

At the end of the leash, Sully tugged harder; tugged with intent. "Hey," Dale said, about to pop a correction, "be polite."

But he didn't, because something in Sully's intently focused posture, something in the whine just now starting to vibrate in his throat. . . .

All becoming a little familiar of late. And cautiously, not giving any clues with the tone of his voice, Dale said, "Find it, Sully—find it."

The whine escaped in a sharp little escalating bark and Dale took a cautious few steps just to see where Sully would lead. Out into the space between the clinic and the deli they went— not with any interest in the scrabbly weeds there or the bugs within the weeds, but still air-scenting, still straining onward.

The deli?

Surely not the deli. Terry's entire family lived behind that deli, the entire local community ate at that deli. . . .

Right. And even the best-kept deli had a transient mouse or two. And the scrubby strip of cinder field between the deli and the woods had its own little rodent occupants. Now that Dale had trained himself a mouse dog, he'd learned a whole lot more about mouse occupancy habits than he'd ever intended.

And maybe later, he'd discourage Sully from such unbridled response. But for now. . . .

"Find it!" he said, much more assertively, and pretty much gave Sully free lead.

Together, they ran toward the back of the deli—the stretch where the old block foundation did a dogleg back to the newer addition of the living area, dark brown siding not quite match-ing the newer materials. Back here, the garbage dumpster sat up against the side of the house; a few crates stacked neatly beside it, a pallet or two beside that, along with the broom and big flat-bottomed shovel the kids used to keep the area clean. World's biggest dustpan. All stark in the afternoon sun breaking through dramatic clouds, glinting light and dark shadow.

"Wow," Dale said to Sully. "A mouse in the garbage? You think?"

The sarcasm was lost on Sullydog, who cast wildly about to find the strongest thread of the scent, tail stiff and wagging tightly with eager certainty, *findit findit findit!* The exhaust fan from the kitchen obscured his eager little noises, but Dale knew they were there. "Hey," he said, his own words also almost obscured by the fan, "Mouse. Garbage. It happens. Let's go see Laura." Okay, false promises, since only one of them would see Laura, but so be it.

Sully's ears cocked forward, wrinkles of deep thought engraved on his forehead, and Dale gave up and let him lead the way around the other side of the bin, sniff-sniff-sniffing, and then back again since they were going that way anyway, and then, to his surprise, to the little moisture vent set into the block foundation, there where, as Dale's eyes adjusted to the shadow of that corner, it suddenly seemed as though the block looked freshly chipped. Not the best place from which to disperse hanta, but if one brought not only the nest but the mice as well. . . .

As he crouched to look more closely, Sully gave a sudden wild shy, spinning on the leash with a fierce and feral warning snarl. "Hey—" Dale said, straightening—but not getting all the way up before the deli reached out and smacked him in the face but that wasn't right because *wham* there it came again from the other side and Sully launched a snarling baying bark the likes of which Dale hadn't known he had in that small body and *wham* there he went, sliding down the side of the deli using his face as a brake and so utterly, clearly aware that he didn't have the faintest idea what was going on, only that wow, it sure did hurt along the way.

muskyduskysicksicksick lookout! dale! badness! bawh! run! dale! bawh!

muskydusky that's a *shovel* that's *bad!* daledaledale! bite— no, run—no, bite! get away-way-way! my dale! bite-snarl-*bawh!*

muskydusky running away man. go away-way-way, hate you! stand right here on dale and hate you! loud! all my loudest!

dale?

"Sully," the voice said in Dale's ear, sounding both patient and exasperated in quiet tones that sounded familiar and ought to have been recognizable but weren't, "if your eyes bug out any wider, you're going to lose them. The guy's gone. Drove off. You chased him away. Very brave. Now let's see what he's done, ey?"

"What's going on?" Dale said. Or meant to say. It came out without the actual words, sending Sully into a paroxysm of happy snuffling at his face that Dale really, really could have done without. "Aurgh," he said, and that came out pretty clearly.

"Got the leash, Dad," said a young voice. Closer to recognizable. "C'mon, Sully."

"Don't try to handle him," the first voice directed. "Just hold the leash." And then a hand landed on Dale's shoulder. "Dale. It's Terry. You in there?"

"Terry," Dale said. "I know you." Unfortunately, those words did come out.

"Yes, indeed," Terry said. "Rena's on the way. Maybe you should just stay there."

But Dale had pinned himself back to reality, putting recent moments back into place. The spigot, the mouse scent, the dumpster, the vent . . . he rolled over, found himself face to face with gritty asphalt, and pushed himself to his knees. "The vent," he said. "Gloves . . . mask . . . check the vent."

"Take it easy, man," Terry said. "You know, when I told you about that spigot, I wasn't expecting a whole big production. Just the hosing was enough."

"What?" And Dale finally looked up, startled to realize they had an audience, an entire ring of ladies gathered tightly around them, all responding to the sight of his face with a choral gasp of horror.

"How do you think we knew there was a problem?" Terry sat back on his heels, his tone dry, his white apron splotched with blood that didn't look as though it came from roast beef juice. Way too fresh. Way too red. Way too Dale. "The ladies here were keeping track."

"Just happened to be," one of them said.

"Nothing else going on outside that window," said another.

"Cute little dog," said a third.

"Round the back of the deli you went," said the first.

"And then that dog made such a fierce ruckus!"

"Whole lotta noise for a dog that size," Terry agreed. "Look, best I can figure it, you surprised someone back here, and he took after you with the shovel."

"All I remember is falling. Well, stopping the fall with my face," Dale said. "Face, building . . . something like that."

"Very pretty," Terry said, admiring the effect. "Your shirt's a mess, too. I think he clobbered you pretty good . . . but he must've used the back of the shovel." And Dale heard what he didn't say. *He could have killed you if he'd really meant to.*

"I surprised him," Dale murmured. He watched a drop of blood splot onto the asphalt with some surprise of his own.

Terry sighed. "Let's get you inside, man. Clean you up. Wait for Rena."

"I'll help," offered one of the ladies.

"I'm a nurse," said another.

"I've watched every single episode of *ER*," said the very first to have spoken up. They blurred together, leaning over him, blocking out the light; Dale had an impression of short permed hair and glasses, clunky earrings and flashy, overdone rings.

"Just show me to your bathroom," Dale said. "I'm headed for the hospital anyway, to see Laura." He put a hand out, caught Terry's arm as the man started to rise. "I'm serious. Don't wait for Rena to get here. Clean out that vent. Use gloves, use a mask. You've got that stuff for the food prep, right?"

"We've got it," Terry said. "C'mon. Rena's already going to give me grief for letting you move. But I guess your back's not broken."

Dale thought about it, pulling up distinct body memories . . . a blow to the shoulder, to the side . . . another to the side. As if the ladder had really just been warming him up for the day. "Didn't hit me on the back."

And then the woeful one couldn't stand it any longer; Sully barked sharp intent and Terry's son gave a yelp of dismayed warning, and Sully came charging through the line of ladies to throw himself at Dale, whine-sobbing his worry. *daledaledale!* until his wet white parts had taken a stain of bloody pink.

"Great," Dale said. "Now I'll have to hose you off all over again."

"Oh!" said the ladies, bursting into spontaneous chorus. "I'll help!"

Rena threw the deli door open and stalked into the diner with on-duty intent. The expression on her face scattered the remaining coffee crowd, all of whom had merely been finding excuses to linger over the dregs of their various fancy flavors. She saw Dale sitting at the little round table closest to the register and stopped short, muttering a word that Dale was able to lip-read with no trouble at all.

Terry had sent for his oldest boy—a fourteen-year-old now working at the vent, gloved and masked— and his oldest girl, a lanky thirteen-year-old who immediately started wiping down the abandoned tables, albeit not without throwing a look of barely masked resentment Rena's way. Hmm.

Rena resumed her table-stalking as if she hadn't interrupted herself, slapped her notebook down across from Dale, and said, "What's going on? How did you let it go this far without getting back in touch with me?"

Dale gave her a moment to think that one through, and knew, when she heaved a big sigh and helped herself to a chair, that she'd done it—thought about the notes he'd passed along, and the reception he'd gotten. "Let me see it," she said, still using Officer Rena voice.

He shrugged, which was stupid because it hurt, and made a big owey baby face, which also hurt. By then she'd leaned over to pry away the towel-wrapped baggie of ice, much more careful than he expected from her brusque movements. Her assessment—a quick, probing examination, a hint of wince, a nod of her head—was also entirely Officer Rena. "You should have that looked at."

"I'm heading in for the hospital anyway," he told her, which was what he'd told everyone, letting them make assumptions. He'd already done his own poking and prodding, cleaning up in the small deli bathroom and using rough towels to wipe away dried blood and staunch the drip from the single cut that seemed inclined to cause trouble. Mostly it was abrasions and ugly bruises and just enough swelling to make everyone look twice. Ditto up and down his ribs, but that was only if someone lifted his shirt to look. He kind of hoped that wouldn't happen too often, but around here he'd stopped making assumptions.

He'd tucked his shirt in.

"Look," he said, and he should have known better than to say anything at all, not with his thoughts still pinballing around inside his head, much the same as his head had pinballed off the deli. "I think the guy who did this is named John Benally."

"You saw him?" Rena asked, and it got Terry's attention as well, fussing as he was over by the coffee machines and flavoring.

"No, that would have been too easy," Dale said before he could stop himself. Because really, he knew this would go nowhere. And really, he just wanted to get on with the day. Go visit Laura, who knew he'd be late but had no idea why. "Look, can we just call this a tip? The man lives in Cameron, and he's got a shed that should be seen." And a lizard rock that got tipped over and maybe that wasn't such a great idea after all.

Rena leaned back in the chair, drummed her fingers briefly on the table. "Off the record, what else is there to it?"

Off the record? No, not even then. Just . . . some of it. "He was working on the clinic remodel . . . had the opportunity to leave the notes, and one of the painters said he'd done that."

She frowned. "Then what's with the shed?"

Dale lifted one shoulder in a shrug. Carefully. And glad, for that moment, that his face throbbed so fiercely, because that made it easier to keep it free of such thoughts as *and you'd never believe it if I said it* and *no, I don't totally trust you right now.*

She dropped it for the moment, though he saw well enough she was only doing exactly what he might have done, coming at things from a different direction rather than beating against his resistance. "And just now? What was that all about?"

"I'm not sure. I was walking Sully . . . I must have surprised him back there." Yeah, that was plausible. Ow. Then again, why did Dale have to have the answers to everything? No one wanted the answers he was coming up with, after all.

Rena hadn't written anything yet. She said, "You don't know why this man was back there or what he was doing, yet you're pretty sure it was John Benally and that he attacked you just for surprising him."

Okay, maybe he would have done this differently if he hadn't just gone one-on-one with the wrong end of a shovel. Maybe he would have done this a whole lot differently. Maybe he especially would have done it outside, so when Terry's son Joe came into the diner and plunked the mask, gloves, and vent cover on the nearest table, Rena wasn't right there to see. Or to see Dale's reaction when the boy grinned and said, "Nothing there, Dad. I did a complete in-vent-igation."

Because Dale couldn't help but sit straight up, feet flat on the floor, dropping the ice back away from his face as he said, "You're sure? You had a flashlight? You really looked? Because Sully—"

And he'd already said enough. Rena, it seemed, didn't live in a vacuum. Rena came to this place almost every day, right next to the clinic. Rena had ears. "Oh my God," she said. "This is about the Hanta Santa. You can't be serious."

"Oh, crap." Joe's gaze darted between Dale and his father. "I didn't mean—hey, he was definitely working on the screws. I think you got there first, is all."

"Rena," Terry said, setting some fancy flavor of coffee before her, "Look at his *face*. Does it look like a joke to you? Did those notes look like a joke?"

"You know better," she said, not rising to the challenge. "But come *on*—you think what? That this John Benally is Santa?"

Nothing to lose, now. "He's got a shed full of mice, Rena; he's got clean-room gear. And his neighbor's son nearly died of hanta. And for the record, none of populations around here have yet to test as carrying the virus." Not with his last batch just reported back in from Stanford as negative.

"Laura's little relative?" Rena said sharply, not slow to pick up on that detail—and not about to be distracted from it. She crossed her arms over her chest. The notebook seemed forgotten . . . the open page still pristine. "So you've found a guy who works at your clinic who lives next to Laura's cousin? That's just a little convenient, isn't it?"

Pain flared in Dale's jaw; he discovered himself clenching his teeth. He forced himself to stop, shoved hair off his forehead, and finally managed a steady voice. "Nothing about this," he said, "has been convenient. *Nothing.*"

They looked at one another for a long, steady moment. Then Rena picked up the notebook and the pen. "So you were walking Sully, and a guy jumped out from behind the dumpster and whacked you with the deli shovel. He hit you—what, three times?—and ran."

"He hit me approximately one bazillion times." Dale rotated a shoulder. "Otherwise, yeah. And no, I didn't get a look at him, or at the vehicle he drove off in."

Rena scratched a note. "Did you get any sense of his height? Whether that first blow came from above you, or—?"

Terry snorted. "Not many around here any taller than Dr. Dale."

"Exactly," Rena said, steadily. "Makes it worth asking."

Dale closed his eyes, thought about that first moment, shook his head. "Not," he said.

But she didn't respond, and when he opened his eyes, he found everyone looking at the deli entrance, and at the man reaching for the door. Another trooper—a thick-set man, older than Rena, an unpleasant set to his mouth. Rena briefly turned back to Dale. "Just let me handle him."

"He's all yours." Dale was done here. "Look, Rena . . . just pretend you got some anonymous tip about Benally, from someone you haven't already decided you can't afford to believe."

Pow. That one hit home. She winced, and Dale didn't feel the least bit guilty. Refused to feel guilty, even if it wasn't Rena's fault that Sheri had poisoned the well with her Hanta Santa decor.

By then the trooper had entered, his ambling strides nothing like Rena's business-like entrance. "Coffee," he said, before he was asked. "Strong and black, none of that fancy flavored crap."

Terry's daughter immediately headed for the back, but Terry stopped her with a lifted hand as he rose from his seat without hurry. "Kati, the take-out calls will be coming in soon." To his son he said nothing, just a lift of his chin, but the boy scooped up the mess from his *inventigation* and quietly walked out the way the officer had come in. Terry himself went for the coffee.

Rena said, "Don't recall shouting out for backup, Stan."

Stan pulled a noisy chair out and sat. Beneath the table, Sully pressed up against Dale's legs. Dale felt his patience suddenly evaporate. It was not coincidence, he thought, that Terry's hand landed on his shoulder just then, a companionable pressure as Terry leaned over to set the Styrofoam cup before Stan. Rena, too, shot Dale a look—a surprised expression, as if she'd suddenly realized he, too, might have limits.

Stan couldn't possibly be as oblivious as he appeared. "So," he said, curling his hand around the foam cup. "Decided to take on one thing too many, did you?"

Dale stood. Oddly, Terry's hand followed him up.

"You're making assumptions, Stan," Rena said, voice low.

"Am I? Whatever happened, I bet he was poking around somewhere." Stan took a sip of the coffee, looked faintly startled—but not enough to remove his attention or his satisfied expression. Smug.

Okay. So that was only the truth. Dale had been poking around. He hadn't intended to take anyone on—never mind from behind with a shovel—but he'd been poking around. As he intended to keep poking around, especially since no one else was doing it. He ignored Stan as he gathered Sully's leash, looked instead at Rena. "It wouldn't have happened if there weren't something to it," he said, which he hoped was both meaningful enough to make his point and vague enough to leave Stan wondering.

Rena nodded, more a movement of her eyes than anything else, and Stan took another, more thoughtful sip of the coffee. He said, "Maybe you ought to stick to putting Band-Aids on people's pets and learn to ask for help when it comes to the important stuff."

A small sound of exasperation escaped Rena. Terry's hand tightened. Dale found he'd shifted toward Stan the trooper to stand over him, that Stan was on his feet and perhaps just now realizing that Dale *still* stood over him. It was Sully's low, unhappy growl that made Dale take a breath—knowing he'd caused that tension. He eased back; Terry's hand relaxed and dropped away. "In fact," Dale said, "I asked for help weeks ago. I've asked several times since. And I'll keep asking. But probably not from you." He dug into his front pocket, pulled out a five from the ever-present careless crumple of small bills, and dropped it on the table. Unlike Rena, Stan, he thought, was not going to pay for the coffee.

Stan's mouth opened, and his glare went from Dale to the money, as puzzled as it was righteously offended. When it did seem as though he might say something, Rena quite obviously kicked him in the shin, her jaw set and her wide mouth grim. Just as quickly, she mastered her expression, looked away, and took a casual sip of her favorite fancy flavored crap.

"I'll be by tomorrow morning for takeout." Dale turned to Terry, cutting Stan out of his personal worldview. No doubt he'd made an un-friend; no doubt if Rena hadn't been there, things could have gone very much differently. Stan had come in looking to gloat and hoping to start trouble, and Dale, battered and throbbing and off-balance, had almost let it happen. "I'm off donut holes for a while . . . I'm thinking bagels and peanut butter. That's protein, right?"

"I heard something about the donut holes," Terry said, expression giving nothing away. Except . . . Dale thought he saw something lingering there, something unspoken . . . something that had nothing to do with his words. "I'll send along some orange juice. And you're making tea for the ladies?"

"For now," Dale said, following Terry's lightning-quick glance toward Stan the un-friend. Toward Stan taking another sip of the coffee, giving it another of those faintly puzzled looks even as Rena clearly savored her own.

A sudden grin took over Dale's mouth; he hastily turned his head away, and just as hastily squelched the grin because damn, that hurt.

But he had the feeling Stan wouldn't be stopping by for free coffee from the deli again.

CHAPTER 17

Ridiculous, to be standing in a line of handlers with that grin back on his face. Dogs in a line against the fence, handlers ten feet away and motionless, taking a wide stance, hands clasped behind their backs. Everyone serious but Dale and his creeping grin. Come to think of it, no one else wore a continent of bruises across his or her face, or had shown up in a torn and stained shirt.

And still, the grin.

Sully waited in his most earnest sit-stay, staring at Dale with every fiber of his being. Dale figured if he worked at it hard enough, Sully would figure out how to telepathically transport one or the other of them in closer, but not accomplishing the deed so far hadn't yet discouraged him.

Yeah, the grin.

Forget about the shovel. Forget about the smug cop. Dale's mind was full of that glimpse he'd had of Laura, sitting cross-legged on her hospital bed, talking with quiet animation to the visitor he couldn't yet see. She looked. . . .

She looked good. She looked . . . *Laura.*

She wore the pajamas Mary had picked out and Dale had brought, and her cheeks had some color over skin that had returned to her normal toasted-almond complexion. Her hair was braided back in fancy pieces that surprised him, but maybe one of the nurses—

And that's when she'd seen him, turning to greet him with a

"*There* you are—" that didn't quite make it all the way out before her jaw dropped, and that's when Dale saw that her visitor was none other than Dru, dressed in one of her scrubs with cartoon breeds scattered all over front and back, and he stopped short in surprise, suddenly understanding the main conduit of information between the clinic and Laura. By then Laura had her second wind and she said, *"Dale!"*

Dru wasn't far behind. "Mr. Dr. *Dale!"*

"Um . . . hey there. I brought pizza." Because by now he was late enough that he'd have to eat and run if he wanted to make class, but he'd been determined to make the visit regardless. But they both just stared, and he added, hope in his voice, "Gourmet pizza?"

Dru snorted. "There's no such thing as—"

"Picazzo's," Dale said.

"Oh," Dru said, bereft of argument in the face of offerings from Flagstaff's distinctly gourmet pizza establishment.

"Meaty lasagna," Laura guessed. "Sit down here with your pizza, then. I know you don't have much time, and you've . . . well, you've obviously got a lot to tell us." She patted the bed, scooting back far enough to tuck her feet beneath the covers.

Dale plunked his sports bottle down on the bed tray table, making himself right at home with his pizza box, even if he sat with care and respect for stiffening bruises. For some reason, everyone who'd seen him in the hospital had assumed he'd lost his way from the emergency department.

Dru helped herself to a piece right away, but not without pointing a finger at Laura. "You tell *him*, first. Because yeah, yeah, he's a mess. But really, what's new?"

Dale would have taken offense, if Laura hadn't laughed—but she did, and it distracted him entirely. That, and how relaxed she seemed. There was a change, although he couldn't say just what. He took a moment, chewing, looking at her, and as usual she absorbed such scrutiny with complete aplomb. "Okay," he said. "Tell me. And Dru—didn't expect to find you here."

"What, you think I haven't been visiting?" Dru sniffed. Not convincing, as she was groping for a napkin at the moment. "Family's family, Dale Kinsall. We know that at Foothills just as much as you do. Even when they go a little nutty. That's a reference to you, by the way."

Dale tugged the pizza box further away from her. His mouth might be wrapped around all the best parts of pizza and lasagna put together, but his face wasn't letting him chew it very fast. "I wouldn't have guessed."

And Laura said, so casually, "I'm going home tomorrow." Then, less casually, talking just a little bit faster, "Would have been tonight, but they couldn't get the doctors coordinated in time. My lung function tests are improving faster than they'd hoped. I'll have therapy and I'll be off work for a while—"

Dale stopped chewing altogether, and swallowed a great big lump of food. "Home?" he said, and coughed, reaching for the tea of his sports bottle while Dru came over and would have helpfully thumped him on the back had she not belatedly noticed his great alarm and shooing motions.

"Oh," she said as he finally got himself sorted out. "Yeah, that shirt does look messed up." And of course she tugged it right up to look, and then tugged it right back down again, and when she came back to her seat her face was tight and her lined mouth was even tighter. "You're going to talk about that after all," she told him. "But Laura, don't tease him. Looks like maybe he's had enough today."

And Laura caught his eye, which should have warned him. It did warn him, in one way, that she had seen Dru's reaction, that she was choosing to let it go for the moment but only the moment. "Not home," she said. "They won't release me unless I have someone staying with me. Or . . . someone to stay with."

Someone to stay with.

"*Me,*" Dale said. So casual, as if he hadn't just almost spiked his pizza. "Sully and me."

Yes!

And then, of course, he'd had to tell her what happened—as well as the other news of the day, about the negative test results from Stanford. She got that right away, no discussion—*the hanta hadn't come from the native populations.* And then he'd run out on them, pizza tucked beneath his arm, nodding his thanks at the several additional people who directed him toward the Emergency Department, and he'd broken a speed limit or two to reach the other side of town for class.

And now he stared at Sully's earnest face, those big eyes gone even bigger, that intense gaze pinned to Dale, and thought about how the guest room was ready, and the sheets were clean, and the guest sink and toilet was clean, but had he remembered to clear the inevitable spiders from the shower stall?

"Dale?" said Elaine the instructor, pert dark hair covered with a ball cap against the slanted evening sun. "Are you sure you're all right?"

And food. She'd want something other than his bachelor fare, even if he did have a batch of fresh fruit from his latest MyWay grocery store excursion.

"Dale? Do you need to sit down a moment?" Elaine touched his shoulder—lightly, lightly, in deference to his battered appearance.

"What?" Dale started slightly. "No, I'm fine, why—?" But he didn't really need her to answer that. Not when he looked around and realized he was the only one still standing out away from his dog; the other handlers had returned, as obviously instructed, to stand beside their dogs and await the completion of the exercise. Gulp the lab had settled into a down position as was his wont; Twig the Sheltie looked as though she might just explode if someone didn't release her soon. Gripper the Aussie had butt-scooted half the distance to his owner, who now stood beside his dog and looked at Sully with a somewhat different expression than he had used on the Day of the Mouse.

Because Sully, bless his little hound heart, still eyed Dale with all the intense focus he could also apply to a molecule of food when it was just out of reach. Dale hastened to his side, walking around behind to correctly place himself in a heel position, and Elaine wasted no time in releasing them all. "Exercise finished!" she said. "Dale, big praise for Sully—that was mighty fine work."

So Dale rumpled Sully all the way down his back and up again, thumping Sully an extra time or two until Sully was so pleased he just couldn't stand himself and woo'd his own importance. *me! me!*

"Trust me, everyone knows." But Dale fed him an extra cookie anyway.

"That's it for the class," Elaine said. "Give your dogs a few moments to unwind and play with you." Which was really code for, *you can chat now.* Dale was new to this class, but many of Elaine's students were semi-permanent, repeating classes with the same dogs, introducing new dogs, or just coming out for the social nature of the experience. She turned to Dale. "It's probably not circumspect to say so, Dale, but you certainly do justice to every rumor I've heard today."

Dale rumpled Sully up again and admitted, "I didn't have time to change." And then, still crouched beside Sully, he gave her a startled look. "Every rumor?"

"I'm a dog person," she said, gentle in breaking this news. "I heard about the thing with the painter before noon. And the shovel at the deli? That probably took about twenty minutes to reach me."

"I heard it from Hank," said the Sheltie's mom, while Twig

herself did an anti-gravity pogo-stick boing at the woman's side, effortlessly reaching waist height. "The ladder part, at least. I'm not really clear why the painter did that. Something to do with notes. I have no doubt why Sheri smacked him down with his own ladder. That woman knows how to protect her turf."

"My friend Delia takes coffee at the deli every afternoon," said Gulp Labrador's mom, apparently not noticing that Gulp had sucked her entire hand into his mouth, happily possessing it as his own. "I'm not sure why everyone was watching when you went back there, but they were."

Dale knew. Dale didn't say.

"Everyone heard Sully," Delia said. "And then that battered old truck roared away."

"They saw it?" Dale quit pulling Sully's ears to look at her—at least until Sully put a firm, reminding paw on his hand. "The guy's vehicle? They saw it?"

"Well, Delia said it was ugly, whatever that means. Noisy and ugly truck, with one of those stupid peeing boys in the back window."

More than Stan the trooper would ever bother to find out.

"I was surprised to see you here." Gulp's mom looked at her slimed hand in mild surprise, wiping it off on her slacks.

The Aussie's dad seemed surprised to find himself in on the conversation. "My wife was there," he said. "From what she said, I didn't expect you to show up this evening."

Now Dale definitely wasn't going to say why everyone had been watching. He did say, "It probably looked worse than it was." He put a hand up to the several butterfly bandages Laura's nurses had forced on him before he'd left the hospital, didn't quite touch anything before dropping it. "And I've got Sully entered in rally Prescott. Don't ask me why. It seemed like a good idea at the time."

"You'll do fine," Elaine said. "You've got a copy of *Rally-O,* don't you? And the list of stations the AKC has available on their Web site? Practice your footwork without Sully, get your confidence up . . . your dog is a lot closer than you think he is."

"One nice thing about that little hound," the Aussie's owner said, looking at his butt-walking dog somewhat wistfully. "I've noticed that once he understands something . . . he doesn't try to make up new rules for it. He's happy to do it as you've defined it."

Dale couldn't help his surprise, enough of an expression to twinge all the way across his bruised face. The Aussie's owner shrugged. "Live and learn," he said. Or possibly even admitted.

"And anyway," Twig Sheltie's mom said, rather brightly, "at least Laura is coming home from—" The look on Dale's face must have stopped her. She drew herself up and said, "It's not *all* about you, you know. Laura is my vet, and I heard it from my breeder, who was in at Pine Country getting dew claws done on her latest litter this afternoon." She pondered that a moment, then gave him a funny look. "Huh. Come to think of it, Libby said something about Laura going to stay with another vet until she's cleared to be on her own. The tall, hand—the tall one on the other side of town, she said. So maybe it's all about you after all."

"Salt," said Sheri. "I asked Terry. Just the right amount of salt. Too much, and you give yourself away. Not enough, and maybe they even like it that way." She scowled. "He deserved it. What kind of fool would do such a thing? You sitting there all beaten up with a *shovel*, and he's doing the gloat? He's lucky I wasn't there, that's what. You look like crap, by the way. At least that shirt's not torn."

Dale pondered all his possible responses and rejected each. *Just not going there.* He set the small, warped wooden tray on the clinic waiting room counter and nudged one of the tea mugs toward Sheri. "Black Irish," he said. "All the caffeine, none of the bitter. And no salt, either."

"That's because you're none of the stupid." Sheri claimed her mug, standing just enough to peer over the counter into the waiting room at Sully and his endless sit-stay. "How long's he gotta stay that way?"

"Until I say he doesn't." Dale Kinsall, cruel despot of the Beagle world.

Sheri settled back into her chair. "Don't seem right."

"I could take training lessons from Hank and Frank," Dale suggested. He sipped tea, perusing the schedule she'd set before him as he gently rotated his shoulder, hoping to convince it that it wasn't really that stiff and knowing he wouldn't. Ha. Just as his face wasn't a big weird stiff piece of painful cardboard, or that he hadn't just lost a little tea out the puffy corner of his mouth.

Well, a busy day would take his mind from it all. There were surgeries this morning . . . a toe removal with biopsy and suspected squamous cell carcinoma. Removal of an eye damaged beyond repair in undefined household accident; chart flagged for abuse alert. Tooth cleaning by Isaac with removal of abscessed molar by Dale. All set for the new surgery closet . . . the inaugural surgeries. Dale savored the satisfaction of knowing the clinic was nearly back in full swing, the newly constructed areas ready for use, the remnants of construction diminishing visibly by the day. The place looked pretty spiff, if he did say so himself. New tile everywhere, new paint, the countertops still gleaming. . . .

No untoward notes pinned to the bulletin board. No oddly out-of-season cutouts of Santa with attached mouse tail or beady little nose and stiff black whiskers. Yeah. That was good.

And when he finished this day and headed home, Laura would be there, dropped off by her cousin Mary and left on her own for only a few hours before Dale got there. Yeah. That was *good.*

"*How* long?" Sheri asked, peering over the counter again.

"He's better at this than you are." Dale deposited the tea, returning to Sully. He walked around to put himself in proper position, then abruptly reversed course and circled from the other direction, and bounced up and down in front of Sully a couple of times for good measure.

"Now you're just being mean," Sheri said, grumbling from behind her monitor.

"It's called proofing," Dale told her, finally slipping back into position to release Sully, who leaped straight up into party mode and a *woo-woo-WOO* of self-congratulation. Dale snatched his legs out from beneath him to roll him fiercely around while Sully paddled the air with his legs and made horrible faces, then leaped to his feet to shoot down out of the waiting room and down the hallway, all scrabbling nails on tile, to pounce audibly on the Sullybed and worry it into submission.

"Speaking of which," Sheri said, standing so suddenly that her chair went shooting out behind her and smacked into the extensive racks of client file folders some distance behind her, "I didn't find any."

"What?" Dale straightened like a creaky old man in payment for his moments of canine party hearty. Then again . . . *shovel . . . ambush. . . .*

Could have been so much worse.

"John Benally. No proof."

"Were we expecting proof?" Dale had been hoping for gossip at the best.

"Dale!" Dru called from the back. "You pick up that salad last night? And the chicken, and the salmon?"

"Yes, ma'am!" Dale shouted back. Because of course Dru had pinned him down in the hospital hallway, exacting promises that he would indeed feed Laura better than he fed himself. And Dale was no dummy. He'd gone straight to the deli section of the MyWay after obedience class, where they knew him well from those occasions when he did actually feed himself.

"Well," Sheri said, "point of fact . . . no, we weren't expecting any fancy proof. But that's what's known as a *segue*, Dr. Dale. And that was a good one. You think I could pass it up? In fact, if I was you, I'd pause to admire it some."

Could have been so much worse. *And why hadn't it been worse, exactly?*

"Dr. Dale!" Isaac's bass voice didn't exactly rise to a shout. Then again, it carried well enough without such effort. "We documenting the eyeball?"

Dale let those words fall into momentary silence, savoring them. But under Sheri's impatient oversight—the lifted brow, the meaningful eye, the soon-to-be-tapping toe—he sighed, and put them into context with the suspect household accident where they belonged. "Yes, please," Dale said, as Jade poked her head out of the procedures room, hunting his response. "Let's have the digital camera on hand."

Jade gave him a thumbs-up and disappeared, various piercings winking in the overhead lights.

If John Benally had wanted to kill. . . .

He could have. Or maim. And he could have done it with one blow, if he'd really meant it.

Sheri cleared her throat. Hard. She said, "I'm gonna be busy today. *Really* busy. So if you wanna hear this—"

Toenails ticked on tile. Sully poked his head around the corner of the right-angle counter, faint puzzlement wrinkling his brow. *cookie.*

"Forgot something, did you?" Dale dug into his pockets, sent a hasty glance Sheri's way. "I *am* listening. And admiring. Definitely admiring that segue. I'm even admiring your use of the word *segue*."

Outside, a muffler-challenged vehicle pulled into a parking space. "*Told* you," Sheri said. "You think I get paid the big bucks to just sit around here? You think I've got all the time in the world to chase down gossip for you?"

Dale did a quick body check—clean scrub shirt, check; sneakers tied, check; jeans clean, check. Not much to be done about his face. Upon arrival, Sheri had pulled out a giant bag of makeup from her giant purse of horrors, but only for a perfunctory tsk. Wrong skin tones altogether, for which he'd given unabashedly fervent thanks.

"Take notes," Sheri said. "John Benally doesn't make friends. John Benally doesn't keep a job long, either. He wasn't with Mountain Air for hardly any longer than it took to do our job, and he didn't even stick that out. He was with some other heating place before that, not sure where—someplace closer to the reservation. Word is he didn't leave that job in good graces, either."

"He left bad feelings behind on this one?" Dale asked, scooping his stethoscope off the counter and wrapping it around his neck, tucking the end away in the scrub shirt pocket.

"Seeing how he didn't bother to give notice or anything." Sheri snorted. "I think he's the reason the contractors played that painter/duct work shuffle when we thought they'd be good and done already, and he definitely messed up with the timing on the new dog runs. And no one knows where to find him, either."

John Benally . . . a runner, not a fighter. Not a confronter. Not a killer? Then *what?* "Sounds like you hit information motherload."

She narrowed her eyes. "Did you doubt?"

"No, no, no," he said, making hasty warding signs. "I just figured it would be more of a trickle thing."

"My excellent instincts paid off." Sheri stacked patient folders, aligning them precisely. "There was this lady contractor here a couple weeks ago, had a beef with him. Turns out she wanted to make good with you, too. Dunno, she didn't look like your type to me, but whatever—"

"Hold on." Dale leaned elbows over the counter. "She with the fence company? Short, thick, speaks her mind pretty much like everyone around here?"

"Ex-*cuse* me," Sheri said, trapping the folders under a hand so firm Dale thought he heard them squeak in dismay, "but *I* am a woman of tact. And yeah, that's the one. Cancer, waiting to happen on the back of her neck. She said she owed you one or something. So she asked around, too."

But that Mountain Air guy still needs a kick in the butt. John something. Or Ben. That's what the woman had said. And it hadn't made any sense at the time, but now suddenly . . . *John Benally.*

Dale closed his eyes . . . had a sudden image of a short man, broad shouldered and barrel-chested, his shirt from Mountain Air and the name *John* embroidered over the pocket, warning him about Sully's interest in the construction pile mice. Warning him about the diseases the mice carried. John Benally, playing games.

Unexpected anger flushed through Dale, hot and hard and hunting a way out.

"Dr. Dale?" Sheri said, suddenly uncertain.

Startled, Dale looked at her, gave a wordless shake of his head. He wanted to tell her never mind, or it's all right, or it's nothing. . . .

But none of those things were true.

And their moment was over. Outside, vehicle doors slammed; shadows fell across the outer door window, muted conversation trickled through the doors themselves. The phone rang. Sheri picked it up, shifting smoothly into her Woman with the Command Center voice as she answered—but her eyes widened as she jerked the phone away from her ear, and Dale's eyes widened right along with hers at the frantic shouting coming through the line. "*—throwing up EVERYWHERE—*"

Okaaay, then. Time to start the day. Time to tuck Sully away while Isaac and Jade took in their first soon-to-be unconscious patients; time to get his mind back into the game, and back to the house guest who would await his arrival home this evening.

But . . . John Benally. A quitter. Not a confronter. Not a killer? Then again, Robert wasn't dead. Laura wasn't dead.

But they could be.

And Dale was back to the question he'd had all along, the one he'd never answered from the time that first note landed on his desk . . . what, then, did John Benally *want?*

And did he yet have it?

Whatever was driving Benally, so far he'd gotten away with everything he'd done. Robert, and Laura . . . and his aborted attempt to seed Terry's café. His notes. His lurking presence.

So far.

And meanwhile, Dale thought he had just enough time to take Sully around to inspect the grounds, inside and out. And he thought this time, no one would mutter about the Hanta Santa as he did it.

find it! o happy find it!

my dale, me, the smells. nothing better. familiar smells, my people, my places, my clinic . . . smells of me! smells of dale! bugs bugs bugs. and ohhh donuts!

i would like a donut. i would like to eat it.

careful at the stinky trash place . . . but no duskymusky. no mouse.

growl at the shovel just in case.

no mouse.
just my place, being mine.
another bug!
i'm for sure gonna eat it.

CHAPTER 18

"Watch this," Dale said to Laura, and casually nudged a puzzle piece off the high, oversized puzzling table.

Sully, on another endless sit-stay, stiffened in disbelief as the piece landed at his feet, just out of reach. He looked at Dale; he looked at the puzzle piece. Ever so casually, he *leaned*. . . .

And then, with an audible sigh, settled back into place. *poop.*

"You are a cruel, cruel man, Dale Kinsall," Laura said. She sat at a chair, a smile lurking at the corners of her mouth, the puzzle table never more obviously custom-made for a tall man who worked on his feet. But Laura, who had been napping when Dale eased into the house an hour later than intended, was clearly not yet ready for working puzzles on her feet. In fact, she seemed perfectly content to watch Dale work the puzzle—or torture the dog—now that they'd eaten a rewarmed meal a la MyWay and dessert a la Häagen-Dazs.

She hadn't eaten much at that, and even now it seemed to Dale that she was smaller than she'd been, some compact version of herself in jeans and a summery top that fit more loosely than they might, her hair straight and thick around her shoulders. Laura Lite, without the energy that had been the foundation of her quietness. Now . . . just quiet.

Except when Dale snatched up the puzzle piece, released Sully and sent him flying through the house after a reward tennis ball, she laughed right out loud, and he thought again that he'd been right to ask her here.

And maybe she thought so, too, for after Sully returned the ball and traded it for a Nylabone, settling in beneath the puzzle table to chew with his elbows grounded and his butt sticking in the air, and after Dale had settled back into the puzzle—this one newly opened and freshly spritzed to keep down the puzzle dust while he right-sided the tumbled pieces and sorted out the edges—she pulled her legs up to her chest, wrapped her arms around her knees, and said, "Thank you."

Lulled into non-speech mode by the grind of canine molars on faux bone, the sultry tones of Amalia Rodrigues in the background, the foreground activity of the puzzling and the pleasant fatigue of the day, Dale said, "Eh?"

She rested her chin on one knee. "I really didn't want to come here."

Dale pulled out a corner piece . . . turned over several upended pieces. "I'm trying to decide if I should pretend this is news to me."

Her dark eyes were serious. "It doesn't bother you?"

Dale leaned both elbows on the sturdy table, stretched over it to level their gazes. "It might," he said, "if I really thought it was about me."

She frowned. Hard to tell, what with the chin on the knee thing, but Dale saw it well enough. "I mean," he said, "I'm not making any assumptions there. You keep your feelings pretty close, Laura." *Says the man who just splooges them everywhere.* "It's just . . . not wanting to stay here comes from a different place, I think. You know, the same place that made it so hard to ask for my help when it came to getting ready for Mary. And just how hard was it, that night you stopped by to see if I could move things around again?"

She frowned more deeply, and turned her head, putting her cheek on that knee so he couldn't see her face any longer. "You saved my life that night."

It still sent tight dread down his spine, thinking of the moment he'd seen that mouse nest. The moment he'd *known*—and still hoped himself wrong. "Maybe," he said, not wanting to define it so baldly—not wanting to believe it had been so close as all that. So close as Dale, getting nosy with an air conditioner. Following a feeling. And then he asked, "So, why did you?"

"Come here?" She laughed, and it made her cough, and they both waited that out. She was a little breathless when she said, "Aside from the fact it was the only way I could get out of the hospital?"

"Aside from that," Dale said, and he couldn't keep the smile from his voice. Had it come to that, Dale suspected Dru would have taken her home on the spot, never mind her Pine Country colleagues.

Laura didn't answer right away. For a moment, Dale thought she might not. For another moment, he thought she might just have worn out and fallen asleep on the spot. But then she lifted her head and sat back in the chair, arms still wrapped around her legs and just a little bit of skin showing through one worn-out knee of her jeans. "I came because of the hataałii."

"The medicine man?" Dale shifted over the puzzle. "Because I agreed with Mary that he should visit, or because of what it did for you?" Beneath the table, Sully adjusted the bone and reapplied himself to chewing. *bone, mine. people, mine. happy.*

Laura shrugged, but it was in no way careless. "It's hard to say. I do feel different, but wouldn't anyone, after an experience like this? Does it have to come from the singing?" But she sounded as though she was trying to convince herself . . . as if she'd had this silent conversation with herself and thought it might go differently if she also had it out loud. And then she caught Dale's faint confusion and said, "The prayers. They're sung. Hataałii means *singer,* not *medicine man.*"

Confused no more, Dale offered, "I guess anyone *would* feel different. I feel different, and it didn't even happen to me. When I think—" But he stopped, jaw hardening on those words. He couldn't go there, not now—not to the anger that stirred so easily at the thought of what John Benally might have done. *Might still do, to someone else.*

Laura's smile went wry. "Right," she said. She took a deep breath, rubbed her nose along the inside of her eye, and said, "Anyway, that's part of it—the different. Whatever it comes from. And just that . . . well, that you did it. Mary told me she pretty much put up a sign, no biligáana allowed. I think she was feeling you out, if you really want to know."

Dale propped his chin in his hand. "Kinda figured." He thought back to the moment. "It wasn't the important thing, though. I mean, it wasn't about me. So none of that other stuff mattered. Just the part that was about you."

"Mm," she said. Her hair had fallen forward again; Dale stopped himself from reaching out to it. For one thing . . . it'd look pretty silly when he just couldn't reach. She froze him in place then, anyway, just with a single direct look. "And that's why I'm here."

He stayed frozen for a long moment, propped there on the puzzle table with pieces pressing into the skin of his elbows and Sully grinding away below, captive to the meaning in those words. And he should say something; he was certain he should say something.

Finally, with great effort, he gathered his thoughts and managed, "Wuh!"

Laura grinned. "Maybe a little of that, too."

And then, while Dale absorbed it all, she was the one who stood, who reached out to tuck his wayward forelock up just out of his eyes, and who leaned forward to kiss him, there and gone again before Dale's mouth had done little more than recognize the touch. Laura's hand lingered ever so briefly on the bruised side of his face in rueful caress, and then that, too, was gone.

Down, boy. Just . . . down.

"Wuh!" he said again, but his voice cracked a little and Laura's mouth tweaked a grin as she sat back down.

"Now," she said. "About this man."

Okay, that was safe. Dale blew out a gusty breath and pushed off the table, peeling puzzle pieces from his forearms along the way, groaning and creaking as his bruises caught. "Gone," he said, and blew out another gust of air. That about had it, he thought. "As far as anyone knows. I haven't checked with your cousin yet."

"I can do that," Laura said, and there was something about the matter-of-fact way she said it that made him look twice.

"You still think I'm not insane," he said, marveling at that a little.

"Nope."

"Huh." He decided to sit down himself, and backed up to the suspiciously dog-hair-covered recliner in the corner of the room, easing down against the bruises. "Nice change of pace around here."

"Dale," she said, "no one ever thought you were insane."

"I have two words for you," Dale said. "Hanta. Santa." He stopped, gave it some thought, and added, "I guess I'm lucky it wasn't Johnny Hantaseed. More appropriate, really."

"Give it time," she told him, and tucked her knees up again, muffling a cough. "They were worried, that's true. But even if it's really not clear how everything fits together, I don't think anyone in that clinic is still worried that you're seeing phantom trouble."

"Rena wasn't the only one," Dale said ruefully, but he was quick to wave off her response. "No, never mind. I get it. I do. If I'd been in their shoes. . . . The thing is, I see what I see. If I don't pay attention, how can I live with myself later? If I'd paid more attention in Ohio—" He hadn't known he was about to say that, and he decided not to finish it. Instead he followed up on what she'd said, and on how confidently she'd said it. "Dru's been talking to you all along."

"There," she said. "You *do* have a deductive mind."

But Dale was still stuck on his own line of conversation. "And not only do you believe me, but you want in on it?"

She gave him a look. He would have described it as fond but exasperated. His very first truly exasperated *look*. Worth a moment.

But she'd gone right on. "If you were me, wouldn't you be? If you're right, Dale, this man touched me in a way that might have killed me. He's for sure touched me in a way that will trickle through the rest of my life. Puzzles like this . . . you know, they're really not my thing. I'd rather watch you build this one than work on it myself. But this man . . . he's made me mad. And that's a different thing altogether."

A lot of words strung together, for Laura.

"So," she said. "You've been to his place. You've found what looks like a breeder shed. You interrupted him from messing around with the vents at RoundUp, and Sully says he smelled of mouse. You've told the police all of that, and you don't know if they're even checking out the shed. So we need more pieces . . . something that ties things together. Just because there haven't been any more notes. . . ." She looked at him, questioning.

"No more notes," he agreed.

"Doesn't mean he's not done causing trouble."

Dale sunk further into the recliner. "I like the way you think." Sully came over to punctuate this thought by dropping his bone on Dale's bare foot. Dale snatched him up, flipped him upside down and gently thumped his recently fed tummy while Sully squirmed as if this wasn't exactly what he'd wanted in the first place. "Thing is, I don't have any more handy pieces to work with. You and Robert were the only—"

And then he stopped thumping, and he stopped talking, and he squinted at nothing.

"Oh-ho," said Laura, straightening—but she looked suddenly tired, as though she'd reached a limit she hadn't expected to discover still existed. "Pieces!"

"I never thought of them as related, but . . . there was someone else from Cameron, a month or so before Robert came down with it." Dale automatically shielded his lap as Sully righted himself and launched to the floor. "And an older man in Tuba City, early in the season . . . but that's stretching it. I found them both in the *Navajo Times* on-line."

"Then I can check into them tomorrow while you're at work, between my copious naps," Laura said. "I'd say tonight, but—"

"Not tonight," Dale said, seeing again how hard the tired had suddenly hit her, and feeling it himself. "I'm too beat up and pathetic. I need my sleep. I might possibly need more ice cream first."

Laura brightened, however briefly. "Maybe *that's* why I decided to stay here. I knew there'd be ice cream."

silly people. dale smells bruised. dale moves funny and hurt. laura smells . . . tired. not sick. not well.

and still . . . *happy*.

silly people. don't even have a good bone to chew.

CHAPTER 19

Lunchtime, and no word from Laura about the family from Cameron, and Dale pretending he wasn't even waiting, just having a day—tapping away on his laptop, Sully snoozing behind him in some anatomically improbable position, a huge traveler's mug of iced tea to hand and that spicy lunch salad still lingering on his tongue.

"Dale!" Sheri's no-nonsense voice reached Dale down the hall. Not Dr. Dale or even that yodeling "Mr. Dr. Dale" which never led to any good when Sheri was behind it, just the no-nonsense version of Sheri at work.

Dale typed a few last words of his E-mail to Aunt Cily and pushed away from the desk, rounding it to cross still-unfamiliar carpet into the hallway—blessedly clear of construction materials—with legs set to *long*. "Our mystery bitch?" he asked Sheri, before he even reached the counter.

She gave one last look out the window. "Coming in. It's a Boxer. Not one of ours."

More than they'd known until now, with only one choppy cell phone call from which Sheri had gathered *bitch, labor,* and *be there soon*. Now Dale knew perhaps the most crucial thing— they hadn't seen this dog before; they had no history on her. They didn't know the owners.

Sheri added grimly, "And there's a kid."

Dale opened his mouth, caught the interested gaze of the older man already in the waiting room for his post-lunch ap-

202

pointment with Brad, cat carrier by his feet, and didn't say the particular word on the verge of making itself heard. "Isaac? Jade?"

"Both warned. They're doing blood and poop, but they're ready."

Checking fecals, running blood samples. Right.

And then the Boxer came in, gathered in the arms of a beefy, sunburnt man with a white-blond little boy tailing at his heels. The man put the dog down and said, "I called—"

But Dale had eyes only for the dog. A young dog, profoundly gravid, her maiden teats tight and bulging with waiting milk, her hindquarters sagging beneath her, her eyes . . . hopeless. He didn't spare the owner so much as a glance as he crouched before her. "How long has the puppy been stuck?"

"Stuck? What do you mean, stuck? She's just taking a while, is all, I thought someone should take a look—"

"How *long?*" Dale's voice took an edge. In so short an exchange, he knew so much . . . that this was a backyard breeding, that the man had done no homework, had no mentor. That he didn't know what to look for, and didn't have any idea how long ago this whelping had gone wrong.

"Well, I guess she's been at it a day or so. A day and a half. I had to go to work—"

"Thirty-six hours? That's when she started primary labor or—" Dale stopped. The man's expression told him he might as well be speaking gibberish. "She needs surgery, and she needs it now. The stuck pup is probably already gone. The others . . . depends on whether their placentas have detached."

The little boy clung to his father's leg, looking blankly at his dog; then his face crumpled. That he understood was doubtful; that he heard the urgency in Dale's voice . . . yeah. The man rested a hand on the white-blond head. "This is absurd! I just walked in with her—how can you even tell me there's a stuck pup? You haven't even looked at her!"

Cognitive dissonance rattled his thoughts. He hadn't, had he? But—

Sheri slapped a sheet of paper on the counter, along with a pen. "Because he's got *the look,* that's why, and around here that's enough." She tapped the paper. "Fill this out." She wasn't using her happy voice; she'd already made up her mind about this one. And Dale couldn't blame her, but. . . .

Dale ran a hand over the Boxer's head, made even grimmer by her lack of response. "It's been thirty-six hours. That's too long, regardless of the cause. She's in distress; she's no longer laboring. Without surgery, she'll—" He looked at the little boy, changed his words. "It won't be too long now."

The man scowled. "Those are purebred pups—they're worth something. Can you save them?"

Dale glanced at the boy and hesitated on his answer, and that was answer enough—and it wasn't what the man wanted to hear. His scowl deepened. Dale looked up to the man, waiting for the decision—half expecting to watch them all walk out the door again.

But the bitch gave a deep, rending groan, her hind legs slowly sinking beneath her, and the man quite suddenly seemed to recognize the severity of the situation. He nodded, and Dale moved into position to ease the bitch into his arms. "I'll do my best."

"This couldn't be much worse." Dale pulled a grim wince at the odor emanating from the bitch's open abdomen. Her uterus should have been taut and pink and bulging with life, not bruised and toneless over unmoving lumps. "Thirty-six hours of unproductive labor. . . ." He shook his head, flexed his fingers within latex surgical gloves sized too large for anyone else on staff, and picked the scalpel up again.

Isaac kept a close eye on the bitch's vitals, standing ready by the anesthesia; Jade stood to the side with a towel draped over her hands, ready to take the first puppy and turn to the receiving table—suction, a warming lamp, extra towels, and a tiny oxygen cone mask all laid out and waiting. The surgery closet was crowded, indeed, but they all knew how to dance this dance. "Do you think we can save any of them?"

"There's no telling how long the one's been dead," Dale muttered, referring to the very first puppy in the birth canal—

Easily found on exam, it had plugged up the works, died, and already begun to decompose inside the Boxer. Barely more than a baby herself, this bitch was too young to have her own; her body hadn't been ready for this. Now Dale was pouring antibiotics into her veins to fight off sepsis and the best he could do for her would be to deliver these puppies and pluck out this dying organ.

A careful incision over the bulge of one of the puppies, and he hooked his fingers behind the jaws of the first little tan lump, pulling it straight into the towel Jade had swooped in to receive it. "Placenta's detached," he warned her, even as she clamped the cord and cut it. "Don't prioritize him if we get a squeaker." No telling how long that limp little creature had been without an oxygen supply.

"I won't." But if her face and various piercings were hidden by a surgical mask and hat, her voice held classic Jade determination, and he knew she wouldn't give up easily.

"Going after another—looks like we've got four here, and the plug. Isaac, you gonna be ready?"

"Ready, boss," Isaac said, snatching a towel warm from the dryer, taking his turn while still eyeing the bitch's vitals.

"This one's—no, never mind. Don't even bother. Already in decomp." Dale kept his voice even as he set the pup aside on the surgical pad meant for garbage and headed back to the uterus, gently manipulating the least damaged horn to squeeze along the pup lying within it. "Hey, hey—got some movement here!"

"Let me—" Jade said.

"I've got yours," Isaac told her, and they did a quick trade, because here came the next pup, tiny tan and white and by golly *pink,* and pink meant life. . . .

Hard to believe only moments ago he'd been sharing a giant salad in the break room, a concoction Jade had brought in and dished up while Dale cleaned mugs from the morning tea. And after that, a few stolen moments with Aunt Cily.

Dear Aunt Cily—

Yup, Laura's out of the hospital and staying with me. She's tired . . . but she's good. Plus, she doesn't think I'm crazy. That's a plus in a woman, I've always thought.

Did I mention the whole thing with the shovel? Maybe not. Yeah, yeah, maybe I was just avoiding it. The Staties say that I interrupted someone dumpster diving behind the deli, though it's not like any of the old donuts make it that far. Anyway, there was a shovel involved but nothing's broken and I *am* telling you about it. . . .

Okay, yeah, you got me. But seriously, I'm okay. And it was worth it. No, don't look at the computer screen like that! Because the Staties are all wrong—it wasn't a dumpster diver. Sully and I interrupted the Hanta Santa as he was leaving goodies for the deli. Can't prove anything, because he ran off with said goodies while I was inspecting the pavement up close and personal, but for a guy who's been leaving dire little hanta packages . . . either he's just not much for face-to-face confrontation or he doesn't really think he's going to kill anyone with what he's doing.

Question is . . . what *is* he doing? What's he want? Why

is he doing it at all? Motive, right? That's what it's supposed to be about? So far Robert seems to have been an accident and the Hanta Santa has gotten Laura and tried for someone random in the deli, and that just doesn't come together. And then there are the notes. Are they taunting, or warning, or what?

You know . . . it's the oddest thing. Because I *have* my answers—some of them—and it hasn't made a bit of difference. I still don't know why, and I don't know how I ended up at the center of it all over again. And John Benally is still running around free somewhere, and for all I know he's got enough material to start his hanta farm all over again. No one's even trying to stop him.

Well, except us. That would be me. And Sully. And Laura. And you know what, I think he's made Laura mad. Not his best move, I'm telling you. Gotta watch out for the quiet ones—

Hold on—

Yup, got something coming in. Gotta go. Sully says "Send me cookies, Dale never feeds me!" (I do too, but that's what he says—)

Love, Dale

PS: Notice I didn't mention the mystery hospital tests you haven't explained yet?

"I got a squeak!" Jade toweled the puppy ever more vigorously even as she gently cupped the oxygen cone around its snub-nosed face. "Oh, if we can save just one of them—!"

"Antibiotics?" Dale asked, sweating even though this room was kept cooler than anywhere else in the clinic. He'd gotten them all but that last slippery pup, the breech stuck in the birth canal and not willing to move in either direction. "Isaac, grab me that cord—"

"Coming, boss," Isaac said, moving swiftly; none of his

hangdog nature came through here in the OR. All efficiency, all expertise. "Not liking her pressure, Dale. Better hurry."

Dale wasn't liking her chances, period. He took the cord, already looped just as he needed, and passed it behind the jaws of the pup within the uterus, wincing as it tightened around that slack neck. "Sorry, baby," he muttered, steadying the bitch as he applied slow and steady pressure.

"Antibiotics," Jade confirmed, grabbing the gap in conversation. A tiny, juicy squawk heralded her proclamation. "Ooh! Yeah! Come on, baby!"

"Whoa!" Dale took a step back to catch himself as the dead pup came suddenly free. "We have liftoff!"

"Good," said Isaac. "I'm pushing fluids here . . . the faster the better. . . ."

And now, Dale could be fast. He cleared the ruined uterus from the incision, found the ovaries . . . tied off the ligaments and blood vessels. Harder than a normal spay with the enlarged and dying organ flopping around in his way, but he moved with swift surety and by the time he cut the thing away, Jade had left the pup under the warming lamp, sucking in oxygen while she came in to irrigate the field—and irrigate, and irrigate. No taking chances with this one.

Dale checked the Boxer's belly . . . he double-checked. No bleeders, no loose ends, no necrotic tissue left behind. Isaac prepared to bring her out of the anesthesia while Jade went back to the pup, setting it up in the tiny intensive-care box they'd prepared in case any of the pups made it this far. A heating pad, plenty of towels . . . if the bitch couldn't feed shortly, then they'd tube feed as well, but with such a young dog, with the pup appearing magically at her side and without the birth process to stimulate motherly instinct, the pup might well end up rejected.

If the bitch even survived.

Stitch her up, first, Dale. Then he could move on to pessimism, stage two. And onto discussing the situation with the owner who had put the dog in this situation, who hadn't gotten her the help she needed during early labor . . . and who nonetheless loved the dog and who had at least one child who loved the dog.

And on to what he'd say if the man again asked how he'd known what the problem was at a glance.

I just knew.

And he'd listened. So why doubt his instincts when it came to the Hanta Santa?

Not that he was the only one.

Jade bustled out with the pup, and suddenly the surgery room—so isolated from the rest of the clinic—became part of the world again. "Dr. Dale!" Sheri called, and from the sound of it, she'd poked her head through the double doors of the procedures room. "Phone call!"

"Stitching!" Dale called back. He'd have to remind Jade to close the surgery door all the way in the future. At least until the stitching was done.

"Laura has errands for you to—"

And just as Dale was thinking that didn't sound like Laura, Sheri broke off, went silent a moment, and said, "Okay, not like that. But the dead guy from Cameron has a satellite office here and they'll talk to you—"

Stitching, Dale thought. Just . . . stitching.

"Oh," Sheri said, apparently to the phone she'd hauled to the double doors, and then, "Never mind! I'm taking a message!"

"She did that on purpose," Laura said, as soon as she picked up Dale's call. She sounded both amused and appalled.

"Of course she did." Dale checked the cloud factor, decided that in spite of the brief, blessed downpour of the afternoon, the sun had made enough of a reappearance so Sully wasn't going to wait in the car even with the tailgate up. "It's her way of staying in charge." He still sat there now, in the abbreviated parking lot tucked in behind the tiny downtown satellite office of Begay Home Balance. One-way streets to get here . . . one-way streets to get out. Dale figured getting lost was pretty much a sure thing. "I ran late after that C-section . . . I hope they're still here."

"She said they'd wait. I think the family is still. . . ." Laura hesitated, word-hunting. "Unsettled. I got the feeling they're still looking for some kind of sense in the way he died. Albert Begay was his name—did Sheri write it down?"

"His daughter is Anna," Dale said, flipping out the silvered windshield screen and wrestling with it one-handed. "That's all I've got."

"That's all I've got, too," Laura said. "The rest is yours—I was surprised enough when calling around led me to a Flagstaff office. Begay Home Balance. Accountants? I know it's a family business. . . ." She shifted, and in the background came a familiar noise that Dale couldn't quite place. "I talked to my cousin this morning, and she checked with her neighbors," she added. "No one's seen Benally. Doesn't mean he hasn't been there, but it does mean he hasn't wanted to be noticed." That noise again. And then her voice, a little worried. "Try to work around to your questions, if you can? The Begays are a reservation family. Direct questions, prying questions . . . they'll find that rude. Assumption of familiarity, too."

Dale grinned. "You wish you were here. You wish you were doing this."

"It's not my thing," Laura said without hesitation. And then she muttered, "Damn it." And made that noise again, louder than before.

"I'll tell you everything," he promised. And realized, quite suddenly, what he was hearing. "Hold on. You're in the puzzle room. You're playing with the puzzle!"

"I'm just turning pieces over," Laura said. A pause. "Mostly." Another pause. "Besides, you hid the cover. How can you do a puzzle without looking at the cover?"

"I don't." Dale grinned. "Purists do, I suppose, but I like to look. I just wanted to see if you'd figure out what it was."

"Oh, please," she said, and sniffed for dramatic effect. "As if I can't recognize another Neuschwanstein when I see it."

"Just for you." Dale's grin widened enough to hurt his face. "Ow," he said. "Face. Ow."

"Try not to scare Anna Begay with that face," Laura said. "Myself, I'm going to take my tenth nap of the day. Tomorrow's a big one, what with the outpatient therapy and all. Better rest up for it."

But he heard the self-recrimination in her voice, and the impatience, and his grin fell away. "Hey," he said. "Give yourself some time. And I'll be home as soon as I'm done here."

But she'd faded fast, as she tended to do, and her good-bye was already distant. Dale flipped the phone shut and tweaked the sunscreen into better position, then went around back to pull Sully from the crate. "Let's go," he said. "And be polite. Go for *unnoticed* if you can possibly pull that off."

Sully responded with a distinctly unquiet *woo-oo*. Dale rolled his eyes, gave Sully a leg-lifting moment, and headed for the narrow alley for the storefront, but only after a brief tussle over direction that he hadn't expected and didn't have time for. "Sully!" he finally snapped at the dog, a rare moment of voice-raising that not only got Sully's attention, but left him subdued, his tail forgotten and hanging, as they finally made it down the alley, stepping past puddles and over the remnants of the gully-washer still draining along the street gutters.

The storefront itself was tucked in beside a New Age–ish

candle and scents store, and on the other side a leather goods store with a corseted mannikin in the narrow front window that made Dale's jaw drop right there in public. It took two tries to snag the handle for the Begay's door; he tore his gaze away from the red leather and took hold of himself, shaking his mind off. Whoa. Maybe that's how Sully felt when he hit the scent of mouse. . . .

The little office was clearly in transition. The sign on the door was a placard taped into place—Begay Home Balance, with a broad graphic of the San Francisco Peaks over what Dale guessed to be the Painted Desert. Inside, one corner held utilitarian chairs and a table; the other held a neat stack of boxes. The space itself was shallow, cut in half by a long standing-height counter and a dividing wall behind it, with the obvious presence of offices behind that.

It looked abandoned; it smelled like new paint and construction—oh-so-familiar—and yet not enough air circulation to keep it to an undertone. Dale's lungs, accustomed to the settling clinic smells, set up an instant protest. A little burn, deep down.

Well. Big Blue II was in his messenger bag, if it came to that.

Sully sneezed, decided they weren't going anywhere, and settled down to rest his chin on his paws, inspecting the room from there with much movement of brow.

Dale was about to call a hello when a short, heavy young woman came from the back section of the office, her long dark hair tied simply at the nape of her neck, her movement as quiet as her voice turned out to be. "Hello," she said. "I'm Anna. Your friend called earlier, I think?"

"Dale Kinsall," Dale said, and when she didn't step close enough for a convenient handshake, didn't offer his hand at all. "This is Sully. I hope he's okay here. I had him at work, and it's too hot to leave him in the car right now—"

She gave him a thoughtful look. Sully sat up to look back at her, tipping his head in query. "He seems okay," she decided, and nodded—and then looked around the storefront, her wide face gone rueful. "Not that it matters so much. We're closing down this office. That's why I stayed for you . . . I don't know when we'll be down here again."

"I thought you just opened?"

"Our main office is in Tuba City," she said, and pulled out a folder from behind the counter, poking through it as she spoke. "My father's dream was to build the business up into the Flagstaff area—create more work for the family. Maybe we can still do that, but not now. Not with what happened."

"I've heard a lot of good things about your father," Dale offered. Stretching it a little, given that he'd read a single brief article about the man, but better than plunging right to the point—*how do you think your father was exposed to the hanta, anyway?* But he lost his train of thought when Sully, still subdued from his scolding, put a beseeching paw on the side of Dale's leg.

want.

"Not now, Sully," Dale murmured. When he looked back up he found Anna smiling at him, though she didn't meet his gaze. She plucked a page from the folder and put it on the counter, then took a step back.

"My father was the last person we thought this would happen to," she said. "He took care of himself. He didn't. . . ." She hesitated, and said carefully, "You may hear about drinking and the reservation. There are some problems. But my father was a healthy man. He was a man who walked in beauty, and he tried to share opportunities with others."

"Balance," Dale said suddenly, thinking of the reading he'd done at Laura's bedside and ignoring Sully's paw as it landed on his leg again. "That's a reference to his philosophy, not accounting."

She laughed; it was light and pleasant and it lit her face up, taking away the shadow of grief he hadn't even realized she'd been holding to herself. "No, not accounting." She nodded at the flyer on the counter. "Heating and cooling. Mostly cooling in Tuba City, but—"

Heating and cooling? Dale all but clamped a hand over his mouth to keep himself from interrupting; it wasn't enough. Beside him, Sully flexed his paw and ran it down Dale's jeans in a manner usually guaranteed to get attention, and let a whine grow to a yodel in the back of his throat.

"You didn't know what we did?" Anna asked, as if she didn't quite know what to think of that.

One glance at the flyer made it pretty clear. *Begay Home Balance,* with images of modest homes, hogans in the background, heating and cooling units. . . .

"I didn't," Dale said, removing his leg from under Sully's paw and fast running out of wiggle room for the indirect approach. "My friend . . . did she mention she's recovering from hanta?"

Anna's expression closed up, grew more wary. "She said you had read of my father and felt saddened by what happened."

"Yes," Dale said, seizing on that. Sully's paw landed on his leg; flexed. Time to clip those nails, for sure. Dale spoke over the new round of whine-to-yodel. "The thing is, my friend . . . she's much like your father. She takes care of herself. She's healthy, and she's young, and she wasn't in a situation to be exposed to the hanta. So when I heard of another . . . I wish your family had been as fortunate as I am, because I still have my friend. But I'm worried that there's something unusual happening, that two such people would catch this disease."

Her eyes widened slightly; she looked directly at him for a

quick moment, and then away. "I'm not sure what you think you can do . . . and I'm not sure how I can help you," she said, finally. "My father worked in the office. He went out to the sites, but mostly he did the estimates and the client visits. He wasn't doing the installations any longer."

Heating and cooling. Cameron. John Benally. Worked for another heating and cooling place before Mountain Air, left in bad graces. . . . *Just ask it. Just take the plunge.* Dale took a deep breath, absently knuckled his sternum where the fumes bit his lungs, and said so casually, "Do you know if your family ever hired a man named John Benally?"

She didn't ask him why. She pulled out a cell phone and moved to the back of the counter space for privacy, and Dale took the opportunity to crouch down beside Sully, who put an earnest paw on his knee and stared at him, goggle-eyed, another whine already building in his throat and looking to be a good one. "Shh," Dale said, cutting it off. "Be patient. We're an hour from dinner time." He put his hand over Sully's face, surprising him and breaking that concentration of *want;* a few repetitions of this peekaboo and a quick scruffle of ears and he figured he'd bought them a few moments of silence. Sully didn't want to be here, no question about that.

He stood as Anna murmured a *good-bye* sounding phrase and turned back around. She didn't waste any time. "We did have a man named John Benally," she said. "We let him go. My father would have handled that, so I don't have details. His file only says that he was not a good worker."

The same impression he'd left with the crews at the clinic. Not a good worker. Didn't get things done, didn't follow through . . . didn't care. Not a stupid man, not incapable . . . but his mind was elsewhere.

Sully flung himself to the floor, sobbed quietly to himself, and began his whine-to-yodel routine again.

"I'm not sure how this matters," Anna said.

"I'm sorry," Dale said, going utterly direct. "I'm not sure, either. That is, I think—I'm *afraid*—this man may have influenced what happened to your father and my friend. Until this moment, I didn't understand how your father might be involved, just that what happened to him, like what happened to my friend, doesn't make sense."

She frowned, shook her head. "I still don't understand," she said. "Hanta isn't something you influence. Hanta is about the weather and the mouse and—is your dog all right?"

Sully had sprawled to his side and escalated into full woeful yodel of want, a whine grown completely out of control and into a soulful, songful life of its own. His ribs rose and fell with the pattern of his whine—but when Dale crouched beside him again, he scrambled to his feet to hook both front legs over Dale's knee and stick his face into Dale's. "He's having a moment, that's for sure," Dale said, and coughed, the one that had been lurking since he walked into the office. "I think maybe the paint and construction—"

And he stopped, because as strong as those smells were, Sully had nonetheless been living with them in one version or another for months now.

And because there was really only one thing in recent weeks that had driven Sully out of his mind.

"Did John Benally ever work out of this office?"

She shook her head. "No one did, really. We were just putting together the office support for a local branch. The only work done here was on the building itself—we put in a new system as a showcase. But my brothers did that work."

And still. . . . "Do you mind if I let my dog look around? I know that sounds strange, but we've been training on. . . ." No, not gonna go there. "Can I leave it at I know that sounds strange?"

Her voice was remarkably without intonation as she asked, "It has something to do with your friend and my father?"

"It could." Dale stood, plunged in the rest of the way. "Or it could be nonsense."

"But you don't think so."

"No." One firm shake of his head, a moment to think back over every single gut reaction he'd had since the notes started coming in, the instant dread that no one else had felt, the slow and grueling bits of information now beginning to make sense of it all, if not enough sense for any truly sane person. And then another shake of his head, and, "No, I don't think it's nonsense."

She thought about it, long enough so he thought she would shake her head, unwilling to involve herself in *it sounds strange* when she still had a couple hours to drive before reaching home for the night. But she lifted her shoulders in the slightest of shrugs, her expression one that he really couldn't read.

"We'll be quick," he promised. Especially if there was nothing to it.

But he didn't think that, either.

"Okay, Sully!" he said, deliberately vague. This time, he didn't want to send Sully after something . . . he wanted to see what the fuss was about. "Let's go!"

Sully jumped to attention, his tail back upright and wagging, and let slip a single sharp *woo!* of excitement, managed a brief moment of grace to look abashed about it, and then headed off right where he'd been wanting to go.

If Dale thought they'd do a quick look in each of the offices, he'd thought wrong. What they did was wind behind the divider, down the hall and past two small rooms with doors open and disarrayed contents open to view, jog right, and straight to a third room at the end of that hall where there was, *aha,* a back exit, which was, *aha,* open. He turned to Anna, who had followed on his heels. "Or yeah, it could just be nonsense—"

But Sully jerked hard on the lead, throwing him off balance, and Dale stumbled right on out the door on the other end of that straining leash, finding himself pretty much back where he'd started—with the Forester off to the side, in close to the inner corner of the building where the mullen had grown up fairly high and nearly obscured the pile of collapsed flexible ducting there, a tangled aluminum and fiberglass octopus.

"Oh," Anna said, chagrined. "There's no telling what's in that mess. We'd just pulled it all when . . . we just haven't gotten it cleaned up like we should have. Be careful, there could be black widows—"

But Dale knew what they would find. And so did Sully, who went straight to the spot he'd been trying to reach since the moment Dale had pulled him from the Forester, jamming his nose into the end of the collapsed duct to whine eagerly.

Not so much with the nonsense. Gently, Dale pulled Sully back, placing a hand under his chest to relieve the pressure on his collar. "Good boy, Sully. Good *find it.*" And to Anna, "It's a mouse nest. If you don't mind"—as if anyone would—"I'll take it with me." Somehow. Not that the virus was live at this point, but taking chances . . . no, thanks.

He should have collected the nest at Laura's, too. Evidence, that. But he hadn't understood the full significance of it at the time . . . and besides, he'd been busy. Distracted and busy. And now the house had been cleaned, the nest removed and destroyed.

This one, he'd keep.

"I don't understand," Anna said, standing well back. "How could it matter, if a mouse built a nest in this mess? My father was never back here. My brothers removed this ducting and replaced it before we began any work on the interior."

Dale hesitated on an explanation. The Begay family was coming to grips with Albert Begay's death as they understood it, and it quite suddenly didn't seem fair to catch them up in the Hanta Santa. Not when it was still his own private Santa hunt. So he answered her with a question. "So no one in your family was ever exposed to air that traveled through these ducts?"

Baffled, she shook her head.

John Benally had been here, it seemed . . . and he'd left a dud, a little package of doom that had been unwittingly removed before it ever came into play. He must have realized his error, rectified it somehow.

Dale had come on a hunch, on the vague need to pursue every possible lead, and he'd found a murder. Before Robert became ill, before Laura's air conditioner had been seeded, before the first note landed on Dale's desk, Albert Begay—the man who'd fired John Benally—had been murdered.

For the first time, there was something of sense about it all—an understandable motive.

And still Anna Begay stood back by the doorway. Dale almost warned her to check the ducts at their Tuba City office, and those at their father's home, if any family still lived there. But the virus didn't survive outside those little mousie bodies for long; anyone who was going to be infected, was infected. And with an incubation period of two to three weeks, anyone who had been exposed also would have become ill by now. John Benally was through with the Begays.

Why he'd started in on the notes, why he'd infected Laura . . . Dale didn't have a clue. But the nest, inactive as it was, was still evidence—and currently in danger of being carted off with the garbage. So he said to Anna, "I could explain this, but I. . . ." He scrubbed a hand through his hair, picked up Sully, popped the Forester tailgate, and crated Sully, dropping in a pressed rawhide and grabbing a garbage bag from his ever-present box o' things in the back. "Can you just think of me as a crazy vet from Ohio doing some esoteric research, and trust that I'll let you know if it turns out?"

That wasn't quite it . . . but it would do. He dug into his pocket for his small folding knife, watching Anna Begay think about it. She didn't shrug this time. She looked at him and she said, "You know more than you're saying."

"I *think* I do," Dale agreed. "I just think it's too important to . . . well, that sounded pompous. I just want to be certain." *I want other people to be certain, too.* "It's a matter of being respectful to your family."

She shook her head. "One day this conversation might even make sense."

"Don't hold your breath," Dale said, relaxing at her acquiescence. And then instantly thinking *on the other hand . . . hold your breath.*

At least, until John Benally showed up.

"She must think I'm an idiot," Dale said, looking up into the high-desert night. Sporadic blue-grey monsoon clouds drifted overhead, silvered at the edges by the moon. They'd be gone before morning, leaving a bright blue sky a clear palette for the daily build-up of thunderheads. "I had no idea what to say to her. It just suddenly . . . I mean, I've always had. . . ." He thought again of the Boxer; he thought of the Wilsons' dog; he thought of all the improbable on-sight diagnoses he'd ever made and how he all but took them for granted.

"Those moments," Laura supplied for him. "The *I had a feeling . . .* moments." She shifted under his arm. It was a tight squeeze, but it turned out that the patio dog bed was big enough for a cozy side-by-side, a certain Beagle curled up on the outside edge beside her.

"It just seems like one thing to act on them as a vet, or to follow my Hanta Santa curiosity on my own turf. But to bring the Begays into it? They've been through enough."

"Mmm," Laura said. Her hand was warm on his chest.

"I just didn't have enough time to think about what I was doing . . . what I might find there. Not the way the day went. Just had some vague notion that I was going to see what I could see. But that they'd be into heating and cooling . . . that Benally had so obviously been at work. . . ."

"You sound as though you're sorry you went." She tipped her head to look over at him—so close, just inches away.

Dale had to recapture his thoughts. "With what I found out? No. But I feel as though I *should* be. As though I crossed some line."

"Or came close," she agreed. She tucked up more closely against him, lifting her outside shoulder as Dale nudged the sleeping bag more snugly around it. Not quite big enough for the both of them, so half of him went uncovered.

A very, very small price to pay.

Oh yeah.

He realized she'd bitten her lip on a smile, was losing that battle so the smile won through. "What?" he asked, and it seemed the perfect excuse to touch her hair, too.

"I'm not sure you're still thinking of this afternoon."

"Of course I am." Smooth and thick and just as he'd always thought it would feel, both heavy and sleek in his fingers. "I'm . . . um. . . ."

Laura grinned outright. Dale sighed, withdrew his hand. There'd be no actual thinking as long as he was touching her hair. With some effort, he pulled his scattered thoughts together—or at least brought them back into the same neighborhood. "I didn't tell her. So she thinks I'm nuts. I should be used to it. It just felt more important than that."

"It *is* more important than that. She's like me. Like *us*. She's been touched by Benally in a way all these others haven't."

Dale settled back on the giant dog bed and dropped his arm

over his eyes, closing out the sky. On the other side of Laura, Sully let out a contented groan. "I can't help but think—if Benally hadn't miscalculated with that first nest, he might have gotten more than just Albert Begay. He might well have infected anyone who worked there."

She shivered slightly under his arm—not from the cold, he knew that much, and gave her shoulders a gentle squeeze. Her voice was remarkably even as she said, "He must have been more selective, wherever he put his nesting material the second time."

"More time to think about it," Dale agreed. They fell back into silence, while he thought about *what now* and *Benally's still out there* and *oh my God she smells good.*

Sully's tail beat a sudden quick tattoo, and Dale had a dislocated moment when he thought Sully had read his mind, and another moment where he didn't care because he was *so* just going to roll over and touch that hair again and see where it would lead, and he sank deeper into the distraction of Laura beside him, the scent of her that close, the memory of touching her hair and the intent to do it again and more, so when Rena's voice came out of the night and into that quiet patio space, he pretty much levitated right off the dog bed.

"You really ought to lock that gate."

"You think?" he gasped.

"No answer at the door," she said, hitching up to sit on the lowest of the stepped adobe patio walls. "But your little SUV is outside . . . figured it was worth a try. Hmm, cozy."

"It *was.*" By now Sully had gotten up to turn happy little circles, not quite certain of his best approach but clearly happy to walk all over Dale and Laura while he figured it out.

Dale gave it up. He rolled out from beneath the sleeping bag and from beneath Sully and from beneath Laura's warm hand on his chest, and he straightened his rumpled shirt as he stood, and tugged his jeans into something more comfortable while Rena waited with something far too close to a knowing smirk.

Laura merely pulled the sleeping bag in close around her and sat cross-legged on the dog bed as though it were a throne. She looked tired yet content, and when Dale flicked on the back porch light, she scraped back her hair to reveal a light flush on her cheeks. Dale decided to pretend he'd put it there.

"You look pretty good," Rena said to Laura. "Considering."

"Hanta's like that," Laura agreed. "Hits fast, leaves fast. I've got some follow-up lung function tests over the next week or so and they said it'll be a couple of months before exercise doesn't bother my lungs, but mostly they just want to make sure I'm not alone this first week or so."

"I'd say that's taken care of." Rena grinned, although it turned to surprise fast enough as Dale scooped Sully up and deposited him in her arms.

"Here," he said. "You woke the sleeping giant. Now pet it, before it bays for attention."

Sully danced, half on the broad wall, half on Rena. *me! pet me! admire my ears!*

"His head is so soft," Rena said, sighing. "I keep thinking . . . but no, it wouldn't be fair. Not with me at work all the time."

"Which you are . . . now?" Dale eyed her uniform in the most obvious way.

"On the way home," she agreed. "I thought you'd want to know. I've been keeping my ears open . . . been in touch with some people. Unofficially, you know, since I'm just your basic officer on patrol and it would not do if I went over heads, got above myself, stepped on toes—"

"Got it," Dale said.

"Good. Well, John Benally's shed burned down this afternoon."

"What? It *what?*" Surely there was a more thoughtful, intelligent response. Dale couldn't come up with it. He couldn't do anything more than stiffen, watching Sully's tail droop in response to the sudden change of mood, exchanging glances with Laura to see her gone just as grim, just as tightly angry at this trail gone cold.

"Nice tidy little fire. Didn't spread—not that rock burns— and it pretty much incinerated the contents, took the whole thing down."

"It *what?*" Dale repeated, in spite of himself. "That thing was the Fort Knox of sheds. Four-by-fours, three-quarter-inch plywood . . . it would have taken a heck of a hot fire to do anything but singe around the edges."

Rena shrugged. "It's gone. Whatever you wanted us to see . . . gone. And there's no sign of him at the house. It wasn't even his house—belongs to a family who went down to Phoenix. So he's gone, too. No one's seen him, and even if he wrote those notes. . . ."

"Annoying notes don't rank too high against drugs, murder, and mayhem," Dale said. And without the shed, without that evidence. . . .

Annoying notes was as far as it went.

"Look, Dale. . . ." Rena shifted on the wall, causing Sully to teeter precariously on his perch; Dale rescued him and set him on the ground, and he immediately went to the wall to stand up against it and investigate Rena from that angle. "I want you to know, I've been in touch with the detective ever since it became obvious those notes were a threat. I passed along what you said after Benally attacked you. That's why they were alert to that fire in the first place, so no one's just been ignoring this thing. But I think we've hit a dead end. Benally's gone, and you haven't had a new note for days. I really think you scared him off when you came up on him behind the deli. I mean, he'd already walked off the job over at the clinic—between you and

Sheri, it probably just got too hot for him."

Dale exchanged a glance with Laura. She nodded, ever so slightly. Rena—stuck between a rock and a hard place—had done her best to come through. And Dale wanted this on the record. He didn't want it said that he'd been holding back. "I think you should know," he said. "I talked to a woman named Anna Begay today. Her family runs a heating and cooling business, and John Benally worked for them before her father fired him early this spring."

"Okaay," Rena said, the voice and expression of a woman who knows there's a shoe waiting to drop.

"Her father died of hanta not long after that."

For a long moment, Rena didn't react. Then, her voice flat and her face still expressionless, she said, "Oh, crap."

Laura smiled without humor from her dog bed throne—as grim as Dale had seen her. *Now you see,* it seemed to say.

And maybe Rena did, but—

She shook her head, and she slid off the patio wall, brushing off her uniform slacks. "Problem is, there's no connect-the-dots here, Dale. And I'm sorry, Laura, I know it's not fair if this guy somehow had anything to do with you getting sick and you can hate me for this, but—he's gone. No one's going to go looking for him with what we've got—vague notes we think he wrote, and three people who could well have been exposed to hanta anyway." She looked at Laura in desperation. "Mice build nests in air conditioners! It's one of the things they *do!*"

In the wake of that, they were silent a long moment. And then Dale said, in his most even and reasonable voice, "None of the mice I caught on the grounds at Laura's had the virus."

Rena blinked, visibly. "What?"

"I've been catching them and sending samples to Stanford for testing."

"Is that *safe?*"

Laura ducked her head for a smile. Dale couldn't help but give Rena an exasperated look. "I took precautions, Rena. And I thought it was important to establish whether the local population was in fact shedding the virus. I've been checking around the clinic, too."

Rena probably didn't realize she was leaning toward him slightly, enough to put one hand on the low adobe wall for balance. "And—?"

"And we're clean. We get a rash of hanta in the clinic or the deli, it won't come from the local mice."

Rena took a deep breath, let it out, and straightened. "Well . . . the shed is burnt. If you *are* right, Dale, then he's done spreading hanta."

"If I'm *right,*" Dale said quietly, "he killed a man."

Rena pushed the heel of her hand against the bridge of her nose. "I know, I know . . . and when I talk to you, I can see that . . . and when I talk to the detective, I suddenly . . . it just seems so . . . I mean, the *Hanta Santa.* . . ."

"It's okay," Laura said, quite suddenly. "We understand. *I* understand. We're glad you've been able to act on the situation at all."

Startled, Dale could only look at her—couldn't even voice the *but . . . but . . . but . . .* so close to his tongue.

"Good," Rena said, her relief profound. "I'm doing my best. I'll *do* my best. If we do come across this guy, he'll be questioned, it's just . . . he's gone, Dale. Seriously."

But . . . but . . . but. . . .

"Thanks for coming by," Laura said. "For letting us know about the shed. About Benally being gone."

"Sure thing," Rena said, and she'd gone back to her normal self, cheerful and a little oblivious and tired at the end of the day. "Let me know if anything else comes up, okay? And Dale—get a lock for that gate!"

But . . . but . . . but. . . .

"But—" he finally said out loud.

"She's doing what she can," Laura said. "She needed to know that was okay. Or she's going to feel bad, and pressured, and you're going to find she's suddenly not around the next time you want to talk to her."

"Huh," Dale said, and leaned back against that same wall, sitting against it with his legs propped out. "When did you put on the Dr. Phil hat?"

"I'm surprised you even know about Dr. Phil," she said, and patted her lap as Sully wandered past.

oh. me! yes! here i am!

"Sucker," Dale said. "See if you get out of here with a single piece of clothing that doesn't have a Beagle hair on it."

"See if I want to," Laura told him, and kissed the top of Sully's head. "Besides, you're just evading the Dr. Phil thing."

"I have one word for you," he said. "Sheri. And Dru. And Isaac."

And Laura was kind, and didn't point out how many words he'd actually used. Instead, her hand absently smoothing down Sully's ears, she looked up at him and said, "Do you think she's right? Do you think that's it? We should let it go, just go back to life as it was before hanta?"

Dale pushed away from the wall and crouched beside her, and before he even knew what he was doing, he'd cupped one hand behind her head, tangled in her hair and brushing her ear and totally ignoring the surprise on her face. "Life as it was," he said, "didn't include this." And damned if he didn't kiss her. Right on the mouth. Just long enough to be more than casual, to feel how easy it would have been to sink down and keep right on kissing her, and to make it one of the hardest things he'd ever done to move away from her again.

Her eyes were wide, her cheeks flushed; he'd taken her by surprise.

But she'd kissed him back.

"Wuh!" he said, and shook himself off, and with further supreme effort he shifted back another notch and got to his feet. He heard the dazed nature in his own voice as he said, "I've got to. . . . I left my. . . . I. . . ." And made a feeble gesture that was meant to encompass the path through the house to the front and the driveway.

"Wuh," said Laura, smiling in a way of someone who'd come across an unexpected goodness. "Go." She pushed the sleeping bag away, including Sully, who had gotten to his feet to investigate the kissing thing in any event, an interest that made it just as well that there was nothing to investigate any longer. "I'll be in frowning at the puzzle."

"Okay," he said. "I'll just, uh." And somehow managed to turn around, although he barely missed smacking into the wall and had to take a hasty sidestep to manage the sliding glass door. *I'll just uh.* Great. *You smooth talker, Dale Kinsall.* And he tripped over one of Sully's bones and bashed into the kitchen counter, but eventually he pulled himself together well enough to grab the car keys from said counter and head out the front door to the driveway, because although he'd pretty much manufactured the need to grab his messenger bag from the Forester *now*—being a big fat coward who needed that distance to get his head on straight—he did indeed have to get himself sorted out for the following day, which included paperwork and journal-reading at the hospital while Laura had her morning appointment.

Back to life as it was before hanta . . . not quite. Not for either of them.

Dale headed out to the Forester in darkness, his feet following a familiar flagstone path to the gravel driveway. A few steps of that crunched under his feet and he reached the SUV, and the cool night air had just about cleared his head. He stopped there, closed his eyes, and let himself linger on what had just happened, found one hand touching his mouth where he could still feel the contact with Laura. That did it—he gave in to the grin that wanted so badly to break out. *Wuh!*

But he'd left her inside alone, and he knew she wouldn't last much longer before she crashed for the night—just as well, given the early appointment in respiratory therapy. So he sighed—happily, at that, a good moment in the midst of Hanta Santa uncertainty—and pulled open the passenger door of the Forester, where he'd dumped his messenger bag. The cab light flooded the interior, worthy of a squinty blink or two.

He'd already cleaned out the other effects of the day—the garbage bag of flexible heating duct—and replenished Sully's water, emergency treats, and the cleanup supplies, all of which had been badly depleted these last weeks. All that remained were the front seats, and if Laura was to ride here tomorrow. . . .

Dale got to work. The bottles he hadn't tossed so he could recycle, the junk mail that had never quite made it into the house or the garbage, the journals and reading he carried around in case he got stuck in traffic or stuck at an appointment or just plain stuck; he jammed those into the messenger bag, ready for tomorrow. And after dumping the garbage, collecting the recyclables, and gathering up the overflow of loose change from the cup holder that seemed to attract it, he hauled up the messenger bag, the other hand already reaching to close the door.

Never made it.

Never got close.

Because there, on the seat under his gear, was an unlined index card. Not his. Not familiar.

But that careful handwriting, this time in marker that took up most of the index card, was instantly recognizable.

Your discoveries may make you seethe
But that doesn't mean you'll continue to breathe.

CHAPTER 20

Dale's sense of serenity clamped down into gut-deep alarm; he fumbled the messenger bag and caught it again, clamping down tight and freezing in the instinctive manner of any prey being stalked.

But no. The note had been put here earlier, before he'd dumped his things onto that seat without looking—rushing out from the office, preparing to drive into town. Benally had proven his mettle—the sly sort, first slipping in notes unseen, then badgering someone else into doing it, and even doing a bash and run when it seemed he might come face to face with Dale.

Your discoveries may make you seethe
But that doesn't mean you'll continue to breathe.

But that didn't mean he hadn't already been here.

Dale slammed the door closed on the note—he'd get it later, when he could slip it into a baggie. He ran back into the house, blind, now, in the darkness, but his feet knew the way. Through the front door, where he dumped his gear off to the side, and then to the leash rack. Didn't matter which leash, this time—he grabbed a one-piece slip lead of thick, soft nylon. "Sully!"

Sully came running from the back of the house, very much his *here I am to save the day!* arrival, and stuck his head out for the lead as Laura called, "Dale? Is everything all right?"

Because of course she'd heard it in his voice, just as Sully had heard it. "Hang on," he called. "I'll be back in a moment.

Save some of those edge pieces for me!" As if he cared about puzzle pieces right now. Sully looked up at him with imminent antigravity about to manifest itself, and Dale rumpled his ears. "C'mon, son," he said. "Let's go find it."

Sully barked sharply. *find it! find it! me!* He led the way outside, lunging against the leash to hunt scent against the foundation, through the volcanic and river rock Xeriscaping. He invested some serious time at the base of the juniper clumps at the corner of the house but moved on when Dale did. Through the backyard gate . . . all around the back of the house, from the foundation to the patio area to the storage nook that Sully called his own. And then around the other side of the house and out to the front again, all damp and sniffy from the heavy rains of the afternoon, the evening cool enough to make Dale wish he'd grabbed a jacket.

Nothing. Happy dog, hunting scent. But no scent.

Dale did it again. And then he went inside and took Sully from room to room, vent to vent.

As he finished the master bedroom—the last of it—he slid the leash from Sully, grabbed a squeaky toy, and flipped it into the air. Sully flipped off after it.

Laura stood in the doorway—leaning against it, arms crossed. She'd changed into her pajamas—she probably thought them staid enough, but Dale had found them adorable—oversized, tan with hoof prints all over them. She'd had to roll up the pant cuffs. Another time he probably would have paused to take note of this chance to observe said pajamas without the light blanket she often trailed over her shoulders. Not tonight. Not now. And she saw that in him, too, for she narrowed her eyes and she said, "What's going on?"

He realized, suddenly, that she'd reached that point—the one where her recovering body had been awake too long and was about to leave her asleep on her feet, and without asking politely first, either. He went to her, slid a hand around her waist, and headed for the guest room in tandem.

At the door to the room, she muttered a grumpy "All right, all right," and pulled away from him, heading for the bed on her own steam. He helped himself to the recliner tucked into the corner, going so far as to pull it closer to the bed as if it didn't really weigh anything after all.

And by then she'd figured it out. "You found another note."

He raised both eyebrows at her. "You're *sure* you don't like doing puzzles?"

She pulled the covers up against the cool night air; Dale had opened the house to it, letting it wash out the closed-up air-conditioning of the day. "Not exactly subtle, all that hunting around the house, outside and in. *Sudden* hunting."

"No," he said. "I suppose not." He scrubbed a hand through his hair, knew from her expression that he'd left it a mess. "In the Forester. He must have put it there while it was at work. He might have burned down that shed . . . he might not be in Cameron anymore. But he's not *gone*." He looked at her a long moment, tucked up under the covers, drawn by hanta and drawn by events. "When we get back from the hospital tomorrow, I'll leave Sully here."

"The mighty guard dog," she mused.

"Biggest mouth this side of Flagstaff."

"Truth to that. What did it say, Dale?"

He felt suddenly reluctant to tell her. "It's a threat," he said. "A pretty direct one."

From behind her fatigue, she gave him an even look. "And what're we going to do about it?"

"Fifteen minutes ago, I was halfway to leaving it alone," he said. "Even without having doubts about Benally and the hanta . . . and even if we don't yet truly understand how it all comes together. But now. . . ."

233

"Even if it means involving other people? Or telling the Be-gays?"

He winced . . . but he nodded. "Now," he said, "we follow the feeling. We follow what we know is right." He'd done it today with the Boxer . . . he'd been doing it all his life. Now, when he suddenly fit into a bigger picture . . . now was when it would really count. And he would either stand up under it . . . or he wouldn't.

"We," Laura said, hitting that word hard. "This is mine, now, too. *We.* Now go away. I've got sleeping to do."

And when Dale leaned over to kiss her good night, it felt entirely natural.

Chapter 21

First came a morning at the hospital with Laura; then an afternoon at the clinic, calling her every hour or having Sheri call her. The tension climbed, the note waited for Rena at the RoundUp Café, the Boxer bitch died and left her single surviving puppy orphaned, and at the end of the work day Dale came back to hunt the monsoon-wet grounds for any signs of sudden mouse inhabitation with no results. At home, Laura read while Dale made great strides on the puzzle and Sully was happy enough to do not one but two rounds of the house and damp yard before bed, leaving them ready for an early morning for their planned expedition north.

"I couldn't get anything else on the Tsosie family," Laura said, setting Dale's phone aside and picking up one of the bacon pieces he'd left out for her. He'd already scarfed down a Saturday morning bacon-and-eggs breakfast, and left what he'd hoped was an enticing portion for her. She still wasn't eating enough, not to his eyes.

Then again, he was used to eating for a six-three guy-type, and not a petite five-foot-something.

Laura snorted, and he smiled to himself where he scrubbed the egg fry pan at the sink. She'd realized what he'd done with the bacon and eggs—the smiley face. But she said, "Our best bet is to drive on up."

Dale grumbled at himself. "I should have asked Anna Begay about it—if they'd done work on that home. I was too gob smacked at learning they were in heating and cooling at all—in putting them together with John Benally." And then, as he rinsed the pan, "Are you sure you're up to this?"

"I can sleep on the drive," she said. "And I don't think you'll get anywhere without me. We might not get anywhere anyway, since I'm not bilingual."

He held the pan up, let it drip off into the sink, sneaking a peak to see that Laura had pulled up a stool and dismantled the smiley face to pick at breakfast. Good. With Sully fed and sunning in the yard as the clouds moved in, the Forester restocked and ready to ramble, and the house and yard patrols completed . . . maybe today, they'd get somewhere. Get some answers.

As if she was reading his mind, Laura said, "It's not likely we're going to learn enough to understand what's driving John Benally. If we find the right Tsosie family at all."

"I know." Dale tucked the pan away in the drainer and turned around to sit against the counter, ignoring the instant evidence that he should have wiped down the edge of the sink first. "At least, I keep telling myself. It's just . . . he went after Albert Begay for revenge . . . that seems clear enough. But why the notes to me? And why you? If we can get any sense of that . . . we can be ready for him. If I'd asked enough questions in the first place, it never would have come this far—"

She stopped eating. She looked at him. She said, "Are you even talking about Benally anymore?"

"I—" He crossed his arms, realized how very defensive he looked, and uncrossed them. "What?"

"Because you said that once before, about Ohio. Or you started to. And when it comes to this Benally thing . . . Dale, I don't know how you could have asked any *more* questions. You took the notes to Rena. You taught Sully to hunt mice on command, before you even knew there was a connection. You took me to FMC when I would barely admit I was sick at all. And I know what you were dealing with at the clinic. What more were you *supposed* to have done?"

Dale crossed his arms again. He uncrossed them. He swallowed his grumpy and he looked away and he didn't think about the fire in Ohio, he *didn't.* "Stopped it from happening," he said. And by that he didn't mean the notes or his inauspicious interlude with the shovel. He meant what had happened to Laura.

She snorted. It wasn't even genteel. "The day you're omnipotent," she said, "is the day I won't be eating smiley face eggs at your counter."

Dale rubbed the bridge of his nose. He thought about it. He said, "Is that your way of telling me to get over myself?"

Laura crunched a piece of bacon. Swallowed. "Did you get that last note to Rena?"

"Left it at the café yesterday—didn't talk to her." Dale sighed, stretched hugely, and scrubbed a hand through his hair. Laura, going after the last bit of eggs, smiled down into her plate. "Never mind," he said. "I've got to brush my teeth. I'll fix it."

And indeed, the early humidity of the day had left his hair in a particularly creative mood. He sorted it out, noted that indeed a haircut might help, swiped a token toothbrush across his teeth, and finished cleaning up in the kitchen while Laura captured her own hair back in a short, thick braid and pulled on jeans and a summer top that made him want to suggest a picnic hike out of Elden Pueblo instead of a long drive to Tuba City.

Not that she was really up for either.

And besides, it looked very much as if they were in for more rain. The clouds had already cooled the day; Dale didn't even close the house up as they loaded Sully into the Forester, but left open the strategic cross-ventilation windows where any rain wouldn't blow in. "Monsoon for real," he said, looking up at the visibly building clouds as he held the door for Laura. "When I was in Ohio, I never thought I'd be this obsessed about getting rain."

"It's not always this bad," Laura told him, settling into the passenger seat. She looked through the windshield, up at the sky. "I guess I missed my first rain this year." Dale caught a glimpse of wistfulness on her face as he closed the door. When he rounded the front of the car and slid in behind the wheel, she added, "I stand in it."

"It's not too late," Dale told her, and she seemed to think on it as they drove out of his Cinder Hills area and still as they turned north on Route 89—and then, after half an hour had passed and they headed past the dramatic geology of volcanic Sunset Crater and Wupatki National Park, she just plain fell asleep.

From the back end, Sully heaved a sigh so loud it was meant to be shared. *waiting.*

Normally Dale would have informed him that he would indeed be waiting, that it would be a day of waiting in one form or another, but this time he glanced over at Laura and kept his silence.

She woke forty-five minutes later as they left 89 for Route 160, heading northeast toward Tuba City—and, if they kept going, Kayenta and Monument Valley beyond. By then he'd turned on the air-conditioning; the seasonal clouds loomed more distantly at this lower elevation, covering only half the sky; the sun still beat against the windows, pushing through the heat. The Painted Desert still lingered on the horizon to the southeast, while up ahead, red and ochre rock formations closed in around the road. "Wow," she murmured. "Different world."

"Monument Valley up ahead . . . Grand Canyon an hour west of here . . . Meteor Crater outside of Winslow, the Painted Desert, the Petrified Forest . . . this place is the ultimate tourist destination. And I *live* here." Dale hadn't realized it when he'd moved out here; still didn't quite believe it.

"Sedona, Montezuma's Castle, Walnut Creek, the Peaks themselves," Laura said. "Have you ever been up to the top of Agassiz on the Skyride?"

Dale cast her a disbelieving look, negotiating an unexpected curve. *Dinosaur Tracks Ahead!* proclaimed the handmade sign propped by the side of the road as the road straightened. *Jewelry!* "There's a Skyride in Flagstaff and I don't know about it?"

She laughed, reaching for the insulated bottle of ice water stashed by her feet. "It's just the highest ski lift at Snowbowl— that's what they call it in the summer. But the view is incredible."

"Then let's do it sometime."

She hadn't expected that; it took her by surprise. Then she nodded. "Okay," she said. "We'll talk about that."

That sounded like Laura-speak for *let's not make assumptions* and *I might need a little space when this is over.* So although Dale winced inside, he just nodded. "Good."

From the back, Sully yawned loudly. *waiting!*

"We know you're there, Sully," Dale said. "When we get up to Tuba City, you can have a sniff-break."

"Is that what the guys are calling it these days?" Laura wiped water from her chin where the uneven road had caused her to miss her mouth.

"Hey," Dale said. "It's Sully. What do you suppose happens more—leg-lifting, or sniffing?"

"Point to you."

Another few minutes and they'd hit the main intersection in Tuba City, where 160 and 101 met to give a brief impression of modern encroachment—fast food and two different grocery stores and the gas station where Dale pulled in for gas and gossip—if one didn't count the little building on the corner cheerfully labeled *Yah-Tah-Hey,* which Laura effortlessly pronounced as *yá-át-ééh* when they entered the gas station's convenience store and Dale didn't dare try to pronounce at all.

Laura also made effortless small talk for some moments while Dale stood around feeling tall and lanky and significantly white—not to mention alarmingly bruised—so eventually he eased off to the side, and, when the timing seemed appropriate, nodded to Laura and eased out of the store altogether, returning to the Forester to take care of Sully's needs. They'd left the tailgate open and the interior of the vehicle was no less toasty than the outdoors, but that was plenty toasty enough, and Sully greeted him with a lolling tongue and much impatience.

"Get used to it," Dale told him. "This day has only just started—and that's if we're lucky." But he pulled Sully out of the crate, leashed him up, and found a weedy patch at the back edge of the parking lot that needed much close and repeated inspection.

When he returned to the SUV, Laura was sitting in the shade of the raised tailgate, enjoying an ice-cream bar. She handed him an unopened one and said, "Be quick."

Dale didn't waste any time. Nor did Sully, as he leaped lightly to the back of the Forester, putting himself high enough to apply his masterful wrinkles of great want. *mine?*

"I'm thinking not," Dale told him, taking a big manly bite out of his and risking the brain freeze to beat the melt.

"We're waiting," Laura said. "Someone's cousin should show up eventually, to take us to the old Tsosie place. Mrs. Betty Tsosie lives there now—recently widowed. They think that's who we're looking for."

"Whoa," Dale said, forgetting about the melt altogether, and getting Sully's hopes up as his ice-cream bar drooped slightly. "That fast? You walked into that store and got what we needed?"

"Luck," Laura said. "Plus . . . it's the center of a very small town. If not here, we could have tried the Yah-Tah-Hey place. Given the number of cases of hanta each year in the whole state and the number of people who die from it in any given area . . . I thought our chances were pretty good."

He remembered the ice cream just in time, salvaging a glacial slough and talking around it as though he'd been raised in a barn. He begged silent pardon of Aunt Cily and did it anyway. "Not the impression I got earlier."

She shrugged. "Didn't want to get your hopes up." She paused, taking a more delicate bite of her own ice cream, savoring it, and swallowed before she added, "Also, I didn't want to look totally hopeless if I was wrong."

Dale choked, recovered; lost a chunk of ice cream from the stick to the ground. Sully eyed it mournfully from the edge of the Forester's back end, and Dale managed an *"Uh-uh"* at him in the middle of it all, catching the remaining ice cream in his hand.

"Sorry," Laura said, looking more amused than sorry at that. As well she could, with her own ice cream finished down to the stick, and no chance of such heat-induced high jinks. But she turned to rummage in his box o' things, and by the time he captured the last melting glob of ice cream from his palm, she was ready with a damp towel and a cookie for Sully, because that was only fair.

Dale took the towel with gratitude and Sully the cookie with unabashed greed, chomping it so mightily as to spray crumbs around and give himself the secondary treat of vacuuming them all up.

"Here we go," Laura murmured as Dale wiped the last sticky spot from his hands and then his mouth and chin just in case. A battered little Dakota pickup truck bumped carelessly through the driving patterns between gas pumps and parking, dingy tan with white pinstriping half scraped off. Inside, two occupants bounced around unrestrained, neither looking terribly large. Dale tossed the towel in the back and hustled Sully into the crate long before Sully was finished hunting the last molecule of cookie dust, garnering himself a baleful Beagle stare. He pulled down the tailgate just as the truck rattled to a stop behind them—and at that, only long enough for the young driver to gesture at them to follow before he zoomed off again.

"Was he even old enough to drive?" Dale asked, throwing himself in behind the wheel and starting the engine at the same time.

"Don't ask," Laura suggested, fumbling for her seat belt as Dale cranked the wheel, backed a few feet, and headed after their guides with much more alacrity than he'd prefer.

"Hold on," he said, hitting the gas to surge out into the highway—but only for a short distance, when the tan truck zoomed briefly into the turn lane and scooted through a gap in traffic to turn left. Dale followed as he could, vaguely aware that they'd taken Peshlakai Avenue, and then that they'd veered left onto Tumbleweed . . . and after that, he was lost, following twisty turns through neighborhoods so bereft of signs and directionals that they all but shouted *residents only*. The roads turned to rutted dirt and the stunted trees faded out and the desert pushed in, a dry sculpted land of striped and layered stone, gullies, and looming formations.

The pickup rattled to a stop at the far edge of one of those neighborhoods, pausing in a semicircle lined with stones that served as a driveway loop before the trailer-sized old house tucked up against a modest sweep of rock. Off to the side, two haphazardly penned sheep nosed at strewn hay. A hexagonal hogan of wooden cross-ties was built to the side of the house, its door facing east. The little house had a sturdy porch with a rocker on it and flower boxes full of sparse herbs, and if none of it was in complete repair, it hadn't gone without attention, either.

Dale pulled in behind the little pickup and cut the engine, slumping back in his seat. "Whew." And yet the lure of answers prodded at him, had him reaching for the door handle even if he hadn't quite decided what he'd say to this woman, not with only the brain-jarring ride between the store and this house to think about it.

But Laura stiffened, and his hand fell away from the door. Right. Gotta wait. Especially here and now . . . if they didn't start with respect, then they started with nothing.

Dale turned the key enough so they could roll the windows down, and hoped he wouldn't have to get out and pop the back gate for Sully before he'd been properly invited out. The clouds were with them, at least, rolling in overhead to announce themselves with an occasional grumble. The heat poured inside nonetheless, carrying enough humidity to promise rain.

The girl slid out of the pickup and ran to Laura's window. Maybe twelve, maybe not quite; her face was still a child's, still soft and rounded, her eyes big and her thick dark hair drawn back into a simple long braid. Her voice, too, was a child's—young and light, and soft in tone. Dale could barely hear her as she told Laura, "I can translate for you. Grandma Betty will understand most of what you say, but she mostly answers in *diné bizaad* and my brother doesn't speak it, so I said I'd come."

"Thank you," Laura said. "My name is Laura. This is my friend Dale, and he got those bruises without even starting a fight—he's a nice guy. We appreciate your help."

The girl smiled. "I'm Gracie." She looked over her shoulder to the house, and waved, and turned her grin back on Laura; she still hadn't looked directly at Dale. "Here she comes!" And as an elderly figure appeared on the porch and carefully closed the door behind her, eyes buried in wrinkles and smile scantily toothed, Gracie waved and called a greeting, then ran to the porch. The boy—and Dale still doubted he was old enough for a driver's license—got out and leaned against the truck, arms crossed, looking as though he was prepared to oversee the visit for as long as it took. His dark hair was buzzed short and a clean old T-shirt hung off his frame over worn jeans, a contrast to his sister in her cute summer outfit, a girly thing with capped sleeves and matching shorts.

Gracie conversed for a few quiet moments, standing beside the raised porch to look up at the elderly woman she'd called Grandma Betty, and then she waved them in. Dale glanced at Laura; she grinned and opened her door. "Let's go see what we can see," she said, and waited while he lifted the back for Sully, who had already figured out he'd be waiting in the crate and had curled up in a resentful ball in the back corner of the crate. "Ha," Dale said, and slipped a thick bully stick through the crate bars.

The ears came up. *mine? for me? i'm going to eat it!*

"Make it last," Dale told him, as if Sully would have any choice. Some things slowed even the mighty Sully jaws.

"You ready?" Laura asked. "You're not suddenly stalling or anything?"

Out of his element, about to involve this dignified older woman with the Hanta Santa? No, of course not. "No, of course not," he said out loud. "Just. . . ."

"I know," Laura said.

They reached the porch side by side, where the elderly woman was clearly taken back by Dale's height. The girl saw it and laughed, and said, "Come sit on the steps," even as she ran up to sit on the wood decking beside Betty Tsosie's weathered rocking chair. "We might not have long before the rain comes."

And so Dale sat, one step below where Laura sat, and as usual all awkward about just where to put his knees. His shirt, a loose weave cotton pullover, already stuck to his back. Laura said, "We came up from Flagstaff today. We both work there, we're veterinarians." *Come at things the long way,* he remembered, and they certainly did, as Betty Tsosie allowed that she had some relatives in Flagstaff, but found she preferred to be surrounded by the people.

"The people," Gracie said. "That's us. The Dine." She looked at Laura. "And you."

Laura said, "My name is Laura Nakai, and I was born to the Castilians, and born for *Taachii'nii.*" She glanced at Dale. "Red Running into the Water People." And as Betty Tsosie nodded, Laura added, "My maternal grandfather's clan are the Castilians and my paternal grandfather's clan is *Todichi'ii'nii.*"

The old woman considered this, her hands folded in her lap. She wore a scarlet shirt over a midnight blue velveteen skirt—not her best, surely, but still looking mighty spiff for an average summer afternoon. A single turquoise bracelet, set in silver, set off her wrist, while her rings—what she surely considered her everyday rings—were of the size and quality to make a collector weep. A bun held back her steel grey hair and her face was weathered so deeply that its original contours were indistinguishable. She spoke in low tones, a gymnastic language of tonal finesse that Gracie had no apparent trouble following but from which Dale couldn't even pick out individual words. "She says her sister married a man from Red Running into the Water, but she's never met anyone from the Castilian clan before."

Laura smiled. "Spanish," she said. "My mother was born in the Castilian part of Spain. But she lived in Cameron with my father when I was a child, before we went to Flagstaff and Phoenix."

Betty Tsosie nodded, and through Gracie she said, "You still carry something of those years."

"So I'm beginning to understand." Laura glanced at Dale,

took a deep breath. "This is Dale Kinsall, and he recently moved to Flagstaff from Ohio. We've come. . . ." She hesitated; to Dale's practiced eye, she looked as though she was tiring. "It's hard to explain. We're on a journey of sorts. We didn't really know it would bring us here. You see . . . I've had Sin Nombre." The old woman's eyes, dark and hidden within folds and wrinkles, widened. Laura added quickly, "I'm getting over it. But it left me with questions. I don't understand why I caught it, and I'm looking for others who have had it . . . I'm hoping I can learn something that will give me peace."

Wow. Dale had to hand it to her, she was good. Nothing but the truth, and yet . . . not a single bizarre reference to the Hanta Santa.

And still Gracie startled a little, and for the first time looked uneasy, glancing up to see Grandma Betty's reaction. She opened her mouth, closed it . . . waited. Finally, Grandma Betty spoke—as quiet and thoughtful as ever, but without excess. Gracie said, most carefully, "When one catches the Sin Nombre illness, it comes from the droppings of mice. Your own people have taught us this. We must look to our surroundings when such things happen." And Gracie glanced over at the goat's shed, a little bisected shelter with hay on one side and a lean-to for the goats on the other. She added, very clearly, her own words. "The shed was cleaned early this spring."

Whoa. Dale was in the company of masters. One side not talking about the Hanta Santa, the other avoiding any mention of the dead.

The older woman spoke again, not quite looking at Laura; Gracie translated. "At times like these, we must look within. If something is out of balance in our lives, we should fix that. Learn to walk in beauty in all things, instead of being mired in the one thing." Then she blushed and looked down. "Something like that. It's hard to do the bigger meanings."

"That's fine," Laura said. "We appreciate your help." And she glanced at Dale; he knew the unspoken words behind it. They'd found the season's first hanta victim, but it didn't mean it would lead them any closer to understanding John Benally. This was the Four Corners area; hanta happened. After all, there was a reason the CDC had first suggested the name *Four Corners virus,* although the Navajo had objected on the grounds that it wasn't the site of the first case. In fact, the first case had come from an area without a name, and so the virus had gone on to become the No-Name virus. *Sin Nombre. Hanta* merely identified the type of virus . . . a lazy man's nickname.

Hanta virus trivia . . . all the reading, all the research . . . for all he'd known before Laura was taken ill, it hadn't been enough. For all he'd learned afterward, it still didn't seem like enough. Maybe Grandma Betty was right. Maybe he was just mired.

In that pensive moment, a sound kicked up in the background. A low hum, a mechanical sound that took Dale by surprise here at this rustic and simple home. Many reservation homes didn't have electricity or running water, although this one was close enough to town so he had supposed it had both. And yet . . . "Is that an air conditioner?"

Grandma Betty smiled, wide and genuine, and when she spoke her words came quickly, and with obvious pride. Gracie did stutter-steps of translation, hunting gaps between the words. "The children had this done for us." This as the old woman gestured to the closest houses along the dirt road—all a little bigger, all a little newer, but built with the same hand and the same eye. "They don't have the cool air themselves—air-conditioning, I meant to say—but they wanted to gift it to us. A true luxury, from our children."

Us. So it had gone in before her husband had died. Or around that time.

"It's a special type," Grandma Betty said, nodding happily. "It's quiet inside, so quiet. And very quiet outside. And it's just the right size for a small home like this. It doesn't waste energy. The workers were also quiet, and respectful. And then, when—" She stopped herself, as though taken by surprise. Gracie caught up to her, waited a moment, and quietly added, "There was illness."

Dale hesitated, and then—even though he already knew, he truly already knew—he asked, "Which company did the work?"

But, for that moment, the old woman seemed caught up in her memories. Gracie gave her a worried glance, then gestured to her brother, who came over from the truck with rather more alacrity than one might expect from his carefully insouciant lounging. She rolled over on one hip to speak to him through the rails of the porch, and he went loping off around the house. Within moments he had returned—which was good, because Dale had become worried about the old woman, and Laura's expression told him she felt the same—that they were now intruding, and needed to find a graceful way to extricate themselves. The kid shot Dale a look that pretty much said the same, but out loud he said only, "Begay Home Balance."

It couldn't be coincidence. It *couldn't*. And yet here they were on hanta home turf, where the death of an elderly man to the disease was tragic but not startling.

Grandma Betty spoke again, just as Dale couldn't quite stop himself from opening his mouth to ask Gracie if she was all right. "They were respectful," she said, in English, and then in her own language again, with Gracie translating, "One of their people even offered to finish cleaning. To make the shed safe. He would be protected, he said, and he came with special clothing and a mask." As Gracie spoke, Grandma Betty drew her hand down over her face, pulling an invisible mask into place. "He burned what was there, and he took some of it away, so I would be well."

Dale stiffened. He closed his mouth on his exclamation and he closed his fist on his reaction, whitening knuckles there where it rested on his knee. And yet he must have fairly exuded the vibrations of that reaction—of a missing piece, gained. For Laura looked at him, full of understanding, her gaze reflecting something of her own horror. And the old woman looked at him, and Gracie, and the kid narrowed his eyes down to become less welcoming than ever.

Here, John Benally had acquired his hanta.

John Benally and his doesn't mean you'll continue to breathe, *still hanging over them. . . .*

"What I've said means something to you," Gracie said, translating for the murmurs of Grandma Betty.

"Yes." Dale wasn't about to lie to this old woman—but nor could he tell her that her benefactor's kindness had been nothing more than a deadly harvest. *This is where it started.* "We know of him, and of his work for the Begay family. They're in Flagstaff as well."

If she suspected it to be a sidestep, it didn't show. Then again, what would he know?

"Thank you," Laura said, shifting. "You've been of more help than you know. I appreciate your time, and what you shared with us."

And Dale murmured something in a similar vein; it must have been pleasing enough to judge by Grandma Betty's face and by Gracie's expression, although a moment later he couldn't remember it, finding his thoughts too full of *this is where it started* even though that got them no closer to *this is how we end it.* And then Laura said, "Oh! Just a moment!" and headed for the Forester at a pace much swifter than Dale thought she could sustain even if it hadn't been in the mid-nineties with the humidity climbing and the clouds grumbling lower; he could do no more than offer Gracie a shrug. When Laura turned away from the SUV, she had a cardboard four-pack of long-necked amber bottles in hand, and Dale hastened to meet her, to take it from her and carry it back, having guessed her intent if not the details.

"Sarsaparilla," Laura said to Gracie as Dale handed the carton up. "At the store, they mentioned . . . we were hoping Mrs. Tsosie would enjoy it."

Grandma Betty's smile returned, size large. She watched as Gracie set the carton beside her rocker and nodded. " *'Ahééhee'.*"

"You're welcome," Laura said. But she looked quite suddenly tired, her face gone flushed and her eyes unfocused, and Dale knew she was done for, had probably been done for since their rough and rattly ride from the store, and just been going on determination once they rolled down the windows and hit the heat.

"Time to get you back home," he said, and added apology to Grandma Betty, "She's only just out of the hospital."

"*Dale,*" Laura muttered, and that quarrely little note in her voice made him absurdly cheerful. *My first scolding.*

But Grandma Betty, rocking slightly in her chair, nodded at him, offering him parting words that hardly needed Gracie's translation. "Take care of her, now."

That he would. That was the whole point. The whole reason that John Benally and his notes couldn't just be allowed to fade away. He'd call Rena when they returned home, that's what—

Oh. Saturday. Well, he'd try.

Gracie stayed with Grandma Betty—Dale still wasn't clear if they were even related, but knew that the Navajo clan system made *related* into something different than he was used to, anyway—while her brother walked them back. "Nice face," he said.

Dale laughed. "Came right out with that, didn't you?"

"Why do you think Gracie came?" the kid asked. "I could have done that much talking for Grandma Betty. But everyone likes Gracie's words better. You get in a fight?"

"Not so much." Dale opened the door for Laura, helped her in, and went around back to close the gate on Sully, who pretended not to notice. A bully stick would do that.

busy.

"Yeah, yeah," Dale muttered at him, and pushed the tailgate down.

"You talking to the dog?" The kid gave him a squinty-eyed look.

Dale stopped to think about it, one foot already in the driver's footwell. "I guess I was."

The kid stopped, then, just looking at him a moment. "Okay," he said. "You were okay. I don't get why you were here today, but . . . just don't do anything to disrespect Grandma Betty."

"Okay," Dale said. "I'll do my best."

"Yeah," the kid said, and grinned. "If you can find your way out of here."

Dale started the car, rolled up both windows, and cranked up the air. "It is our solemn duty to make sure that kid and Sheri never meet."

Laura laughed softly, already looking better as the cool air washed over her face. "Good point." And then, as Dale pulled out to the road, a much more sedate pace than they'd taken on the way in, she said, "I don't think Grandma Betty would countenance a killer, no matter how nicely he cleaned her shed."

"I hope not," Dale said. "Because *I* don't. And if I get the chance, I'm going to do something about it."

Big talk from the man with shovel bruises all over his face, a collection of increasingly threatening notes, a collection of cops saying to let it go. . . .

And absolutely nowhere else to go with it all.

CHAPTER 22

When Laura opened her eyes again, they were approaching Cameron. Dale had turned the CD player on low—one of his sultriest chanteuse collections, one he'd listened to with a deepening appreciation over the years.

"It always surprises me to hear you listening to this music," Laura said, yawning. "Are you hungry?"

yes! hungry! That answering whine came from someone in the back who had just been waiting for the question.

"I thought we might stop at the Trading Post," Dale said. "I've never been."

"The food is wonderful," Laura said. "And there's shade; we can probably pull Sully's crate out and tuck him away . . . if you've got a lock for the crate."

"Got a lock," Dale said. And then, although she hadn't pushed, he added, "My parents listened to this music. They danced to it, out in the front yard. Old Ohio farmhouse . . . corn in the fields, a couple of cows in the barn, the barn cats teasing the old dog, lightning bugs in the yard, and my parents dancing." He could close his eyes and see it all, as clear as if he was there. Smell the green growing things, hear the crickets and katydids. . . .

Except, of course, he was driving. Much better to keep his eyes open. "Anyway, I've always listened to it. Seems like one of the few things I have left of them. My uncle never quite got it, but Aunt Cily understood." And if at first it was just that, a comfort to a young boy full of loss, now it still settled him, even as he'd come to recognize the talent and beauty and sometimes raw nature of the voices.

Settling was something he could use right now.

Because although Aunt Cily was right . . . although sometimes he'd just have to learn to live without getting the answers he wanted, this time around, it looked as though he'd have to get the answers he wanted in order to live.

And heading home to open-ended yard and clinic patrols wasn't how he wanted to end this thing.

But Laura . . . Laura was the one who closed her eyes at his words, at his memories. Laura was the one who said, "I can just about see it . . . the dancing. The yard. The cows. I'm having a hard time imagining all that green, though."

He grinned at her. "Then one day I'll have to take you there, so you can see for yourself."

She didn't respond. He had the startling impression that she was considering it. Too bad for his wishful thinking that her cell phone rang. Dale turned off the music as she fumbled around in her saddle-leather purse and pulled out the phone, looking at the display. "Mary," she said to him, "They're heading home today," before she answered.

Mary and Robert were home already, that much was evident from the conversation. And then Laura got tense, and she got quiet, and she listened. And then she said, "I need to talk to Dale. Will you be there?" And then a nod, and murmured good-bye, and she cut the connection, resting the phone in her lap rather than putting it directly away. She took a deep breath; it got caught on a cough, and by the time she worked her way through it, Dale was about ready to pull over to the side of the road, no longer prepared to drive right on through whatever was going on.

She didn't keep him in suspense. "They're home. She found

a going-away gift from Benally—a packet inside her screen door. It adds up to thanks and apologies."

Dale did pull over. Checked the rearview, found himself nearly alone on this stretch of two-lane highway, and slowed down to the broad gravel shoulder, letting the engine idle. Sully moved restlessly within the crate, quite certain that *stopping* meant *unloading*, and after a moment went so far as to run his claws down the crate wires. Slowly. And again, when no one paid attention.

"Later, Sully," Dale told him, and turned to face Laura.

She couldn't quite look at him, but instead looked at the phone in her lap. "He left a note. She describes it as similar to your notes—so neatly written the printing looks drawn. But it's a normal note, no rhymes. He apologizes for Robert's illness, says that wasn't supposed to happen. And he thanks her for her help." Now she glanced up at him, and she looked miserable. "Dale, he came after you—after *us*—because of Mary."

Robert ran around with Sully in the backyard in full view of the burnt-out shed, dutifully keeping hold of the six-foot leash Dale had snapped to a flat collar. Sully had no idea what this new game was all about, but he joined it wholeheartedly, matching Robert's movements with his tongue lolling and his laughter bursting out in sudden barks and bays.

"They won't last in this heat," Mary said, looking out the living-room window at them, and then up at the sky where the clouds were now breaking up, their promise of rain unfulfilled. "But it's the first time my son has had the chance to be a child again since he became ill. I don't have the heart to call him in."

Dale sat on the edge of the old couch beside Laura. Everything about the house was in similar shape—worn, but neat and clean; cared for but overdue for replacement in this decently affluent neighborhood where everyone had electricity and running water. Mary's house had a small wood stove in the corner of the living room instead of central heating, and the heavy window AC unit cut into the wall of the home that he'd already inspected from the outside.

And while Dale knew he should be making small talk and circling around the real issue, he had eyes for nothing but the small pile of material on the otherwise empty coffee table just barely touching his shins. He could see some of it at a glance—an old newspaper with the front page story of the eco-killers and the vet who'd tracked them down—literally—in the Cinder Hills woods. A key to the house next door, for whoever should care to come pick it up. Oddly, what looked like a carefully typed resume.

And the notes.

"When the story broke about the Flagstaff killers, it was big talk around here," Mary said. She turned away from the window, her hands folded in her lap. Quiet, as her voice was quiet. "John Benally seemed especially interested; he talked about it every time I saw him. Maybe I was looking for a way to feel important . . . because even though Laura and I haven't been closely in touch, she is still my sister."

Dale nodded. He got that; Mary meant it literally enough, in Navajo terms.

Laura said, "No one is blaming you."

"*I* blame me," Mary said. "I've been part of this without even knowing. If I hadn't given him all that information, told him of your friend Dale and how he'd outsmarted the biligáana police to solve the murders, would he have thought to go to Flagstaff? Would he have continued to keep the sickness in that shed right beside us, so my son became ill? If I had been in better knowledge of myself when he first started talking about the murders, I could have spoken more appropriately."

But as Dale and Laura exchanged glances, each hunting for

the right response, Mary took a deep breath and smoothed the material of her slacks. "That is my journey, now, I think. But this is what you need to know." She knelt beside the coffee table and pulled out a sheet of paper, touching it gingerly. Not just a simple index card, this. First the apology . . . then some bits about people in general not taking him seriously enough, but she always respected him and he appreciated that . . . and then the good part. *Kinsall didn't pay enough attention, and now it's too late for him.*

"Okay, not literally too late," Dale said, and looked pointedly at himself. "Still here. Still in pretty good shape, in spite of all the donuts and even that whole shovel thing."

"Dale . . . ," Laura said, dark eyes worried.

So much for keeping it away—that thump of reality coming home, the solid weight and reverberation of it inside him. The *knowing* . . . and knowing that no one else heard it.

No, not true. Laura heard it. Not at first, and not as loudly . . . but this time, Laura heard it too.

Dale couldn't sit still any longer. He stood, abruptly enough to startle Mary, and paced out past the confines of the coffee table. "Can we—do you mind—can we take this? The things he left you?"

"You're welcome to them," Mary said. "I wasn't careful about handling them, not at first. But I'm the only one who's touched any of it since we got home." She pulled a large manila envelope from beneath the papers and scooped the papers inside. "This is what it came in."

"Thank you," Dale said, somewhat more fervently than she'd perhaps expected; she stopped what she was doing to look at him. He shrugged, hunting words. "I know you feel bad about all of this, but from my perspective, you've just made sense of things."

Almost.

They knew where the hanta had started. They knew what had motivated its collection, and the first case—the only death at Benally's hands. And now they knew how Benally had targeted Dale.

Why Benally had written the notes, *why* he'd pursued Dale, they still didn't know.

Really, really want to know. Want. To. Know.

Dale unclenched his jaw. He unclenched his hands. He unclenched his toes.

And Laura stood, joining him, glancing out the window to where Sully and Robert were winding down, and where Robert hunkered down on the hard caliche to receive big sloppy kisses and offer clumsy pats in a boy-dog mutual admiration party.

"Do you think," Mary started, and it was the hesitation in her soft voice that got Dale's attention, "maybe you shouldn't go back, Laura? Maybe you should stay here, with us? Let us open our home to you, now?"

"Oh!" Laura said it in surprise—Dale thought both at the notion that perhaps she shouldn't go home, and that Mary had made the offer. And then she looked at Dale and said, "I think we're okay. We're together. We've got a mouse-sniffing dog. And I—" She looked at Dale, shook her head. "I couldn't just be here, worrying."

An astonishingly silly grin would be wrong at this moment, just plain wrong. So Dale didn't. But he didn't miss the moment, either—didn't miss the choice she was making, and how it so thoroughly finished unclenching his tension. Oh yeah. Nice. He cleared his throat and said, "Rena's detectives seem pretty convinced that Benally has moved on, for what that's worth. Anyway, we'll get this stuff to her as soon as possible, and spend tomorrow watching out for each other. I've got this great puzzle that needs work—perfect for the convalescent."

"You build," Laura said firmly. "I'll read *Harry Potter* again."

Dale zipped back into the driveway from town, the mighty hunter bearing food in the wake of their adventurous day. "Anything?" he asked around car keys dangling from his mouth, balancing the pizza box on one hand and about to lose the day's mail all over the floor from the other. He'd dropped Laura—and his cell phone—at home, done a quick Sully patrol, and gone right back out again while she called in the order for pizza.

This was one pizza he wouldn't have to inspect for UFOs. *Unidentified Fertility Objects.*

"Not yet." Laura hesitated before him, uncertain just which burden to relieve him of. He solved her dilemma by letting her close the door behind him, grateful for the nominal air-conditioning as he strode for the kitchen, spat the keys out on the counter, and deposited the box pretty much at the same time the mail spewed from his hand. In the background, loud Scottish drums and piping reverberated through the house. Laura, it seemed, had been exploring his CD collection— Wicked Tinkers, this one was, acquired at a recent Flagstaff event.

His shirt still stuck to his back where the driver's seat had plastered it into place, and he let everything sit where it had landed while he reached for the perpetually handy giant desert-sized travel mug and stuck it in front of the fridge icemaker, once more blessing the day he'd decided to pay for that luxury. "If I'd known the day planned to clear up, I'd have left the AC on while we were gone. By the time this place cools down, the sun will set and it'll drop twenty degrees and be cooler outside than it is in."

"Probably," Laura said, pulling a smaller mug from the cupboard. She'd already gotten out plates and napkins, and now as she waited for her turn at the icemaker, she pulled two flavored waters from the fridge and set them on the counter by the pizza box, then rescued a stray piece of mail from the floor. She'd recovered quickly from the morning's adventure; compared to several days earlier when she'd been released from the hospital, she was practically hale and hearty.

She'd be going home soon. Maybe even Monday. Dale traded places with her, snagging one of the flavored waters, and poured it over his collection of ice before snapping the lid on the mug, gone pensive as he watched her move—that quiet self-confidence that had always fascinated him, that quality of self-possession.

Truth was, if it weren't for John Benally, she'd probably be gone tomorrow.

His phone rang, faint beneath the pounding syncopation of a particularly drummy Tinkers cut. Both he and Laura straightened, looked around. "Where?" he asked. He'd left it here for Laura to answer so he wouldn't miss Rena's callback while on the road. And possibly so he wouldn't succumb to temptation to call her yet again, leaving yet another message. Two was enough on a Saturday when she was either at work or off doing her own thing, and would return his call when she could. Most likely, when she couldn't be overheard.

The phone riffled through another ring tone; Dale started tossing mail—magazines and ad circulars and unwanted catalogs, recycling fodder all. It was Laura who snatched up the canted pizza box and held it high so Dale could grab the phone, barely taking time to glance at the display before beating the next and final ring tone. "Rena!"

"Geeze, Dale, you'd think you wanted to reach me or something." Rena laughed at her own humor, just a little bit of a bray there. "Hey, that sounds like Wicked Tinkers!"

"I hit the Celtic Festival last month." Dale met Laura's gaze and nodded, an exchange of mutual relief. The pizza, the cold clear water . . . forgotten. "Listen, I went out to the reservation today—"

"Geeze," Rena said, in an entirely different tone, "you didn't start any trouble, did you? Tell me you didn't start any trouble."

"Hey!"

"Like I'm not right to worry?"

Dale gave it a moment of thought. Okay, maybe. A *little*. "Laura was with me," he said, as if that was answer enough. "And we know where Benally got his hanta. And we know where he connected with me. In fact, I've got a whole big envelope of new stuff here from him—and if that last note looked threatening, you ought to see what he says here."

Rena didn't quite say anything. Almost, because he heard her take the breath to do it, but she just held it a moment. Finally she said, "I got that last note at the café. It's a beaut, all right. But it must have been sitting in your car for a couple of days, because Benally's in Phoenix."

She said it with such certainty that Dale grew wary. "What do you mean, he's in Phoenix?"

"Pretty cut and dried. His truck was involved in a one-vehicle accident—a hit-and-run with a lamppost. Not only is it registered to him, it fits the description of the vehicle witnessed leaving the café after you were attacked—right down to the peeing-boy sticker. And get this—the kiddie is peeing on the words Begay Home Balance. Who knew you could get those things personalized? Anyway, the Phoenix cops have an eye out for him. The important thing is, he's down there. Sounds to me like he left a couple of notes as good-bye presents, just to keep you looking over your shoulder."

"Yeah, well, it's working." But Dale didn't say it very loud. He scowled at the pizza box; he scowled at the counter. He was careful not to scowl at Laura as she came closer, moving into his field of view to give him a questioning look. "You're gonna want this stuff anyway, right?"

"Sure," Rena said. "But I'm off-duty—just got in from a security gig at the fairgrounds—and you probably need time to copy it anyway." Her voice took a dark tone, as if she knew he'd darn well copy the stuff regardless of what she said. And he would, too—because he knew darned well everything he'd sent over would soon end up in a giant *Raiders of the Lost Ark* warehouse, lost for eternity, no one knowing or caring. "I can pick it up next week, okay?"

"Works for me." But before he hung up, Dale caught himself. "But hey, Rena—this'll do it, right?"

Puzzlement practically oozed from the phone. "How's that?"

"This whole thing. The eco-murder-solving vet gets nasty notes, gets laughed at, gets bashed with a shovel for being nosy, ha ha ha Hanta Santa . . . you think they've got it out of their systems, your Officer Stan and Friends of Stan?"

"*T'óó hashtł'ish,*" Laura muttered in the background. And, when Dale glanced her way, added, "Merely mud."

On the other end of the phone, Rena had gone from puzzled to abashed. "Let it die down, Dale. Just let it all die down. A year from now, who'll know the difference?"

"Right," he said, and said his good-byes—but only to stare at the phone with frustration after he cut the connection. "*I* will," he told it. "*I* know the difference."

And then, with determined composure, he pulled out several pieces of pizza and put two on a plate for Laura, and pulled out the napkins she hadn't found yet. He poured absurdly expensive kibble for Sully, who came flying in from who knew where out in the yard, *thwip-thwap!* through the dog door fitting right in with the music, to present himself at Dale's feet. And Laura was very, very patient, and finally Dale took a deep breath and said, "Benally's in Phoenix. He's lost his truck. The End."

Laura pulled up a stool and thought about it long enough for them both to get through a piece of pizza and for Sully to finish his own meal and commence coveting everyone else's. She drank a long chaser of water, and she looked at him through entirely noncommittal eyes. "What do you think?"

He didn't trust that expression, that's what he thought.

He'd come to understand that it meant she darned well had her own opinion, but she was keeping it to herself. He'd been reaching for his second piece of pizza; he closed his hand into a fist instead. Not so very long ago, that hand and wrist had been in a cast, courtesy of a showdown with the eco-killers. They'd taken Sully; he'd had no one but himself to find them. Laura beside him . . . but Dale's hunches. Dale's instincts.

Benally's in Phoenix.

It's over.

Let it go.

"I don't think so," Dale muttered.

And Laura smiled.

Dale made it halfway through the second piece of pizza and got restless. "Not just no," he said, still responding to the general official conclusion about John Benally, "*Hell,* no." Sully wagged his tail, hopeful at the animation in Dale's voice. But he'd become distracted, wandering the living room, coming back to ponder the possibility of food—approximately none—and wandering away again. Dale's voice brought him in from the bedroom, but didn't hold him for long.

Dale put the pizza down, headed for the bedroom with decisive steps, and slipped the lock on the dog door as Sully pondered another visit to the yard. Sully looked up in offended surprise, and Dale leaned down to pat his chest. "Sorry, son," he said. "Chalk it up to my squirrely overprotective nature. We'll go out together, later on. For now . . . come on back in the kitchen, and you might even get a piece of pepperoni."

As it happened, he got one piece of pepperoni from each of them, leaving him in quivering expectation of more once he'd finished sneezing. "Probably be a week before he can smell well enough to do mouse patrol again," Dale said, giving Sully a rueful rub on the head as they retreated to the puzzle room— dishes stuffed in the dishwasher, pizza box stuffed in the fridge, and plenty of pizza stuffed in Dale's stomach.

Laura, true to her earlier comment, had come up with one of the early Harry Potter books, and she helped herself to the recliner in the puzzle room, curling up with just the right amount of space left over to share with a modestly sized Beagle. Sully took the invitation without second thought, and Dale swapped the CD out for one of Craicmore in keeping with the Celtic theme, checked the outdoor temps, and decided to wait until sundown to turn off the AC since the house still oozed warmth around the edges, chiding him for guessing wrong about the day's weather.

Okay, maybe John Benally would be back for him. Maybe it wasn't over. But for the moment . . . didn't get much better than this.

Laura coughed, looking surprised at herself, and then looking amused at her own surprise. "That can last for months, they said. And it's been a busy day."

"Welcome to my life," Dale told her. "Though with the rain damping down all the dust and the construction done with, I'm doing pretty—" And he, too, coughed, and felt his own surprise clear on his face. Laura laughed at the timing of it, and he pointed a warning finger at her, working through the cough and realizing then, that he felt the faint burn of irritation in the back of his throat. "I could short-sheet you. And I just learned this great trick with coffee, not too much salt, not too little . . . you're not quite sure, you just wonder about it. And then there's the very good chance that Sully could tear around the house in the morning and find your door open—" But he started coughing again, and then it wasn't quite as funny anymore.

He held up a finger, and he went to pull Big Blue from the master bath, taking a quick couple of hits. And when he returned, still holding his breath and counting off the seconds, his face pulling its usual quick flush from the wash of the drug through his system, he found Laura with book open but going unread, concerned . . . and pulling the same shallow breathing he knew so well from trying not to trigger his own coughs.

"Do you smell pepper?" Laura frowned. "Maybe it's just pepperoni."

Dale let out the breath he'd been holding in his lungs, tasting albuterol on the way out, and had to shake his head. "Tasty inhaler."

Sully sneezed, and looked surprised at himself.

Dale, still flushed by albuterol, suddenly flooded with something else besides. *Fear and certainty and bone-deep anger. . . .*

Benally.

He reached the window in two long steps, shoving it open; he reached the hallway and the thermostat in a quick reverse course, flicking off the air-conditioning. And then back to the puzzle room, where Laura had half-risen from the recliner and Sully was about to bail, if only he hadn't stopped to paw at his nose. Dale scooped him up. "Over here," he told Laura, who—much to his relief—didn't stop to say, "But what—?" or "Why?" or demand explanation of any kind. He took them both to the window, breathed of the fresh air . . . found it a relief to his lungs and nose. "Hang on. I'll be right back."

Now she did stop him, with the *buts* and the *whys* clearly on her face. "If there's something wrong with the house—?" and she tipped her head toward the window, at the clean outdoor air.

"Benally," he said, out loud this time. "We don't know that it's safe out there." He put Sully in her arms. "Keep him up by the window?"

She nodded—and he could see she was still thinking it through, that she hadn't quite capitulated. But he left them anyway, taking in that clean air and holding his breath on still-burning lungs as he headed for the front door. He'd always been too tall for natural stealth, too lanky and maybe just a little too far from his feet—not one of those cat-like military guys. And yet he managed to slip through the door quietly enough, immediately breathing in the good outdoor air and tasting, in retrospect, the difference. But *what—?*

Nothing looked amiss in the front yard. A quiet traverse to the corner of the house showed him not a rock out of place, not a thing gone unusual. A mockingbird scolded him from a pine by the road; house finches fled the corner poplar at his approach, twittering madly. Still in quiet mode—as if the birds hadn't totally given him away—Dale eased around the corner and confronted the gate.

Yeah, maybe he ought to get a lock at that. Even if he was out in rural Cinder Hills and didn't want to think of people here that way. He flipped the latch open—much more casually, now, with no signs of encroachment anywhere. Possibly just a matter for the home warranty company, air conditioner gone mad after a summer of unusual heat.

The house shadow stretched long over the backyard . . . Sully's domain, marked by careful collections of favorite sticks over here, dust wallows in the best heat-of-the-day shade spots, and a dead horny toad gone leathery and stiff, and one futile, clandestine starter hole at the corner of the fence, thwarted by the chicken wire Dale had laid in upon moving here. The newly cleaned shed sat off to the side, smug in its pristine interior; now that the rain had started, Dale would have to haul out the lawnmower. And one of these days he'd have to remember to turn off the hose when he finished grilling—it still hung stiff and full over the western patio wall.

And as he rounded the patio, thinking about mowing weeds and getting Laura out into this clean air and throwing open all the windows and doors, he found the gaping dark opening at the foundation. There, just the other side of the air conditioner. The crawl space opening.

Whoa.

He slowed abruptly, patting his pockets—but no, those keys with their LED flashlight were back on the counter, and meanwhile he saw nothing, no movement, no sign of anything other than this open crawl space. If it wasn't for the smell, for the coughing, he'd call it mind games. And for the first time he stopped, took the moment to think again what he'd known way back in the puzzle room—that whatever the cops believed, John Benally wasn't in Phoenix at all.

And John Benally liked to play games.

But Dale heard nothing. He saw nothing. And he smelled the faint sharp odor of pepper and pineapples, something so familiar and yet so much stronger than he'd ever encountered, strong enough to be warped beyond recognition.

He should have brought the phone. Nine-one-one and a suspected gas leak would have gotten him company fast, a damned sight faster than a call to the sheriff. But the phone sat where he'd left it, right beside those keys with their LED flashlight.

Dale eased up to the crawl space, putting himself on the upwind side; he sank down to his knees and then his elbows, finding in the shadowed lighting nothing more than the glint of ductwork, the tangle of cable and wires, the stolid pipe running to the nearby outside spigot, the canister of—

The what?

Movement blurred in the corner of his eye; Dale had just enough time to roll away, thrusting out a deflecting arm and hunching his shoulder against—

Wham!

Flat metal against flesh, all too familiar. *Not another one!* His entire arm buzzed and went numb and Dale scrambled aside as a second blow bit sharply into the side of the house and sliced aside and *would have taken my arm right off.* Benally wasn't playing around now, he came back around again, careless in haste, slamming into Dale with less force and giving Dale the chance to grab the handle where it melded into the blade, using his one good hand to wrench at the weapon even as he quite suddenly recognized it. *Hey!* "That's *my* shovel, dammit!" Out of *his* shed!

Benally didn't care, apparently—and Benally it was, that same short, strong man Dale had seen the day Sully nosed out his first mouse—and Benally wasn't playing fair, either. He wrenched Dale closer via their mutual grip on the shovel, and at the same time drew back a mighty kick. Pointy-toed cowboy boots slammed against ribs; ribs lost. Dale made a visceral noise, a wounded noise, and fell back. Just that fast, Benally stood over him, the shovel raised, a guillotine ready to fall.

Eyes watering, vision blurry—speech impossible—Dale gasped something entirely unintelligible even to himself, shoving up a hand that was demand as much as entreaty.

"What?" Benally snorted. "You think I'm going to stop, now, and explain it all to you, like some dumb crook in the movies? You had your chance. You didn't figure it out. Now you die."

Celtic music became suddenly louder. Toenails scrabbled.

mine mine MINE BAWH! and Sully launched to the low patio wall, touching down only long enough to springboard away, soaring at Benally's shoulders—only to quite suddenly lose his fierce grace upon landing and turn to all scrabbling feet and big alarmed eyes, clawing his way down from his landing point on one ear to neck and shoulder and side and disengaging somewhere around the belt, which was just about when a sharp, hard stream of water hit Benally directly in the face—

Which was just about when Benally dropped the shovel over Dale's neck.

Dale made a strangled noise, still half-paralyzed by kicks and blows and shock, and managed to roll mostly out of the way so his shoulder took the remaining half of the shovel instead of his neck—and then, with Sully dancing around in the background baying his eyes bloodshot with fury *minemineMINE daledaledale!* and the water still blinding Benally, Dale grabbed the shovel and swept it around to knock Benally off his feet, reversing roles so quickly that for a moment he was the one getting wet, until the water abruptly cut off and there he was, sitting on Benally's chest with the shovel handle pressed against the man's throat and discovering it really didn't take two good arms to keep a man down, so long as you had that shovel handle.

And Dale, taking a cue from Sheri not so long ago, *leaned.*

Benally's eyes widened. Sully, grown even braver, danced closer to bark at his face. *badbadbad!*

"Sully." Laura, by the patio, just now setting aside the hose nozzle. She crouched and Sully—quite suddenly grateful for an out—ran to her, abashed and happy to hide in the circle of her arms—if not without one final scolding bark at Benally.

And Dale, somewhat hoarse and strained, said, "*Now* you talk."

CHAPTER 23

Dear Aunt Cily—

Yes, we have our answers. And I swear, if I'd known you were keeping track of the local paper on-line, I'd have mentioned something about the chlorine gas before you read it there. But we're okay—all three of us. Between my asthma, Laura's recovering lungs, and Sully's nose, we were pretty quick to catch on.

Oh, I am *too* taking it seriously. But it's done. And we're safe, and Benally is in jail. He was only ever trying to get my attention, so I could admire his handiwork when it came to Albert Begay. I was supposed to figure it out and be felled with awe. Every fine craftsman likes to be appreciated. I suppose. In some sick, dark, twisted. . . .

Maybe I wasn't his best target fan base after all.

He must have come to the same conclusion . . . decided to cut his losses, laid a trail down in Phoenix, doubled back up to Flagstaff to take care of his loose ends—because I *had* finally figured it out. The irony of it is, it still never would have come to anything, if he'd actually taken off.

Anyway, they say yeah, broken ribs are a bitch and they should heal in two months. (Can you pretend I didn't say "bitch"?) But Laura's doing better. She'd say not—she's impatient. But she is.

Sully goes to the Prescott show in a few weeks. He would like you to know that he's feeling especially handsome.

AND he sniffs a good mouse, too.

Love, Dale

PS: Could be a trip to Ohio in my future if you don't start talking about those tests.

"Wow!" Sheri said, loudly enough to turn heads in the crowded dog show grounds parking lot—people rushing here, dogs rushing there, hustle and bustle and hurry. Ordinarily, Sheri's clothes alone might have already turned heads, but today she was dressed conservatively, in fine pale slacks beneath a mint green summer shirt that might have looked a bit toothpastey on anyone of a lighter complexion but on Sheri looked just plain breezy. Besides, it matched the streaks in her highly coiffed hair with a vengeance. "Wow!" she said again. "You totally *owned* that show ring!"

Not that she spoke to Dale. Nope. There, at the end of Sully's show lead, her eyes sparkling and her face alight, Laura still also wore an expression of faintly stunned surprise. "Dale!" she said. "Did you see that?"

Since Dale had been at ringside, and had taken the ribbons Laura thrust at him upon exiting the ring, and had walked back from the bustling grass show grounds with her, he could only give her a silly, affectionate grin. "As a matter of fact," he said. "I did." He gently removed the braided leather show lead from her death grip, slipped the other end over Sully's head, and lifted Sully to his crate—there waited water, a particularly fine cookie, and shade. Sully grabbed a quick lick on the way up, still wagging his tail—still in complete show-off mode.

me. handsome me. special ME.

"Yes, yes," Dale said, and deposited an unmanly kiss on Sully's head before guiding him into the crate. "You are definitely all of that." And then he sat at the Forester's back end—for unlike the others who'd come to see Sully at this show not so far from Flagstaff—Dru, Hank, and Sheri—Dale didn't quite fit

271

beneath the canopy he'd set up off the SUV's back end. A luxurious spot of shade, complete with the early morning tea he had brewing—courtesy of the small battery generator tucked in behind him, and later, as the day heated up at this lower altitude, he'd plug in a fan. But it was still early and cool; Beagles had been on at eight a.m., and that had meant an o-dark-thirty departure from Flagstaff for all of them.

"But I don't understand," Hank was saying. "What's it *mean?*"

Dale opened his mouth to answer, then closed it again—grin back in place—when Laura beat him to it. "He won his class, which means he went up against the other boy dogs who won their classes. It's by age, mostly. And other things, but never mind that. And then he won against them, which means he earned points toward his championship. And his second major! Those are important, the two majors—now he just needs points." She turned to Dale. "When's the next show? Are you entered? And—but . . . oh. I guess your ribs will be healed by then."

For Benally had done it this time, gone and broken several ribs. Ribs Dale had personally been very fond of, and found himself no little bit put out at just how much their damage limited him. Moving Sully around the show ring . . . not a problem. Lifting him on and off the table for examination by the judge . . . well, he could do it. But he invariably made a lot of strange noises in the process. And so Laura had, reluctantly, offered to stand in—had gone to handling classes, had practiced the various handling patterns in Dale's backyard . . . had taught Sully to kick into his show gait for her. And had now come out of the ring in a state of stunned excitement. Not just the winning, she'd told him—just the woot! of being out there with Sully showing off for her, the two of them working together, the friendly nature of the breeders and handlers also clustered around the ring.

"My ribs," he told her solemnly, "will never heal well enough for me to deal with the show ring. The doctor told me last week. It was a terrible blow. I was trying to hide my pain from you, but now I find I can no longer—"

She silenced him with a big quick kiss on the lips, soliciting noises of appreciation from Sheri.

Dale just figured the silly grin would be a permanent fixture on his face. He turned to the tray behind him—*ow, ow, slowly*—and checked the tea. Ohh, yes. Just right. Irish breakfast tea, just like at the clinic, tea bag tags still dangling. He added the final touches while Dru talked about some French Bulldogs she'd seen and pondered if maybe those could be the dog for her.

"About time," Sheri said, taking her tea. "I hope those food vender places aren't open yet. Tremayne will talk my mother out of a donut for sure, and he don't need to be starting his day with no sugar. You put sweetener in this?"

"Two packets," Dale said, indicating her mug. Dru took hers straight, and Hank pulled a little cup of creamer out of his breast pocket as though maybe he just always kept one there. Laura pulled off the fancy stitched vest she'd been wearing—like Dale, she was dressed for her time in the ring. But where Dale was headed for rally, tidy and pressed in dark khakis and a tan polo shirt with a nice narrow dress belt, Laura had come in a rich brown pantsuit that set Sully's colors off to perfection in the breed ring.

An unexpected natural, that Laura Nakai.

Dru took a sip of her tea. She'd come on her motorcycle, and her brillo grey hair still showed signs of the helmet effect; she'd draped her black leather jacket over the frame for the tailgate canopy. "You know, Hank, that dog of yours shouldn't be here. No dogs on the grounds unless they're eligible for the show."

"Aw," Hank said, looking down at Frank. Frank sported a

new collar in patterned neon, clashing brightly with his sparse terrier frizz.

"It *is* a mighty fine collar," Sheri said. "And besides, we're in the parking lot. So that doesn't count. And boy, this is a nice setup you got here, Dr. Dale. All rigged up for showing, now, are you?" But she had a glint in her eyes that Dale wasn't sure he liked, and a moment later when Laura went around to the front seat to stash her vest and that glint notched up in volume, he was sure of it.

"Dale!" Laura said, her voice tense, coming to him from within the vehicle as opposed to around it. He leaned back, then rued it and caught himself on one arm. And then she relaxed a little and said, "Oh." And sighed, and handed him an index card with carefully printed lettering on one side.

His heart beat faster in spite of himself. Even though Benally was behind bars, even though Laura had already relaxed, even though Sheri had already given herself away . . . he sat up, turned the note right side up, and read it.

Hanta Santa gone bad
Made Mr. Dr. Dale mad
Johnny Hantaseed swung his shovel
But whoa! He ended up in a grovel!

Go Dr. Dale GO!

"That last bit doesn't rhyme," Sheri explained.

"I hadn't noticed," Dale said dryly.

"It's a cheer," she said, taking him seriously. "Now give me that. I want to put it up in the clinic with the others."

Because of course she'd gotten hold of his copies. Of course she'd put them up in the clinic. And of course the Flagstaff newspaper, desperate for headline news at the best of times, had taken this new "murder-solving vet!" story and run with it, so those clippings were all over the wall as well, and it had done no good to remind her that they'd just paid to have those walls painted. "Then we've got a good supply of matching paint on hand if that tape makes bare spots," she'd said, and smoothed down the Hanta Santa she'd just added to the shrine.

But Rena hadn't stopped by Terry's café for weeks.

"She'll be back," Dru said, watching him—correctly interpreting his wistful expression. "She just needs to work past those hardheads." And she snorted. "Nice bunch of egos they've got going there. They drop the ball on this whole hanta thing, ignore your notes, ignore all the information you give them along the way, convince themselves that the bad guy—who *you* identify—is down in the Valley with his tail between his legs when he's actually up here conspiring to hook—what was it?"

"Chlorine gas," Dale murmured. Because Benally's brother, who'd loaned him an old junker, worked down in Phoenix at a municipal pool maintenance business. And because with Sully on hand, the whole hanta thing was busted. "And it would have happened sooner, if the rain hadn't kept the temps down and the AC off."

"—Chlorine gas into your ductwork," Dru said, as if she hadn't been interrupted, her voice rising steadily with indignation, "meaning you were lucky to get out of there alive at all, never mind that you *catch* the guy for them and get all bashed around for your efforts—"

"We were lucky," Laura said, leaving Dru at the end of a perfectly good rant. She returned to the shade to pull her hair into a ponytail and then pull the ponytail through the hole at the back of her ball cap. It had a Beagle on the front.

Oh, yeah. She was hooked.

She said, "Between Dale's asthma and my lungs, we reacted so fast to the gas that they figure it hadn't even built up to fifteen ppm yet." And at Sheri's scowl, she added, "We reacted before it could do any damage. Another couple of minutes, and that wouldn't have been the case. Not with the two of us already compromised." And boy, didn't that sum up a whole lot of fuss and bother in one fell swoop—the sirens, the fire department, the EPA, the emergency room. . . .

"But *why?*" Hank asked, and it fairly burst out of him. He'd been pretty good, actually, hanging around the clinic at mail delivery, lingering at Frank's weigh-ins, dropping little hints . . . and Dale just hadn't wanted to talk about it. Because. . . .

"It's stupid," he said. "It's beyond stupid. And a waste. The man's brilliant, and he kept waiting for someone to notice."

"Resenting it when they didn't," Laura added. She'd been there—she'd seen it on his face. "Resenting his lack of opportunity . . . resenting the boredom of his work. . . ."

"Bored and resentful," Dru said. "Not a good combination."

"He was fired during the job at the Tsosie place," Dale said. The Begays knew the whole story, now; Laura had called them from the emergency room—before the cops could get to them; before they could read it in the paper or hear it in the news. "Went and cleaned up the hanta shed on his own time. And got a very clever revenge, too. He would have gotten away with it if he hadn't heard Mary talking about her cousin's new friend—big-shot vet, solving the eco-killer murders."

Sheri's jaw dropped; she stabbed a finger at her note. "Those notes! You were supposed to figure out what he'd done so someone would be impressed!"

"Too bad for me I was so slow. Too bad for *Laura.*" Dale glanced at her, felt the guilt down to his toes. She shook her head. *Don't go there,* that look said.

"You *did* figure it out," Dru said. "A lot sooner than any of us let you."

"I forgot to be impressed," Dale said dryly. "I forgot to be impressed *loudly.*"

"Brilliant," Laura said, "and quite probably sociopathic." She glanced at Dale, and at Sully—lounging in his crate and quite clearly wallowing in his own importance. "Were you going to warm him up, get his gears switched to rally?"

Dale glanced at Sheri's half-empty tea, and at the squint she'd just given the mug—at the look she exchanged with Dru. Yeah. Now might be good. Without hurry, he pulled out Sully's short leather obedience lead and the serpentine chain collar that went with it, clipping a bait bag to his belt. Sully jumped to his feet within the crate. *more me! more us! daledaledale!*

"Absolutely," Dale said, and opened the door to slip the collar on and lower Sully to the ground. "It's not quite as nice as Frank's," he admitted to Hank, "but we're trying not to draw attention."

Hank puffed up his chest a little, which had the noticeable effect of making it less sunken. "It *is* a fine new collar, for a good dog like Frank."

Frank said, "Grr." But Dale thought he puffed his own stout chest out a little bit. Hard to tell. Most of Frank was puffed out to some degree.

Sheri looked more closely at her tea. "Hey," she said.

Dru hadn't had nearly as much of hers, but she'd caught Sheri's concern and she'd caught her own suspicion of something not quite right, and she reached for her tea bag tag about the same time Sheri reached for her own, and Dale bent down to smooth Sully's ruffled coat—his whites still totally white from their pre-show grooming, the arch of his neck revealed to perfection through stripping and clipping and thinning shears, his flanks and haunches similarly trimmed. And so, as Dale stood, he had the perfect view of Sheri's face as she pulled up the tag and string to reveal not a tea bag, but the shriveled, preserved little object tied to the tea bag string, a perfect match to the one Dru pulled from her own tea.

He'd warned them. . . .

"Dale Kinsall!" Sheri shrieked, flinging the testicle tea bag away as though she couldn't possibly get rid of it fast enough.

"Dr. Dale!" Dru bellowed, dropping hers to the ground with distinct disdain.

"Dale!" Laura laughed, face in hands.

Ahh, yes. Life was good. Dale grinned wide and large and knew he'd pay for this later. And didn't care. Here he was with friends and Laura and a darned fine dog, a puzzle solved and a prank well-played. He looked down at the darned fine dog, caught the waving tail, the wrinkles of interest and readiness. Well, Dale was ready too.

Or at least, he hoped so. "Sully, heel!"

ABOUT THE AUTHOR

Doranna responded to all early injunctions to "put down that book/notebook and go outside to play" by climbing trees to read and write. Such quirkiness of spirit has led to an eclectic publishing journey, spanning genres and form over nearly twenty-five novels to include mystery, SF/F, action-romance, paranormal, franchise, and a slew of essays and short stories. But after all that, mostly she still prefers to hang around outside her northern-Arizona home with the animals, riding dressage on her Lipizzan and training for performance sports with the dogs (including a certain Ch. Cedar Ridge DoubleOSeven, AKA ConneryBeagle). She doesn't believe so much in mastering the beast within, but in channeling its power. For good or bad has yet to be decided. . . .

You can find her online at doranna.net, where she keeps a collection of gorgeous high-desert sunsets and scoops about new projects, lots of silly photos, and contact info.